Praise for
Hard Skin

Melissa Llanes Brownlee's collection *Hard Skin* invites readers of all ages to Hele mai and listen in the same manner that oral histories and traditions of Hawai'i have been passed down. The speaker in these personal narratives describes how family members and kolohe neighbors shape one's identity growing up on the Big Island of Hawai'i.

Readers will be smitten with the speaker's quest to define what does it mean to be good, as well as how to avoid getting "dirty lickens," as the speaker sifts through ethnic stereotypes, racism, and fairness, with poignant, but sharp wonderings: "How come we aren't on welfare, so I can buy lots of candy, too?"

Readers need no prior knowledge as Llanes Brownlee deftly places us in a field with a loving Aunty Haole who educates a young child about Pele's many lovers like Kamapua'a, the pig god, or candidly asks, "Whachu smell?" besides cow doo doo: "With the wind blowing so hard that you'd think you'd huli off your horse, seeing where the ocean touches the sky, the dark meeting the light, it somehow makes you just want to be quiet without being told to."

Llanes Brownlee's narratives encompass a gentle tension deciphering truths from tales and finding faith in the not perfect family, yet growing up in a world with much incongruity, lessons of love and loss, as well as being strong enough to carry their generational legacy with all the complexities of how we define home.

— **Shareen K. Murayama**, author of *House Break* and
Hey Girl, Are You in the Experimental Group

Melissa Llanes Brownlee possesses a voice of singular fierceness and beauty. With these stories, she takes you into the life of her characters, into the life of the islands, into the life of old gods. And once you have seen this life for yourself, it is hard to leave it behind. You will carry these stories with you, and you will carry this powerful, stunning voice.

— **Cathy Ulrich**, author of *Ghosts of You*

Melissa Llanes Brownlee's prose is a gift to readers! In the way she uses the senses, allowing us to taste and smell and touch the worlds we're reading about. In the way her characters are so believable, so beautifully human in their flaws. What they want, we want. What they can't have, we long for. Llanes Brownlee pulls us into every story, humor and grief mixing in a compelling series of family portraits. This collection takes your heart for a ride.

— **Hannah Grieco**, editor of *And If That Mockingbird Don't Sing*

In *Hard Skin*, Melissa Llanes Brownlee exhibits breathtaking fearlessness as she lays bare the realities of coming of age on the Big Island of Hawai'i. With exquisite authenticity, she paints stories of poverty, loss, anger and modern colonialism alongside natural beauty, connection, and ancestral power, establishing herself as one of the great new voices of contemporary fiction.

— **Liz Prato**, author of *Volcanoes, Palm Trees, and Privilege: Essays on Hawai'i*

Melissa Llanes Brownlee's debut collection of a dozen stories is at once exotic and familiar, identifiable and personal. Llanes Brownlee immerses readers in the lives and backdrop of her characters with an often-poignant and always-believable voice. From the titular "Hard Skin" to stories like "Pele's Daughter," "Any Kine Boy," and "Talking Story about Kilauea," each one is like listening to a master storyteller sharing stories. Cultural aspects, family connections and sensory details shine under Llanes Brownlee's hand with a lyricism that is infused throughout. The powerful closing line looks forward: "I pick up my pencil and trace it over and over, making a space for myself." It becomes the culmination of the characters' and Llanes Brownlee's life journey through the creation of a well-deserved space for herself and these memorable stories.

— **Amy Cipolla Barnes**, author of *Mother Figures* and *Ambrotypes*

Hard Skin

Juventud
Press

by
Melissa Llanes Brownlee

Juventud Press
Copyright © 2022 by Melissa Llanes Brownlee
ISBN: 978-1-953447-38-8
Library of Congress Control Number: 2022938687

Published by Juventud Press
in the United States of America.
www.flowersongpress.com

Cover Art by Melissa Llanes Brownlee
Set in Adobe Garamond Pro

For all the island kids dreaming of more.

Acknowledgements

I want to thank the many teachers and professors at Boise State University and the University of Nevada, Las Vegas, including but not limited to, Anthony Doerr, who first workshopped "Uncle Willy's Harbor" at BSU, Richard Wiley, who read it and accepted me into the MFA program at UNLV, Douglas Unger, who also accepted me into the program and offered me many grains of sage advice on the lanai of my first Vegas apartment, Felicia Campbell, who opened my eyes to the possibility of being an adventurer, Pablo Medina, who chaired my MFA thesis committee and gave this collection its final title. I would also like to thank the friends and fellow writers I gained in the program. Your continued friendship means the world to me. I am grateful to all of the literary magazines and journals for giving all of my stories a home. Finally, I am thankful for my husband who has spent our many years together supporting my writing. Mahalo Nui Loa to all of you!

Table of Contents

2   Uncle Willy's Harbor

16   Dirty Lickins

22   Da Pier

29   Pele's Daughter

36   Opihi Tales

46   Tita

50   Talking Story about Kilauea

62   Ulu's Gift

72   Any Kine Boy

76   Hard Skin

85   Ku's Aina

89   My Kuleana

Hard Skin

Uncle Willy's Harbor

Dad caught a wild pig up mauka for my sister's baby luau. I could hear it screaming behind the house. A sweet smell blew past me into the mango trees. The pig's legs were tied with skin rope and I wondered why there was pink toothpaste foam around its mouth. Flies swarmed around the hole that dad's gun had made.

"Kawika, no worries, it not going hurt you."

They held it down on the plywood he'd put over the sawhorses in the backyard. I watched them slit its throat and blood squirted in the air. It was squealing one minute, quiet the next. Well, as quiet as it can be through the drunk laughter and the talk story of the men.

"Eh Kawika, come help us clean da pig."

Uncle Willy's long hunting knife slid down the pig's stomach like he was cutting through cooked taro. I wasn't sure what came out. It wasn't like cleaning fish. Fish is easy. You scrape off the scales. You slice through the belly. You pull out the guts. Fish guts don't look like food cooking on the stove. There's no steam rising off the insides. And, everything isn't pink and red. I just stood there as they rinsed out the inside with the hose, the water swirling around their bare feet.

Dad helped Uncle Willy hang the pig on the corner of the house. The fur had been scraped off and it looked funny with all of it gone. Like the negatives of pictures. You know like when my older sister Pi'i had her birthday party and she blew out her candles. Her hair is black, and when I looked at the negatives, her hair was white. That's what the pig looked like. They had wrapped it in a white sheet, so the flies couldn't get at it. Blood dripped from the bottom and it looked like a haole woman's painted fingernail. They were going to imu the pig in the backyard before taking it down to Uncle Willy's house on the beach.

After a couple of hours, Uncle Keala and Uncle Willy took it down and wrapped it in chicken wire so they could put it in the imu. They had been burning kiawe all day to heat up the rocks. It smelled so good. They covered the pig with ti leaves and huge banana leaves. Then, they threw big brown empty sacks over the leaves and buried everything with dirt. I remembered when my cousin had died and they had stuck her in a fancy white satin box and then threw dirt on her, too. I wondered if the obake had eaten her, its anthurium-shaped head pushing through the dirt, digging down to her white coffin. Dad told me they had to cook the pig for twelve hours so that's why they had to do it today instead of tomorrow when the party was supposed to happen. I wondered what it felt like to be buried, to be underneath all that dirt and leaves. I wondered if the pig felt anything, whether my cousin felt anything. I think about the movies where the dead people come to life and start trying to eat the people in the town's brains. I could just see dead people digging their way out of their graves in the cemeteries on Mt. Hualalai and then coming down to eat the people here in my neighborhood. Brains. Brains. Brains.

My neighborhood was full of houses that looked the same. They just painted them different colors and put them facing all kind different directions. Some houses had their garages facing the ocean. Some had theirs facing the mountain. If you counted them, you'd see that every fifth house was the same color. You know what was really funny? How different everyone's yard was. My house had plenty of fruit trees with no grass. My mom had made my dad go down to the beach to find flat coral stones that she could put into our yard as walking stones, so, there are big, flat white rocks making a path around the tangerine tree, up to the mountain apple tree, and down to the starfruit tree. My mom has the craziest ideas. She has a little garden under a roofed area, where she grows crab grass, anthuriums, and ferns, but I never really thought of crab grass as real grass, you know the kind of grass they have on TV. The kind a kid mows to make money.

The only people who had that kind of grass lived down the street from us, the Morrises. Mr. Morris had threatened to call the cops on us because he said we had poisoned his dog. Stupid haole. Why would we poison his dog? It's not our fault that his dog wandered into our yard and drank water out of our buckets. None of our dogs do that. They're not that stupid. I thought it was really funny that his dog would dig up his lawn all the time. You never see that on TV. Good dogs don't dig up nice lawns.

Now, the Kanazawas across the street were really nice. Their house was green which was the same color as the Rodriguez' down on the corner, and they had a rock garden in their yard. My mom thought it was a waste and that they should have fruit trees in their yard instead. I think that my mom didn't like Mr. Kanazawa's wife because she was a haole, but I thought she was nice. She would always give us kids peanut taro. The sticky sweetness was worth going into their stuffy house. Mrs. Kanazawa collected Japanese dolls. She wouldn't let us touch them. She said they were Mr. Kanazawa's family heirlooms because he was an only child and his parents had died in a bombing in Japan. I didn't really understand but I liked how real the dolls looked. They stood in their little glass cases staring at you with their dark eyes and red lips. They all had really fancy kimonos, even the guys. One time Pi'i told me of this Japanese doll that would come to life and eat people. Its long black hair would whip around its face as its fingernails grew really, really long so it could chop up and eat its owners. And when it was done, it would just go back into its case until it ate its next owner. She told me it was a true story. I didn't believe her but I didn't like looking at Mrs. Kanazawa's dolls after that.

The Kanazawas' were invited to the luau, which surprised me because I didn't think my mom would want them there, but parties make people do stupid things to each other. The last party we had, Uncle Willy threw his beer can at Mr. Kanazawa, calling him a slanty-eyed prick. Everyone started laughing but I didn't know why. I asked Pi'i and she said it had something to do with some war and since Mr. Kanazawa came to Hawai'i after it, then he was just a stinkin' Jap. I told her that didn't explain the laughing. She said they were laughing because Uncle Willy was making an ass of himself.

"What about Mr. Kanazawa?"

"No worry about him. He been here long enough to know Uncle Willy gets stupid wen he stay drinking. No worries, Kawika." Pi'i rubbed my head.

Uncle Willy was a really old man. He wasn't even related to us as far as I could tell. I think my parents said he was my grandpa's hanai cousin or something like that. He lived on a beach off to the right side of the harbor. The house was built on stilts over the water. To get inside, you had to walk over a wooden plank underneath which the honu liked to swim, their green shells reflecting the sun, flippers pushing against the current. His house didn't look like any of the houses in my neighborhood. For one thing, it wasn't only made with wood. There were metal pieces on the sides, on the roof, even on the floor. Uncle Willy even had plastic sheets for windows. I asked my mom why he lived in the house on the beach and she told me he was claiming his rightful place. That this was the land of his family.

"Why he no live in a nice house like we do?"

"He stay on welfare."

"What? Like Aunty Mahealani?"

"Yeah, but don't you let me catch you saying anything about that in front of her, or else you going get lickins."

"Why come, mom? How come I no can talk about it?"

"Because your aunty stay shame, that's why."

"But why, it's free food right?"

"Yeah. But there stay more reasons than that. Go help Pi'i straighten up the bedrooms."

I thought about what she said. People are ashamed to be on welfare? Then, how come I see people use it all the time at the grocery store? They buy steak and shrimp and lobster. The kids get to buy tons of candy and it's not fair. How come we aren't on welfare, so I can buy lots of candy, too? Maybe I can get some from Uncle Willy at the baby luau.

When we got down to Honokohau, we set up the picnic tables and put up the decorations. Dad strung up the blue tarp between a couple of coconut trees to keep the sun off the tables and mom spread out her rainbow of Tupperware, holding all the food that didn't need to be put in the huge fish coolers. Mom had made squid luau and shoyu chicken, and they were sitting in big pots next to the charcoal bbq Uncle Keala was starting. We were going to pulehu some chicken and teri beef. I liked Uncle Keala because he always took me cruising with him and he never took my sisters.

Sometimes, he'd take me for a cruise down Old A's. He told me it was the old airport before Keahole Airport was built. I had never ridden on an airplane, but I see plenty of them take off when I'm surfing at Pine Trees because it's right next door to the airport. There's nothing cooler than seeing an airplane right over your head while you're riding a wave into shore. The sound just goes through your body. Uncle Keala said that the planes that came into Old A's had propellers. I couldn't imagine propellers on planes, except in the movies. The Red Baron flying through the clouds, guns tat-tat-tatting. The planes I've seen are huge monsters that scream. Uncle Keala likes to stop down at the end of the strip and talk story with the braddahs that hang out down there. Sometimes they smoke pakalolo. Sometimes they just hang around drinking beer and looking at the cars that drive by and honk. Mom doesn't like me to go cruising with Uncle Keala. She thinks he smokes too much pakalolo and doesn't want me with him if he gets caught. Get caught? How can he get caught? What's wrong with pakalolo? It just like cigarettes, that's what Uncle Keala says.

Uncle Keala gets the bbq started and everyone's drinking beer and laughing and joking and talking story. Mom had made Spam Musubi for pupus and there was futomaki sushi and my Uncle Willy had caught some ahi for sashimi and poke. I couldn't wait to eat.

And then Merna showed up. She's so lolo. I don't like hanging with her. She's always trying to play house or doctor. I laughed when her mom said that if she doesn't behave she was going sell her to the old Filipino man who lives on the other side of the bay. She shut up real quick. I don't blame her. I wouldn't want to be sold to some old man, either. Merna's my stupid cousin, so I have to be nice to her, when all I really want to do is take her over to the old Filipino man myself—but I can't, I have to watch her and now I have to take her boogie boarding with me.

"Merna, why you gotta come with us? Can't you just stay here and swim with da other kids?"

"I no like. I going come with you or I going tell your mada you being kolohe and you never like take me."

"Oh sorry, eh tita. No get all lolo. I going take you. No worries beef curry."

"Wen you going?"

"Bumbai, wen we pau eat."

"Den we go?"

"Yeah, I tole you already. Now scram before I tell your mada you like play doctor all da time."

She ran off kicking up sand like the roadrunner does when he's running away from the coyote. Beep. Beep.

Robert finally showed up.

"Hey wassup? We going go surf or what?"

"Garans babarans, but I no can yet. I gotta wait til they pau with da party. Get one nice break over there." I pointed to some lava rocks the tide was trying to climb.

"Man I knew I shoulda stayed home. I coulda been watching Robotech."

"What, you no have to stay. Go home if you like."

"Nah, nah, nah, nah, was only joking. What you like me do?"

"We going help Uncle Keala with da chicken."

"Shoots, brah."

We walked over to the fire and Uncle Keala was talking to Uncle Willy.

"Someone gotta go Taneguchi's and pick up some moa beer."

"I stay go. You like come Kawika?"

Uncle Willy drove an old blue Datsun pickup truck. He let me ride in the back and I stood up the whole way into town to the grocery store. I jumped off the back and begged him for some money for ice cream. He smelled like beer and salt and he had dark red skin. You know like how you would imagine Indians looked like long ago. Skin darkened and tanned, sunburned so long that it had no other choice but to be red all the time. Mom said he was a fisherman. He took his canoe out and he caught fish, like ahi and aku, without any poles. He caught them like the Ancient Hawaiians did by hand. Using just line and handmade hooks to reel them in. His hair looked like an aborigine. I saw a picture of one in my class one time and I thought they were brothers. Sometimes I wonder if Uncle Willy came from there. You know, crossed the ocean in his canoe, landed on the beach and got adopted into our family. I can imagine him like Momotaro, the Peachboy, drifting along until a nice old couple takes him in.

"Well, ah dunno Kawika your mada not going like if I give you money for buy ice cream."

"Please uncle, I can go help you later with da kine fish, if you like."

"Ah guess you can have one dollah food stamp, but no tell your mada and you betta eat 'em before we get back to da baby luau."

"Garans uncle, much mahalo."

He smiled at me and gave a wrinkled brown slip of paper that almost looked like a real dollar. I walked over to the ice cream case. There were so many choices and I had a whole dollar to spend. I picked out a Neapolitan ice cream sandwich, which was forty cents, and a drumstick since I had enough left over for it. Uncle Willy was already at the cashier with a couple of cases of Budweiser. I remember the first time I ever had it. We were at Aunty Mahealani's wedding and Uncle Keala gave me a sip of it and it tasted yucky. It tasted like how he smelled. Kind of how Uncle Willy smells now. Uncle Willy looked really tired and I asked him if he was okay.

"Eh, I stay fine, no worries. Da kine ice cream looks ono."

"You like one?"

"Nah, nah, I get beer. No worry about me."

The cashier recognized me and asked about my dad and how he was doing and I said we were celebrating my sister Kahealani's first birthday and we were having the baby luau down at the harbor.

"You should come wen you pau work."

"Sounds good. Mahalo nui loa Kawika."

"Mahalo."

I hopped up front with Uncle Willy on the way back to the harbor so I could eat my ice cream. Uncle Willy was shaking out his arm, his hand flapping.

"You alright uncle?"

"I tole you no worries Kawika, I just neva eat yet."

"Okay uncle, mahalo for the ice cream."

He smiled at me and started the truck. I tried not to get the brown stuff from the ice cream sandwich all over my fingers.

"Uncle Willy, how come you live on da beach?"

"Cuz."

"Cuz what?"

"I live on da kine beach cuz dat's my family's aina."

"But how come your house stay so kapakahi? It looks so hamajang."

"It no stay hamajang. One house is one house. Why for you asking?"

"Ah dunno, I was just asking."

"Why you so ni'ele?"

"I not ni'ele. I was just wondering why you stay live at da beach. Dat's all."

He looked at me. His red face was dripping with sweat. He looked like he was really hot. He lifted his Budweiser up to his mouth and drank his beer. I wished I had bought a soda instead of that second ice cream. I was so thirsty. If my house was just like Uncle Willy's, would I one day have dark red skin and white hair like him?

"Bumbai, you going come fishing with me?"

"Shoots uncle, I going come. Come get me wen you stay ready."

We got back to the luau and all the family had shown up. Uncle Willy had a little trouble carrying the cases. His arm kept giving him problems and he was having trouble breathing. He put the cases near the coolers and sat down next to the bbq. That's where mom's side was, and dad's side was by the coolers. Someone passed Uncle Willy another beer and he cracked it open. I always thought the sound of a beer can opening sounded like bones breaking. I wondered if every time a beer opened someone broke a bone. You know like how an angel gets its wings every time a bell rings. If that's true, then there must be a lot of bones broken in the world because my family drinks a lot of beer.

Mom's family had brought their ukuleles and guitars and had started a kanikapila. Uncle Keala was singing Pua Hone with Aunty Mahealani. She was a really good falsetto and Uncle Keala wasn't too bad himself. Dad's family was talking story and drinking all the beer. Lucky Uncle Willy and I went to the store. Robert came up to me.

"We going go surfing or what? And how come you neva take me to da store with you."

"Cuz we was just getting beer. Why bada you? You know we no can go surf til we pau eat, so just cool your jets."

"Shoots brah. I neva like go anyway. Your sister Pi'i is one sweet honey girl."

"Eh, no talk about my sistah dat way! She way too old for you."

"What she one junior right?"

"Yeah, and you stay in da fifth grade! What you think she one cradle robbah. You lolo."

"Eh, I can handle da ladies."

"Yeah whateva. Let's go grinds."

We sat down at one of the tables near the bbq. My dad started talking. Everyone stood up and Uncle Willy began to pule, thanking God for all the wonderful food and for having us all together to celebrate Kahealani's first birthday. I peeked out over my fingers and saw that everyone had their heads bowed.

I never understood the whole praying thing. I know there's a God and a son named Jesus Christ who died for our sins, but I never felt anything and I knew I was supposed to. Sometimes I think that God is like the emperor's new clothes. Everyone says they can see it, but they're just lying because they don't want to be the only ones who can't see. That's how I feel sometimes about God, and yet I pray every night for my mother and my father and my sisters and the whole world in the name of Jesus Christ, Amen.

My dad finished and everyone started lining up at the end of the food table. Since we're the kids we got to go first. I was so hungry even after eating ice cream and the Spam Musubi. You know I did feel kind of bad that Robert didn't get any, but oh well, you snooze, you lose. The smell was so ono. I couldn't wait to eat the kalua pig dad had pulled out of the imu this morning. I piled my plate with rice, potato salad, kalua pig, pulehu chicken, teri beef. I wanted to put more on top but I didn't have any room. So, I got a second plate and put some squid luau and shoyu chicken on it. Me and Robert sat down on the sand away from the other kids so we could talk story about school and surfing. Merna wanted to come and sit next to us but I stuck my tongue out at her and she sat down with my sisters and some of my other cousins. We could hear the older folks laughing and joking. Aunty Mahealani was still singing and my sister Pi'i was dancing the hula. I think the song was He Aloha Mele. My sister was always dancing that song at parties. She liked the attention. She looked really pretty with her black hair blowing around her waist as she swayed to the rhythm. Someone was yelling we should've brought some pahus and ipus and someone yelled out that's too much work, and then someone started a beat on the back of a guitar. Oom pa oom pa pa. Oom pa oom pa pa. Robert started tapping his feet to the beat. I knew he was part of a halau.

"You should go dance."

"Nah, I stay shame. Surf first. Nah, nah, nah, eat first, then surf."

"Alright brah, sounds good."

I could hear Uncle Willy laughing and talking to my dad.

"So, Kawika said he like go out with me on the canoe today."

"Really?"

"Yeah he wen promise he going come out with me for catch

fish for eat later on."

"I thought he was going surf."

"Ah dunno. He said he was going come with me. Eh, Kawika? You going come fishing with me later on?"

"I like go, but I wen promise Robert we was going surfing after we pau eat. Maybe bumbai we can go."

"If das what you like do. We can go bumbai wen you pau surf."

He turned back towards my dad and took a big drink of his beer.

I felt really bad, but I didn't really want to go fishing with him.

"Man, you almost had to go fishing with your uncle, shoot dat was close."

"Nah, I wanted for go, but I said I was going surf with you too."

"Whateva."

We finished eating and sat around listening to the old folks drinking and singing. I watched my little sister being passed around as everyone kissed and bounced her. I think mom was surprised she wasn't crying. I couldn't remember my first baby luau, but my mom said that I cried so much that they ended up giving me some whiskey in my milk to shut me up. She said I knocked right out after that.

We walked over to Merna. She was giggling with some of my other cousins and pointing at Robert.

"You pau eat or what? We going go show you where we going surf."

We went to the edge of the sand where the lava rocks started and I pointed to the break.

"You guys lolo. I wouldn't surf dat if you paid me. No way, Jose. You guys can go by yourselves. I not lolo, I not going."

"What? You stay chicken?"

"No. I not crazy."

"We neva like you come anyway."

"I going tell your mada you wen say that."

"So. Go. I no care."

"I going tell on you Kawika. Den your mada not going let you surf."

"You betta not or I going give you dirty lickins."

"You and what army, uku boy."

I lifted my fist and she ran. Beep. Beep. Robert laughed and we started climbing over the lava rocks, heading toward the short break. The sun was burning my neck but it felt really good to be away from the family. All that pinching and groping and kissing. I just wanted to eat and surf.

We jumped off the rocks into the water, careful not to put our feet down on the coral, didn't want to get cut up or have to pee on our legs because of the wana. I duck dived under the first wave, swimming out to behind the break. I pushed myself up on my boogie board to look at where the wave was breaking so I wouldn't end up crashing into the lava. Robert was right next to me, pushed up on his board looking for his first wave. Robert was a pretty good boarder. He could do a couple of 360 spins before he came into shore. I wasn't too good with the 360 but I could shred through any wave and still be able to pull out before wiping out.

He paddled into the first wave of the set but didn't paddle fast enough so he dropped off and came back towards me. There was no one else out at this spot so we pretty much had the whole break to ourselves. I hit the third wave of the set, paddling hard to get on it. I barrel rolled, flipping off the lip, getting ahead of the barrel before it closed off. I finished carving up what was left of the wave and flipped over the top, dropping down on the backside.

"You wen shred, brah."

"No joke? Phew, I thought my 'olos was gone for sure."

"Nah, not you. You stay cool as a cucumber."

We floated there waiting for the next swell to come in. I stared at the reef below me. I saw the manini picking at the limu on the coral and the yellow tang darting from rock to rock.

"Eh brah, that's not your Uncle Willy's outrigger out there, is it?"

"Looks like it. I wonder where he stay? He no dive and there's a one mile drop right outside da bay."

"Maybe he wen drink too much."

"Nah, he no go out like dat. We betta swim in and see if he

stay on shore."

"Man, we just got out here."

"You can stay if you like, I no care."

"Brah no be like dat. I stay coming."

We paddled back to shore. We walked quickly over the hot lava rocks back to the party. I couldn't see Uncle Willy, so I went up to my dad and asked him where he was.

"You know he wen go out to catch some more fish for da party."

"But I thought he wasn't going go if I neva go."

"Well, he wen go."

"He no stay on da canoe."

"What you said?"

"Me and Robert wen go surfing and we wen see Uncle Willy's canoe way out past the bay markers. We thought someone wen let his canoe loose."

"We betta go check 'em." My dad pushed himself up from the picnic table.

"Eh braddah Keala come get the other canoe. We gotta go check on Willy."

They pulled the other canoe into the open water. I watched them paddle out to the markers. We couldn't see Uncle Willy's canoe from the beach, but we saw my dad and Uncle Keala pull to the left of the markers and soon they were behind the lava rocks where me and Robert were surfing. We all waited. I hoped nothing was wrong with Uncle Willy. Robert put his arm around my shoulder.

"No worries, brah. He stay all right. No worries."

We saw my dad and Uncle Keala come back from behind the lava rocks towing Uncle Willy's canoe and paddling as fast as they could. They were shouting. I saw one of my other uncles run off to the payphone near the dock. Mom started shouting. Aunty Mahealani put her arms around my mom who started to cry. I started to get scared. Why was everyone so worried? This was Uncle Willy. The guy who looks like an aborigine and an ancient Indian and threw beer cans at Mr. Kanazawa. There was nothing wrong with him.

My dad dragged his canoe onto the beach while Uncle Keala

pulled Uncle Willy's canoe on to the sand next to dad. Inside the canoe was Uncle Willy, just lying there. He didn't look so much like an Indian. He looked like spilled fruit punch wiped up with a paper towel. Dad pulled him out of the canoe and I could hear mom and the aunties crying. Dad laid him on the sand next to the plank that leads to his house. Nobody touched him after that, not until the ambulance came. Even the men's cheeks were wet. I didn't know how to feel. I even saw Merna crying and I wondered why. She didn't even like Uncle Willy because he liked to hug her a lot. I wondered what happened. Was he sleeping? Was he dead like my cousin? Were we going to have to bury him, too? I should have gone fishing with him. I said I would go. He could have waited for me.

The ambulance showed up. The whirring sirens and flashing lights reminded me of TV cop shows. A shoot out at a bank. The crooks' bodies being taken by the ambulance. The guys in the ambulance came out carrying bags, running up to Uncle Willy. They were asking questions and I didn't really understand what they were saying. Uncle Willy was still just lying there in the sand. I couldn't see the sweat on his face. I could still hear my mother crying. I could see my father holding her.

The men from the ambulance were pushing Uncle Willy's chest and hooking him up to something. One of the guys went to the back of the ambulance and got a stretcher. The guy near Uncle Willy looked mad, like my uncle had done something bad. Uncle Willy was like the crooks at the bank shootout. They did something wrong and they got to ride in an ambulance, and now it was Uncle Willy's turn to ride in the ambulance, his red skin covered in a white sheet as they put him into the back. Wee ooh. Wee ooh. Wee ooh.

Dirty Lickins

Sherri and I were walking home from school when we saw Roger playing in the street. We always walked through Kaimalino Housing. That's where all the people on food stamps lived. Kaimalino was old with paint that looked like black lines dripping down to the concrete and skinny louvered windows that stared down at you as you walked by. Roger was in Mr. Chee's class with us, but we knew he was lolo because he went to a special room for lolo kids. His hair was always dirty, he probably had ukus, and his clothes were always ripped up and holey. Even his slippahs had holes in them. Kaimalino had a huge monkey pod tree that dropped pods all down the slanting street, getting squished by cars, and sometimes we would throw the pods at some of the kids that lived there because they were on food stamps and my mom said that people on food stamps were lazy.

"Teri, dea stay Rogah. Let's go make fun of him. Let's try make him cry."

"Nah, I no like."

"How come? You chicken?"

"I no stay chicken. I just like go home watch She-Ra. Let's just throw some monkey pods at him and go home. I still gotta cook rice and clean da bathroom before I get dirty lickins."

"Shoots, we go."

I liked Sherri. She lived two streets up from me, and she was in the same Ward. We played together at school and sometimes at church, if we could get away with it, and told people that we were calabash cousins, even though we really wanted to be sisters. Walking over to where Roger was playing with his Transformers, I wondered where he got them because his mom was on welfare and both my parents worked, and I never got toys to play with. I didn't even have a Barbie doll. Sherri bent down and picked up a pod from the ground. It looked like a long curving claw that belonged to one of those monsters we read about in school during story time. She started to sing Rogah is lolo, Rogah is lolo, and she threw the pod at his face. She missed, but Roger looked up and smiled.

"Why you stay smiling? Stupid haole. Don't you know wen people stay making fun of you?"

I picked up a pod, the sap sticking to my fingers, and threw it at his head. I didn't miss, and he started crying.

"Rogah is lolo. Rogah is lolo."

"Why for you stay crying, haole? Stop crying, or else we going beef you. You like me give you something to cry about? I going, you know, if you no stop crying."

He just kept crying. Hanabata was hanging down his nose, and he wasn't even wiping it off. I just wanted to keep throwing monkey pods until he knew how stupid he looked. I bent down to pick up another pod, but my hand grabbed a rock. It felt sharp in my hands and the gray dirt stuck to the sap between my fingers and on my palm. I saw Roger's head, and all I wanted to do was throw that rock as hard as I could. Maybe then he would stop being so lolo and I would stop wanting to hurt him.

"Rogah is lolo. Rogah is lolo."

All I wanted to do was stop her and stop him. I knew if I threw it hard enough, they would both shut up. I just wanted to throw and throw. Stop crying, stop crying, stop crying. I lifted my arm over my head and let fly.

"Rogah is lolo. Rogah is lolo. Rogah is lolo.

The rock hit him right in the face and Sherri shut up. He just sat there, not crying, and I wanted to tell him, what, one rock finally shut you up, but I didn't. Then, he started to cry, but it wasn't the loud cry from before. It was a quiet cry. His body just shook, and I didn't like it. I wanted the loud cry back. Sherri touched my arm. We started walking and I could just barely hear Roger crying and I wasn't mad at him for being lolo anymore and for having Transformers when I couldn't even have a Barbie. I just wanted to go home and watch cartoons.

I got home and cleaned the bathroom and straightened up my room and cooked the rice and did my homework in front of the TV. He-Man was fighting the evil Skeletor and She-Ra was lost and the SDF-1 was stranded out towards Pluto and had to fight its way back through the Zentradi fleet to Earth. I heard my mom's car in the garage. She was home early. I quickly turned off the TV and sat at the kitchen table, pretending I was doing my homework. 9 times 9 is 81. 8 times 9 is 72. I hated the times tables, but we got gold stars if we finished the fastest. My mom came in and I got up and gave her a kiss. She smelled like the bank she worked at, like money, or how I thought money smelled like.

"How was your day, mom?"

"Teri-girl, how come you didn't change out of your school clothes? Didn't you clean the bathroom today? I thought I told you to clean the bathroom."

"I did clean it."

"Don't you talk back to me."

She turned me around and pulled at my school clothes. Then, she walked into the bathroom and lifted the seat.

"I see you did clean it. Well as long as you didn't ruin your school clothes. Go change right now and come help me with dinner."

"Yes, mom."

After I changed clothes, I walked back into the kitchen and my mom was standing by the sink, washing lettuce.

"Teri-girl, where's the Tupperware you took your lunch in?"

"In my backpack."

"You never clean them out yet?"

"No, I neva."

"You come here, right now."

"Why?"

"Don't you make me ask you again."

I walked over to her at the kitchen sink and she had the big wooden spoon in her hand. I knew I was going to get it because I forgot to clean out her Tupperware when I got home. She hit me on the head real hard because I have a real hard head, at least that's what she says, and I started crying.

"No cry or I going really give you something to cry about."

She raised the spoon above my head. I tried to stop crying, but my head really hurt. I rubbed my nose on my shirtsleeve and she hit me on the head again. I was grateful that was the first thing she grabbed to hit me with. Could've been my dad's army belt. One time, she got so mad at me and my baby sister because we ate all of her Oreos that she made us pull down our pants and she had my dad give us lickins with his army belt. That belt had ridges on its buckle to keep the belt in place and when my dad whacked me with that part of it, it would catch and yank skin off. My 'okole was sore for weeks. I even had to go to a slumber party, where all the girls showered together, and I couldn't because I didn't want them to see the bruises and scabs. So, I was pretty happy it was just the wooden spoon and not the belt, or the vacuum cord, or the cast iron frying pan, or the back of a knife. I rubbed my face on my sleeve again.

"Go get it, now."

She hit me on my 'okole as I walked to my backpack by the kitchen table. I pulled out the yellow square as big as my hands. There was still food inside and I knew my mom would know that I ate school lunch instead of home lunch and I was really going to get it but it was hamburger day and that beats mushy canned corn beef any day.

"You kids, you neva appreciate anything. Dad and I, we work all day. Your dad, he gets up four o'clock in the morning to work at the hotel and for what? So his kids no appreciate what he works so hard for buy?"

She raised the spoon again. I tried to duck out of the way when I gave her the Tupperware, but she pulled on one of my braids, yanking me back towards the sink. I almost yelled out but I knew if I did, she would pop me one in the mouth.

"What is this? You neva eat your lunch?"

I didn't want to say anything, but I knew that she would whack me if I didn't.

"I neva like eat 'em. Was hambaga day at school, so I wen eat that."

I was crying. Her hand was still pulling my hair. I wondered if my older sister hadn't braided my hair, would mom have been able to grab me so easily? I hated my sister. This was all her fault. She should never have braided my hair. I wouldn't be getting lickins from my mom if it wasn't for her.

"So you wen eat that, huh? You wen waste good food, so you can eat hamburger? Well you going eat it now."

She opened up the container, a stinky sweet smell reached my nose. She shoved the Tupperware in my face.

"Eat it. Eat it now. I want you to lick it clean."

"I don't want to."

She hit me across the back and then on the head again.

"If you don't, I'm getting the belt. Eat it."

The smell made me want to throw up. I didn't want to eat it, but I knew that if I didn't, she would really give me dirty dirty lickins. I lifted the mushy sandwich to my mouth and shoved it in because I really didn't want it in my mouth. I held my breath as I chewed, and my mother just stared at me with that look. I swear she just wanted to break me into little pieces and dump me in the ocean. I was trying so hard not to cry. I wanted to really throw up because I had to breathe and the mushy sandwich was so gross but if I spat it out, she would get the belt. I swallowed and she hit me hard on the head again. I ran to the bathroom and threw up. She came running after me.

"Why are you throwing up? Don't you dare throw up!"

I couldn't stop. I just kept throwing up and crying and I was glad I did change into my home clothes because there was hanabata and mushy corn beef and Roman Meal bread down the front of my t-shirt. I couldn't breathe. I tried to put my hands over my head, but she just kept hitting me again and again, and I couldn't stop heaving. I wanted her to stop. I wanted her to be a good mother. I wanted her to bake cookies. My hands felt broken as she hit them out of the way. Finally, she stopped hitting me and sat down next to me.

"I'm sorry. Sometimes you kids make me so mad."

She rubbed my back right where she hit me and I tried not to move.

"Why don't you go ʻauʻau, and then go to bed. I'll bring you some milk to settle your stomach."

She got up and walked out. I tried to stand but my legs wouldn't hold me up. I crawled into the shower and took off my home clothes and tried to clean myself up. I couldn't stop crying. On TV, parents don't make their kids eat rotten food. I wiped myself off and picked up my clothes. I tried to rinse them but pieces of bread and corn beef stayed stuck to my t-shirt. I squeezed out the water. I tried to clean the tub and the toilet but my head and hands hurt. I knew I was going to get it for messing up the bathroom.

I walked to my bedroom and put on my sleeping clothes. I wiped my eyes and nose on the towel before wrapping my hair because I'm not supposed to sleep with wet hair. It was heavy and made me feel like my hair would come out. I tried to stop crying. I went back to the bathroom to brush my teeth. I couldn't go to bed without brushing my teeth and my breath smelled like throw up. I didn't look in the mirror. I got my toothbrush and put toothpaste on it. I looked at my arms and hands. I wondered what I would tell Sherri.

I knelt down by my bed. I ran a finger along a single raised stripe. I put my hands together, bowed my head and closed my eyes. Dear Heavenly Father, please bless my mother and father. Please bless my sisters and Sherri, and also please bless Roger. In the name of Jesus Christ, Amen.

I pulled off the bedspread and folded it neatly. I got under the blanket and pulled it up to my chin. I closed my eyes. I imagined a mother tucking me in and kissing my forehead and telling me she loved me and to have sweet dreams. And I prayed.

Da Pier

We hemo our shorts and t-shirts and kick off our slippahs. We throw 'em on my backpack and I run off da pier. I pull up my legs to make the biggest splash. My little sister, she stay right behind me. I hit the water hard. It's cool but feels good after walking in the sun. I kick myself up and take a breath. I dive back to the bottom so I can touch it. My ears ache and my eyes burn as I look at the hazy shapes of the coral, rocks, and big tires around me, little groups of striped manini picking the limu off of them. I turn over. I can see my sister above me. I swim up and grab her leg. She kicks me in the head, and I come up coughing and laughing.

"How come you wen try scare me?"

"Cuz funny das why."

"I going tell mom."

"Why? I was just kidding. You know she going give us dirty lickins."

"I no care."

"Fine. Be lidat. Go tell mom. See if I care." I swim away from her towards the little sandy beach against da seawall.

We wen leave our mom where she wen park the car behind World Square. She wen give us five dollars each and told us to come back by six and for not bada her at work. She'd been wearing her short work mu'umu'u. She hated it. She always kept pulling its pink flowers away from her. She worked at the Pearl Factory. They made all kine bracelets and necklaces from freshwater pearls, because they were cheaper than the real ones. They sold real ones, too, but they were really expensive. They had one tank with oysters inside and you could pick one and cut 'em open, and if you found pearls, you could keep 'em. They were like five dollars so you could score big time if you got any kine pearls. Mom had to talk story with the tourists and try get 'em to put their pearl in one setting, you know like one ring or one necklace. She got a good commission if she could do that. And if neva have one pearl, she'd try talk story with 'em and get 'em for buy something else. She'd give 'em one discount, so the tourists no feel like they wen get scammed. One time she got one tourist for buy not only da oyster that neva have pearl but also a real pearl necklace and one ring to match. That was one good day. She wen take us all out Sizzler for steak and all you can eat shrimp to celebrate. Was so ono.

I try catch one small kine wave onto the beach but it isn't big enough for bodysurf. I dunk my head back into the water so my hair not all hamajang and walk to the stairs on the side of da seawall. I want for climb the rock wall next to the dock but I still small kine angry at my sister and I neva like hassle with her. I can see her scrambling up it like one monkey. She going jump in the water before me. I hope she try flip and land on her back. I know she going cry but I not going be looking. When I climb to the top, da pier stay busy. I can see one boat dropping off da tourists from the big cruise ship that stay out in the bay. Just great. They going be throwing coins in da water for us for dive. I know my sister going dive. She neva like spend any kine money but she sure like getting free kine money.

"Hey lolo get tourist stay coming. You going dive?"

"What you think? And no call me lolo or I going tell mom."

I can hear them talking about us.

"Oh look at those cute little brown kids."

"Aren't they adorable? Look at them jump off the dock."

The kids who like money always wait on the dock for see if da tourists going throw money or not. The kids who still stay in the water climb up so fast when they know they stay coming. I just sit on the side and wait for 'em to pass. Some of the kids show off doing flips. I just roll my eyes.

"Should we throw some money in the water for them?"

"Do you think it's safe?"

"Look at them. They are practically fish."

I listen and stare at the dark steeple on top of Mokuaikaua Church. I don't want 'em talking to me.

We wen cross Ali'i Drive before mom's work. We neva like get dirty lickins for bothering her. We wen walk under da big banyan tree next to Hulihe'e Palace, trying not for step on the squashed and stinky seeds all over the ground. The palace used to be the home of the ali'i wen they wen stay in Kona. Now it's one museum. I wen go there for one field trip. The beds stay huge. My tutu said da ali'i were really tall. He wen tell me King Kamehameha was over seven feet. I wen believe it. The palace stay across the street from the church. My dad said the church was the oldest one in Hawaii. We went to the Mormon church up Hamburger Hill so I never been inside. The outside was covered in lava rocks and cement like they wen just scoop up all da rocks around dem for make their church. The roof stay white but the steeple stay brown. I wen hear that the buildings in town no can be higher than the steeple. I was pretty sure da hotel was taller but maybe I stay wrong.

We wen walk along da palace's rock wall before we wen get on da seawall. There was one baby beach but we neva like swim over there. It stay too shallow and we like jump. I wen try for help my little sister climb da wall which was higher than her. She was my kuleana but she really was one brat.

"I no need help."

"Shoots."

I wen watch her try lift her leg up over the top. She look like she was trying for climb out of the pool. Wen she almost wen make 'em, I wen try push her okole up for help.

"I get 'em. I get 'em." But she neva get 'em. So I wen push her okole anyway. I was going laugh at her and ask her why she always neva go up da easy way, but I neva like make her mad because I neva like get hassle all day. She neva even wen say thank you. Then she wen start running.

"Ho slow down. You going fall in da water."

"So what? I can swim"

"Not if you hit your kolohe head on da rocks."

"I no stay kolohe. I going tell mom you called me kolohe again."

"Kule kule. You know she going give us dirty lickins if we stay bada her."

"Then no tell me what for do." See what I stay mean? Kolohe.

"Whatevas. Go drown den. I no care."

"I going tell mom you wen tell me for drown."

"You stay crazy. You like run. Go den. Da wall stay slippery. You going fall. You going hit your head. You going drown."

Lucky calm the water today so no stay slippery but she was too kolohe for notice. Sometimes get big waves and no can walk on da wall. When that happens, we sometimes sit across from it under da big banyan tree next to the Banyan Court Mall and laugh at da stupid tourists that walk on the sidewalk next to da wall. All the locals who stay working in the restaurants and shops just laugh wen da tourists get hit by big waves. I remember one time one guy was walking on the top and he neva even see da wave coming and he got hit so hard he fell off da wall onto Ali'i Drive. They wen have to call the ambulance. I neva wen laugh then.

"Hey little girl."

I hope they aren't talking to me. I look over and, of course, they are talking to my little sister. She smiles at them. Her teeth stay white in her dark summer skin. Her long brown hair stay wet against her back. She stay the perfect little Hawaiian. I see an old haole man waving a big quarter at her. I like tell her for no go but she neva stay listen to me.

"Would you like this quarter?"

I can see my sister's smile get wider. She one shark now. She not going be one tiny manini. He throws it way out into the water. My sister's eyes stay follow it until she knows where it's going for hit and she runs and dives off da pier.

"Look at her go. I don't know if I could swim half so well when I was her age. These kids must be born in the water."

I like tell him that we wen learn because our dad wen throw us in and wen tell us for swim. Sink or swim. Not really hard for learn. My sister's head pops out of the water and she's holding the quarter.

"Hot damn! I can't believe she actually found it."

She puts the quarter in her mouth, swims back to the rock wall and crawls up it like a spider. She takes the quarter out of her mouth, smiles and shows it to the old haole man. His old haole wife looks at my sister with stink eye. "Thank you." She says to the old haole couple.

"We better get going Herbert. We've got a lot of sightseeing to do and we have to be back at the boat by sunset." She pulls her husband hard as he stay staring at my little sister's wide happy smile.

Another tourist walks up to her. He's holding a quarter too. "Would you like to dive for this one too?" She nods. She stay smiling still. I know what she stay thinking. She can buy one ice cream now or play two video games and she not going have to spend da money our mom wen give us. He throws the quarter way past where the old haole man with the angry haole wife wen throw his. Again, my sister, she stay watch it until it's about to hit and she runs as hard as she can, jumps and dives as far as she can.

"Just look at her."

He's just staring at where my sister is swimming under the water. He's not as old as the old haole man but he's still old. He's by himself. No more old stink eye haole wife. No more friends. He stay tall, wearing long white shorts and an orange striped shirt. He watches my sister. She's taking her sweet time. Finally, I see him smile. His teeth stay white in his gold skin. I look out and I see her little head floating on the blue water and her arm is in the air. I neva going hear the end of it. She going brag about how she got both quarters all day. He waves at her, gives her a big thumbs up and walks along the pier to the seawall. I watch him go down Ali'i Drive, his shoulders and blonde head disappearing behind the wall as my sister climbs back up.

"You wen see dat? I da best!"

"Yeah yeah. No need get all high maka maka."

"You stay jealous. Cuz you neva get free money."

"I no stay jealous. I just no like tourists."

"You stay crazy. Tourists stay give us money."

"Yeah they stay give you money but it no stay free."

"Why? We stay already swimming."

"That no stay da point."

"You jealous is why."

I neva like keep hassling with her. "You stay pau swimming? I like go already."

"I like try get more money."

"No more any more tourists." She looks around and they had all moved on to wherever tourists go when they come visit our island.

"Shoots. Let's go."

I pick up our clothes, our slippahs, and my backpack, and we walk across da pier to the other side where the hotel's tourist beach stay. It get one shower we can use. We pass where one of the canoe clubs keep their canoes. They look ready for get in da water. Neva have too many tourists on da beach yet. We walk past the beach to the pool and I try not for listen to da tourists around us.

"This beach is very cute."

"Yeah but it's too small. Too bad it isn't bigger like Waikiki."

"Those tiki look strange. You'd think they'd be scarier."

"I think that's a temple but it's not a very good tourist attraction. Why don't they just tear it down and make something more interesting?"

"We went to the hotel's luau last night. They pulled out a cooked pig from the ground."

"Did you see those poor saps get pulled on stage? They made them wear coconut shell bras and grass skirts."

There's a big sign next to the pool entrance. Hotel Guests Only. I hate that sign. I neva like go swimming in their stupid pool anyways. I turn on the water and rinse all the salt and sand off of me. I think about sitting on the lounge chairs by the pool or soaking in their hot tub.

"Hyaku. You taking forevah."

"Kule kule. I trying for get da sand out of my suit."

I get out and my sister gets in. I dry off and wait for her.

"Now who stay taking forevah?"

"I getting out already." She dries off and we go to the bathroom nearby. It's still clean. Neva have all the sand from all the tourists and locals yet.

"One day I going get so much money for diving. I bet I going get five dollars."

"You going have to dive like twenty times. You stay crazy."

"Why bada you?"

"What tourist get twenty quarters for throw you? You so lolo."

"I not lolo." She gives me the stink eye as she walks out of the bathroom. I wen follow her because I know she stay getting ready for do something stupid like call mom on da payphone.

"Hey where you stay going?" She neva answer me and I knew she going try for get me dirty lickins.

"Fine den. You not lolo." She stops. "You know tourists no care what kid go dive for them, right? They just like watch you get their money."

"So? It's free money. I no care. I stay like diving." She looks at me. She neva have stink eye so I know I stay safe.

"I know dat but it no stay free. You like diving but you stay diving for tourists." I look at all the tourists sitting on the beach in front of da hotel. "They no care. They just want one show." She looks at them.

"Maybe I no care. Maybe they stay lolo for giving me free money."

We walk past the shower by the hotel pool, the beach that get too many tourists, the canoes that stay ready for da water, back to da pier and all the kids that still stay diving and swimming. We climb up on da seawall leaving the pier behind.

Pele's Daughter

The ocean. I can hear it, even here in the church. I want to be out there, but Aunty Haole is dead. I try to peek at her through the pukas between the heads of the aunties and uncles I haven't met. She is lying in a white coffin, her ehu hair spread over a white satin pillow and she is wearing a white mu'umu'u I've never seen before. I shift my sore okole on the hard wooden seat and try to hear what the bishop is saying, but all I can make out is Heavenly Father this and Heavenly Father that. "Stop being ni'ele or I going pinch you," my sister, Ui, whispers to me. So I try to sit still.

Yesterday we drove all the way from Kona to Naalehu. We had to stay with my Uncle Eddie Boy's family. I hate staying with them. My cousins are so lolo. I wanted to stay at Aunty Haole's house, but because of the funeral, Aunty Noe and Uncle Junior were staying there instead. The funeral is at the Mormon Church closest to Aunty Haole's house. We're Mormons, or that's what my mom says. On the wall of our dining room is a little picture with two hands in prayer. It says the family that prays together stays together. I don't get that. We pule all the time. We pule at breakfast, at lunch, and at dinner. I even have to pule before bed. All I want to do while I'm puleing is run away, but I can't. Where would I go? It's an island, and I can't swim to the mainland.

I hate the mu'umu'u my mom made me wear. I'm itchy. It's hot, and I feel trapped. Ui gives me the stink eye. She's three years older than me and she thinks she can boss me around. I give her the stink eye back and shift my okole away from her pinching fingers and wonder why Aunty Haole is dead.

"What stay Leukemia?" I ask her.

"Wen one evil spirit entahs da body and stay make you real sick and den sometimes da evil spirit stay very strong and you end up dead."

"How come get one evil spirit dat do dat?"

"How should I know! I not one kahuna. How come you asking all kind questions? Kule kule or I going tell mom you stay making any kine."

I'm not making any kine but I don't say anything because I know if I talk back, she's going to tell on me, and then I'm really going get dirty lickins for being kolohe in church. I don't know if an evil spirit caused my aunty to die, but I know plenty of people who have problems with evil spirits and they don't die. What about New Year's Eve when we light the thousand firecrackers at the front door to our house. Isn't that to make sure the evil spirits don't get in? And every time we clean the house, mom goes around blessing everything with ti leaves and Hawaiian salt water. Did Aunty Haole not bless her house or light firecrackers to scare off the evil spirits?

The Bishop pules and we all say amen and then people start getting up from their seats. I think they are going to look at Aunty Haole. I hate having to wear this ugly mu'umu'u and the haku on my head. The damn bougainvillea flowers keep falling out, and the little branches keep poking me. At least Ui has to wear them, too. I hope she's just as hot and itchy as I am. I give her the stink eye again, but she doesn't see me. I wish I didn't have to sit next to her. She pulls my hand away from where I am scratching under my bra strap. I just had to start wearing them, and they are so annoying. Ui pulls me up from my seat and drags my brother by his elbow. He doesn't want to go, but she pinches him under his upper arm just like mom does, and he moves. She drags us out into the aisle, "Hayaku! Move it or you going lose it."

As we walk, I remember when we used to visit her during the

summer. She would let me play Pac Man and Pong on her Atari. She had cable, too, HBO, while all we got back home was The Movie Channel. She used to take me horseback riding around the ranch where she lived. It was on the edge of a cliff. There were huge pastures and little lava hills. I always wondered why the cows never ran off the edge. Aunty Haole used to let us sleep in. My mom never lets us do that. We always get up early, even if we don't have school, because we have to clean house or do yardwork. I hate yardwork. Aunty Haole, she let us sleep in, and then she would French braid our hair. She would let us eat the good cereal with marshmallows or the chocolate cereal that made chocolate milk while we watched cartoons. My mom would never let us watch TV while we ate, and she would never buy us good cereal. One time, mom ran out of milk and she made us eat corn flakes with evaporated powdered milk. I never want to do that again. I remember, one time, Aunty Haole made us taro pancakes. They were big, purple and fluffy. I spread plenty of butter all over the top and then drowned them in coconut syrup. They was so ono. I ate like ten.

When she took me horseback riding, she would tell me stories about Pele, the fire goddess. She said that Pele wasn't really one of the original Hawaiian gods. She came from somewhere else and tried to settle on each of the Hawaiian Islands. First, she tried Kauai, but it was too wet. Then, she moved over to Maui, but she got bored too quickly. Finally, she settled for the Big Island. That always reminded me of Goldilocks and the Three Bears, not too wet, not too boring, but just right! Some say she was a beautiful pale woman with bright fire hair, brighter than Aunty Haole's. Some of the people around Kau believe that they are her children. I bet Pele looks just like Aunty Haole. She would talk about Pele's many lovers, like Kamapua'a, the pig god. There's a place in Puna, south of Naalehu, that's all kapakahi called Ka lua o Pele. This is where Kamapua'a finally caught her. Aunty Haole told me that Pele would kill most of her lovers because they couldn't survive her anger when she'd throw her lava at them. Kamapua'a was the only one who could call on the rain to stop her. He also had power over the plants and the wild boars. Every time

Pele tried to cover the land with lava, he would make everything grow again.

Aunty Haole stopped our horses to look at the horizon. Even with the wind blowing so hard that you'd think you'd huli off your horse, seeing where the ocean touches the sky, the dark meeting the light, it somehow makes you just want to be quiet without being told to.

"Whachu smell?" She asked.

I took a breath and all I smelled was cow doo doo.

"Besides that, you kolohe kid."

"I dunno."

"Try think!"

So, I closed my eyes and took a deep breath. I thought about the ocean and the horses and the grasses we were riding in. I felt the wind and heard the surf. I opened my eyes and looked over at her. I wanted to tell her that I really didn't know what I was smelling, but she looked so peaceful. Her eyes were closed and her ehu hair blew across her pale smile.

"No worries," she said as she opened her eyes. "Just remember, you can always stop to smell the cow doo doo." She laughed. You know she's got a pretty laugh, not like my other aunties, whose whole bodies shake when they laugh. Aunty Haole's laugh floats in the air, falling on your ear, soft as plumeria petals.

We continued riding back to the stable as she told me about a Maui ali'i named Ai' wohi ku pua, who was very handsome. While on his way to the Big Island to visit his lover, Laie, he met Pele. Of course, he didn't realize it was her, because she was in one of her very beautiful human forms. He watched her surfing and he just had to have her. They made love that evening and he left her the very next morning. When he reached the Big Island, he was seduced by Polihau, the goddess of the snowcapped mountains. He took Polihau to Kauai with him, but Pele followed them. Being very jealous, she chased them until she got him back. When Ai' wohi ku pua dumped Polihau, she threw snow all over him and Pele until they separated. Then poor 'Ai wohi ku pua was all alone. Aunty Haole said that's what you get when you mess with the gods. I think the stories are funny because gods act just like they're in soap operas. I told Aunty Haole that Pele sounds like she belongs on TV, on As the Ahupua'a Turns.

Even though we are Mormons, we still pay attention to the rules, especially Pele's. Always pick up the old lady in white if you see her walking by the side of the road. Don't carry pork over Saddle Road. Don't remove any lava rocks from the island. We laugh at this rule because tourists think that they can get away with it, but every year they mail all the rocks back to Volcanoes National Park. They don't believe us when we say that it's bad luck to take lava. And they do it anyway. I giggle and my sister gives me the stink eye. Man, I'm gonna get it now. I look around and see that everyone is crying. Why am I not crying? I don't really want to see Aunty Haole in her coffin. Should I start crying? It's our turn and I see she has makeup on. She never wears makeup. She has too much blush on and there's a light brown smudge on the short lace collar of her mu'umu'u. I want to wipe it off, but I'm afraid to touch her. We move past the coffin and turn around, and I see Aunty Noe, Aunty Haole's mom, and she's crying. She's crying so much that her mascara is running down her face. Uncle Junior is trying to help her but he is crying too. I've never really seen adults cry, and to see Uncle Junior crying makes me start crying too. It hurts to cry. We walk past my mom, her brothers and sisters. I hug Aunty Noe and Uncle Junior. My hanabata starts to drip down to my mouth, and I rub it on Uncle Junior's dark aloha shirt. It's rough against my nose. I don't mean to do it, and the people behind him stare at me. I move away and follow Ui back to our seat.

I need Kleenex, but there isn't any. I try to rub off the hanabata onto my mu'umu'u sleeve, but I know that if I do, I'm going to get it for messing it up. I try to stop crying, but I keep thinking about Uncle Junior's face when I finished hugging him. I heard that they had a son, too, but I've never met him. I think they said that he was in prison. I try to ask my sister if she has Kleenex but she says to kule kule as she pinches my brother to make him sit still. I wipe the hanabata with the back of my hand. We have to drive to the cemetery after the service. Where are they going to put all the bodies on the island when there is no more room? I guess they can dump them in the ocean. I wonder why they don't do that now.

The funeral was pau in the morning so that the luau could be in the evening. That, of course, means more work for us kids as the adults sit around drinking Budweiser. One time they let me try a sip. It tasted like shi shi, not that I ever drank my own shi shi, but it sure tasted like what I thought shi shi should taste like. I never understood why they drank so much. Most of the time it was okay because they would talk story and kanikapila, singing about the stars, the wind, the ocean, the land. Sometimes they would beef over stupid things, like when tutu died and no one helped pay for the funeral except for Aunty Noe and my mom. And dad would get so mad when Uncle Kainoa, mom's little brother, would say dad's not family just because he married my mom and that helping to pay for my tutu's funeral didn't make him part of the family either. They would almost throw blows, but some of the uncles, the ones who hadn't drank too much, would stop them. I don't understand why Uncle Kainoa would say that. He's always coming around our house, asking for money, at least that's what mom says.

After we get back from the cemetery, Aunty Mamo makes me sit next to a big ice chest and scoop opihi. I don't mind it so much. Their shells look like little black Chinaman's hats. I just don't like it when they curl up to grip my finger. Scooping opihi is easy, getting them is hard. Sometimes people die trying to pick opihi off the lava rocks. To get the really big ones, you have to climb out and hope the tide doesn't drag you out. My mom says that the best opihi comes from our side of the island. I pick up a spoon and start scooping the little buggahs out of their shells, dumping the opihi into one bucket and the shells into another. Sometimes the aunties would dry out the bigger shells for jewelry. When I was looking through my mom's jewelry Tupperware container, I found an opihi shell as big as my hand. It was all white, and I wondered how they got a black opihi shell to turn white. I asked my mom, and she said that they bleach in the sun. I never understood how people get red, brown, or black in the sun, but black opihi shells turn white. I want to change out of my mu'umu'u but the aunties won't let me because it's still a party, and girls needed to look pretty. I can't even take off my haku and I am still itchy.

When I am done with the opihi, Aunty Mamo makes me scrape coconuts for the haupia. She brings out a board that looks like a broken canoe paddle with a metal scraper on its end. Taking one of the open coconuts from the pile next to me, I bring the white meat to the sharp edge and start to scoop out the inside. My hand feels the loose hairs and rough texture of the shell. My haku shifts to the side as I lean forward to get a better grip. Little red petals drift down into the coconut meat. I'm gonna get it if I mess up the haupia. The petals turn see-through and I see Aunty Haole's pale cheeks covered with blush and her still too pale skin turning it from red to pink. We all stood by the grave. It was deep. I couldn't imagine putting her beautiful white coffin in all that muddy dirt. What will she do when she has to get out of it? Her beautiful white mu'umu'u will be stained and so will her white, white skin. I have always thought it was funny that we called her Aunty Haole even though she wasn't. I try to get the petals out of the wet coconut meat, but I feel something move and I can't breathe and I'm not sure I want to. As I stood above her hole in the ground, I wanted to be riding with her out in the pasture, listening to her stories, smelling her scent. I cry into the haupia, and I know that I will get it, but I just keep scraping the soft white meat from its hard brown shell while red petals fall.

Opihi Tales

Every summer, we'd pack up our camping gear and head to Opihihale, grandpa and dad sitting in the front of dad's beat up truck, me in the back, holding on tightly as we swing around the windy road down south. We'd leave Kona behind as we drove along Queen K Highway, heading towards Mamalahoa. After we'd pass Honaunau, the rainforest would rise up, towering above our heads, and I'd pretend that I was Indiana Jones, riding through caves in a mining cart, trying to beat a wall of water. Sometimes, I wondered if Indiana Jones could surf. Wouldn't that be something? Catching that wall of water right out of the mountain? Dad loved to take the road a little fast, especially when mom wasn't around. I'd always know that the turn off to Opihihale was coming up when dad started to slow down. It was just a little driveway with a gate. If you didn't know it was there, you'd probably miss it. As we pulled up to the gate, dad would hop out and open the lock, swinging the gate open as he did. Then, he'd set his tires to 4WD, so we could make it down the bumpy road to the beach.

Opihihale is our family's land, an ahupua'a stretching from the tip of the mountain out to the ocean, which had belonged to my bloodline for generations. As I was growing up, bits and pieces had to be sold just to pay for the property taxes. Since we could not afford to pay the family lawyer, he and his family owned the beach. Luckily, my family retained the right to go there any time we wanted. To protect his investment, the lawyer had installed another gate where his piece met ours, just in case someone had made it past the first gate. I had always found it interesting that a lawyer would own the very land, where, supposedly, my ancestors are buried.

As we drove slowly down the mountain, the truck rattling as it was jostled by the unpaved road, we passed through a rainforest filled with guava, papaya, and mango trees before passing through a field of spear grass. I hadn't envied the person who'd have to clean that mess up. Once, we'd cleaned an acre of it, bending down in the hot sun, trying to pull that crap up by its roots, our ungloved hands pricked and bleeding. When we cleared the grass field, I could see our campsite. There were tables and coconut trees and the outhouse seemed to be standing which was good. The last time we had come down, a couple of drunk cousins decided they wanted to see if they could move it and it ended up rolling down the hill and breaking against the lava rocks. Dad had to build a new one and he wasn't too happy about it. I could see the whole coast. I would always imagine I could see all the way to Kona, on the one side, all houses and hotels, and Kau on the other, all lava deserts and pastures. There were no boats on the water yet. I knew that come nightfall divers would be trolling our waters, trying to swim up to our shores, searching for spiny lobsters. Sometimes, we would throw rocks into the water to try and scare them off since they always caused the fish to disappear, disturbing their natural feeding grounds. I had always wondered what they thought as they made their way back to their boats. Damn crazy Hawaiians! Our campsite wasn't a traditional campsite, at least not in the way most people expect. Even though it was a beach, there wasn't any sand. Not really. It was mainly crushed lava rocks and gravel that had been trucked down to make the ground even. At least that was one good thing the lawyer did.

We'd spread out a tarp high over the tables and string it up between the coconut trees and the truck. I could see dad and grandpa scanning the tide to see when it would be a good time to go fishing. I loved going fishing with them, especially at night. We'd sit out on the point with our poles dangling bait in the water, waiting for the schools of menpachi and 'aweoweo to start feeding. As we sat, dad and grandpa would take turns talking story. They'd always talk about work or fishing. Who was getting a promotion. Who was getting fired. What season was the best for which fish. Whether it was good to use fresh, real, or fake bait. They seemed to always have something to talk about. Yet, sometimes, they would just sit. I wasn't sure which I liked better, but quiet can be nice. I could hear the water lapping against the rocks or forever flowing in and out of the caves to our left. We were lost in our own thoughts as the stars passed overhead when grandpa asked, "You see that light out over the ocean?"

"Yeah. What stay dat?" I asked.

"That's a fireball from one evil kahuna."

"There's no such thing. Dat's probably an airplane."

"Airplanes don't fly that low." Dad said.

"Maybe it's a star." I hoped.

"Wen I was one keiki, I saw three right at this spot." I wanted to laugh, but I knew that he was serious because he wasn't looking at me. He was staring at the horizon.

He was just a few years younger than me when it happened. He talked about how you have to be very careful. You never know when someone will curse you. He was raised to never cut his hair or fingernails at night and that he must always burn them when he did. He was taught that if he didn't, the Kahuna 'ana 'ana would use the pieces to cast an evil spell on him. He really didn't believe it, but some superstitions are hard to break.

"One night, I went fishing with my father, your Great Tutukane. We were throwing nets into the water over a school of menpachi wen three big, green fireballs went right over our heads." His free arm cut the air above him.

"What happened?" I leaned forward.

"I thought for sure we was going get it, but Tutu, he told me not to look up, so, I closed my eyes really tight, and I prayed."

"So, what did it look like?" I was trying not to rush him.

"You'd think that it was really hot, being one fireball, but it wasn't. It felt like we were up on Mauna Kea. It got real cold, real fast.

It never even look like fire, not really, but I wasn't sure what else for call 'em." He took a swig of his beer. "Even though I wasn't supposed to, I looked up real fast and the fireballs were hovering right above us." His hands went to his crotch, "I really thought my 'olos was gone for sure, but Tutu just yelled 'Auwe! Don't you think you can scare us! I know who you stay and I going find you in the morning!' Then, one funny thing wen happen. The fireballs went straight up, turned mauka, and disappeared."

"What? How come there was fireballs after you?"

"I never know this at the time, but Tutu had one girlfriend in Miloli'i and he wen try break it off with her because he was married and he knew if Tutu Wahine found out, he was going lose his 'olos for sure. Anyway, his Miloli'i girlfriend never like listen. She told him that he was hers and her father was one kahuna and he was going make sure that Tutu would never leave her, and if he tried, she was going make sure he ended up dead." I could see my dad nodding his head. I wasn't sure, but I think he had heard this story before.

"How you wen find out about all of this?" I had never heard about Great Tutu having girlfriends before and I had wondered what else they'd never told me.

"Wen I was a little older than you stay now, Great Tutu wen sit me down and told me what really happened with the fireballs. He said he had thought he wen fall in love with one pretty wahine in Miloli'i. Her family were fishermen, too. He came down to her village one time to get some opelu for Tutu Wahine, who was pregnant and craving dried opelu. He said she had the prettiest smile he had ever seen and he couldn't resist, so he spent the night with her. He left her the next day and went back to Tutu." Grandpa looked over at dad, but dad was staring into the surf below.

"Did she know?" I couldn't imagine dad trying to have a girlfriend. Mom would've probably cut his 'olos off with the meat cleaver.

"He never tell her nothing, but you know how it is. Everyone knows everyone's business. Plus that crazy wahine started talking to everybody about how they was going get married and have one big family. Wen he heard all of this, he was so afraid that Tutu was going kill him, but she told him to go and make sure this wahine knew that he was married and that she better stop telling stories, or else. So, he went down to Miloli'i again to tell her that it was over and she just went lolo. She started screaming, trying to scratch and throw blows. Then, her father came out and looked at him, and he knew that it wasn't over. He wasn't afraid, but he was worried. He knew the father was going be trouble. He went home and told Tutu everything. Then, Tutu told him in that voice, you know the one your mother use on you wen you being kolohe?"

Of course, I knew what he was talking about. He looked over at me and smiled, but it was a strange smile, one that didn't travel up his face.

"She said, 'I will take care of this and bless the house and the kids, but if you ever do this again, you going wish she had killed you.' And he knew this was no joke."

"I don't get it. How did the fireballs find you?"

Tutu leaned over to me and whispered, "She kept one piece of him." I had shaken my head trying to wrap my mind around what he was saying.

"So, he had left some hair or toenails behind?"

My dad laughed, "Hey, maybe we shouldn't be talking about that kind stuff." Tutu shrugged his shoulders, and I waited for the rest of the story.

He cleared his throat, "She had a piece of him and she had given it to her father. He could not help her because Tutu Wahine had blessed us all, so he waited. He knew Tutukane would be alone, especially on a moonless night as that was the best time to fish for menpachi."

"So, he waited until he knew Tutu would be going fishing again? Not even." I just couldn't believe it.

"Oh yeah. He waited and that's wen those fireballs came after Great Tutu and me, but Tutu knew what it was wen he saw it and he wasn't scared."

"I would have been shitting my pants." I said this before I

realized what had come out of my mouth. Dad and grandpa laughed, their eyes watering, their bodies doubling over.

Grandpa wiped his eyes on his shoulder. "True. True. I felt that too." He sipped his beer. I think he was trying to decide what to say next. "The very next morning he went back to Miloli'i and told that lolo wahine and her kahuna father that his family was ali'i and that their mana was more powerful. If they ever tried to hurt him or his family again, he would burn down their hale and he didn't care if they were in it." I was very shocked by this. I never really thought that our family could be violent, but I saw that my grandpa believed that his father had meant it, and sometimes, I think I did, too. I had never really believed in evil kahunas or evil spirits, no matter how many times my mother threatened that the obake would get me if I didn't clean my room, or do my chores, but I realized that maybe there was some truth to all of it after all. Maybe, I shouldn't discount a thousand years of beliefs. I mean I don't really cut my hair or toenails at night even though I know that nothing will happen to me. I preferred to be in a blessed house, especially after a thorough cleaning. I can still remember my mother whispering as she walked through the house, a ti leaf doused in Hawaiian salt and water, sprinkling, "Send this back sevenfold. Leave our house evil spirits. Send this back sevenfold."

"You know that they buried King Kamehameha here?" Grandpa asked.

"Not even. He no stay here." Like anyone that important would be buried in Opihihale I thought to myself.

"No joke. A part of him stay in one of the caves here. We don't know where he is because the chief that wen bury him never told where exactly he stay." He cast his line out again.

"No worry. He no stay believe you, but you can still tell him how you wen find out." Dad said, baiting another hook.

So, grandpa opened another can of Bud and settled into his chair and started telling us about when he used to sit with his uncles listening to their stories about how all of their fathers were warriors in King Kamehameha's army as they chewed on awa root.

"I really didn't believe them, but it was still good talk story."

One of the uncles brought out a club with shark teeth, which was given to him by his father. His father told him that this club had killed many warriors and to keep it safe. And as he promised to, his father began to whisper to him about the story of how King Kamehameha's body was hidden away. As was tradition in Old Hawaii, special family members would hide the body, so that no one could steal its mana, but because he was so important, they decided to split up his body. They took some of his bones to the place of his birth. Some were kept near a Temple of Ku, although Queen Kaahumanu would not have been very happy to hear that her husband still believed in the Old Ways as she had forced everyone to become Christian by eating bananas with her son, Prince Liholiho. The last place was kept a secret from everyone but the person who hid it. The uncle told Tutu that it was his father who had the responsibility of hiding the bones of Kamehameha at Opihihale. He didn't help prepare the body as that was the job of the kahunas, but he had heard of what they did. They would boil off the meat because the mana was stored in the bones. So, when Tutu's uncle's father received a part of the king, it had already been wrapped in a white kapa cloth. He was told not to open or look at it, and if he did, the worst evil would visit him. When he heard this, he became afraid. He did not dare open it and he hid the bones away in a sack so no one would know what he was doing. He began to walk on the King's Trail to Opihihale. When he got there, he searched for a sign of where to put him and a mist fell over the area and he heard a voice tell him quietly to follow it, and he did. He followed the voice because he had become blinded by the mist and finally he came to an opening in the cliff. All his life he had walked along his family's land and had never noticed this particular cave. He didn't question it, but quietly walked as far as he could to the back of the cave, searching for a puka to place the bones into. Then, the voice whispered "Look to your right," and he saw an opening hidden by a boulder that protruded slightly from the face. "Put it in there," the voice whispered, and he did. He walked back to the light of the cave opening, trying to find his way back to the trail, when the mist lifted and the sun shone as hot and bright as if there were no mist. And, when he looked back the way he had come, there was nothing but a field of smooth pahoehoe lava. He tried to find the cave on several occasions, but no matter how hard he tried, he could not.

"So that's why no one knows where it is? Some mystical mist came down and he found some weird cave? How is that true?"

"I know. I know. This is just one story I heard. You like hear the rest, or not?"

"Sure, sure, I was just asking."

So, every day for a month he searched for the cave. He didn't tell anybody about what happened, not even the kahunas. He was just curious about where the bones were. He walked up and down the King's Trail, searching for a cave in the cliff that can be entered without climbing but he never found it. He started walking home, defeated, when the mists fell again. He knew what was going to happen, and he stopped and calmly waited for the voice, but it wasn't the woman's voice from before, but the strong low voice of an ali'i, and he immediately put his forehead to the ground. He didn't look up but he sensed a powerful presence.

"I know that you have been looking for me, but you must stop. Our family must protect our mana and if anyone should find the places where I rest, they will have our mana and power over us."

He wept to hear those words and knew that what he had been doing was wrong. No one should look for the dead once they have gone. And his searching had caused Kamehameha's spirit to awaken.

"There will be many lives lost and many lives given and one day we will be a great people again. Stop looking for me and you will be found."

I had looked at grandpa and wondered why he was telling me all of this.

"All the uncles started to laugh. 'You lolo. Kamehameha never speak to your father. He just wen drink too much awa and wen scramble his head.' He looked up at them in silence, his eyes burning as he shifted the club in his hands. The other uncles quieted down and shifted uncomfortably in their seats.

'I never say you had to believe me, but this is what my father told me, and you know what? I carried his bones along the trail, too. The mists came for me and I placed him in the same cave as Kamehameha. I walked out and never looked back. I have never looked for that cave and I never going.'"

Grandpa stopped talking and looked over at my dad. "I have never looked for that cave either, and even though we cannot bury our dead as our ancestors did, I think that I would like for what's left of my body to be placed here. I would like to join the many relatives that have passed here. I would like to join my son."

"Son? What son?" Again, I had wondered what they weren't telling me.

"My brother," dad sighed. "You weren't born yet and we were both barely teenagers." He sat back. I could see that his eyes had closed and I wasn't sure if I wanted to hear what he had to say. "It was the baby luau for your aunty and we were in charge of getting the opihi for the party. We walked down the mountain to the point, where we knew there would be plenty of opihi, really big ones. Your uncle wasn't afraid, but he knew that I was. We scrambled out over the rocks, our opihi bags hanging from our belts, knives strapped to our legs. We had come down at low tide and we had a couple of hours to scrape them off the rocks before high tide started to come in. We knew that the further out we went, the better the pickings. We tried to outdo each other, hanging by one hand, our toes clinging to little pukas in the slimy lava rock. Soon, our first and second bags were filled, but we needed at least 10 bags total to feed all the people at the baby luau. So, out we went again, each time coming back with a full bag as the tide slowly came in. The crashing waves didn't seem to bother him. He kept going further and further out. I hung back trying to see if I had missed anything closer. I wasn't being chicken. I just didn't want to get slammed by the waves or get caught in a blowhole, my body trapped, the water forever pushing my body in and out, no family even able to get me. I just couldn't handle that. I just stayed close to the shore, but my brother just kept going lower and lower, below the tideline, scraping off every big opihi as if it mattered what size those little fuckers were. All anyone would do was eat it and what was that worth? I think it was his pride that pushed him to go out to the edge of the point, to brave the incoming tide. As he reached down to grab an opihi sticking to the pink underbelly of a limu crusted lava rock, a massive wave crashed him into the rock he was clinging to and I saw just his hair as the water dragged him under. The very thing I feared for myself was happening to him. I wished I could have saved him but I knew that if I tried to save him, I would be caught in the same blowhole. I was so afraid, I couldn't move. I started crying because I knew that I could do nothing to save him. I have always carried that with me."

Grandpa had looked at dad with what I think now was sadness and regret. I had thought at that moment that grandpa would hate dad for letting his son die, but I realized that death is just a part of our lives. As we fished and took the lives to feed ourselves, sacrificed our lives to protect our families, risked our lives to get that perfect opihi, I wondered if our trips to go fishing was a way to connect to my uncle and for me to know that maybe one day I too would be talking story to my children and grandchildren, letting them know the strength of our history and the convictions of our beliefs. I knew that one day I, like my father before me, would spread my father's ashes hoping that the mist will come, letting me carry my father to the place of my ancestors.

Tita

Our mango tree died the day Tita was born. It was not the slow death of starvation, but a quick moment of green, turned to scorched leaves and rotting fruit. Pulp blackened as foul waves filled the yard, strangling the soft, sweet perfume of tuberose. We believed the tree had died from blight, festering deep before bursting forth. As its neighbors, the tangerine and mountain apple, did not suffer a similar fate.

A source of comfort, our tree had provided many a May Day pickle, filling bazaar tables with mayonnaise jars of green and pink. The time spent creating these pre-summer delicacies reinforced family bonds, smiles and laughter filling the warm air. Children climbed outstretched limbs. Less adventurous adults grabbed branches with hooks on long bamboo poles. Each reached for clusters of unripened fruit. "Watch out! Don't fall! Don't break the branch. Pull gently." Branches shook as clusters quivered and fell, crashing to the dirt. Kids, too small to climb, dodged plummeting fruit. "Be careful! Stop running around! Help pick the mangoes off the ground."

Overflowing sacks sprawled on clean linoleum floors as we washed, peeled, and sliced. We treated ourselves to a quick bite of shoyu and vinegar soaked pieces, the tart saltiness filling our mouths. Jars and their blue lids waited, still hot from the stove. A gallon jug that once held sticky red syrup now carried pink vinegar, which we poured into mango-filled bottles, as stained fingers pressed down firm green slices. We'd line them up in the icebox out back, "Now, make sure you don't touch any of the pickle mango."

After a few days, we would pack them up and bring them to the school's playground. Our table sat next to the royal court's stages. Each stage, an island decorated in its royal color: red for Hawaii, yellow for Oahu, white for Niihau, upon which princesses sat, adorned in lehua, mokihana, and hinahina blossoms, their escorts dripping in maile leis, fragrant green vines brushing against knees. With people lining up to buy our family specialty, we prided ourselves on selling all of our pickles every year.

Tita's birth overshadowed our loss, for a little while. When she came into the world, she was a bundle of stillness, and she did not greet us with a hearty cry to prove her existence. When we took her home from the hospital, the nurses admired her silence, "What a good baby." She never smiled. She didn't even cry, her pink limbs flailing to be comforted. We could not bring ourselves to admit, to pierce the air around her with a suggestion of abnormality. We wanted a giggle, a gurgle, a goo. We searched for any sign of the ordinary.

In her crib, she would stare beyond her tropical fish mobile, lazily spinning in the afternoon breeze, out the louvered window at some imperceptible point. We could sense her concentration, a palpable entity next to her once thoroughly examined, now unused and unloved toys. We wondered, and we waited. We hoped she would respond to our attempts at cajolery, distorted faces and high-pitched noises "Look at daddy. Smile at mommy. Who's got cute little feet? Aunty's going to eat those cute little feet," all competing with an alien indifference.

She did not acknowledge her bodily discomforts. She accepted our ministrations without compliance or complaint. When we changed her diaper, decorated in ducks and butterflies, she would shift her eyes and meet ours, briefly, no kicking legs, wandering hands, or urine-discharging arcs, just a simple lack of acknowledgement. We never knew when she was hungry. A cry never woke us in the middle of the night. There were no struggles for who gets to sleep and who has to wake up. When she did eat, we saw her tongue, methodically exploring the bottle's nipple, her hands moving over smooth sides. We wanted her to take pleasure in phenomena, in consumption and excretion, but she gave us nothing.

Finally, we took her out into the world, her fine dark hair in pink bows. Her little feet in white frilly socks and black mary janes. Anxiously, we awaited some signal, a message of appreciation from her. Passersby would coo and tickle as we walked through a store. She would give each admirer a cursory scan, never consenting to demean herself with the expected giggle or hand grasp. "Isn't she a cute baby? How many months? Is she alright?" We hoped.

We began to avoid her. We didn't want to hold her. We would walk past her room, denying her existence. No peek-a-boo. No sweet lullabies. No make-believe. We were afraid.

Then, one day, Tita began to walk.

She picked herself up and walked out of her room. No wobbles. No suddenly swift sit downs. Just her little legs walking as if it were the easiest thing in the world, as if man had never once walked hunched over, knuckles dragging through the dirt. She strode along the hallway, through the bedrooms, intently examining each item. Her hands were not the clumsy tools of an infant but skillful instruments sliding along edges and around corners. They did not linger or pause. We thought what an exceptional child and welcomed her genius as if her actions were a result of our own manufacture. Deftly, she lifted and replaced the substances of our lives as if their nature were fleeting. "What is she doing? What is she looking for?"

At last, she walked into the kitchen, her bare feet slapping against the floor, her hands gliding along cabinets and the icebox door. She stopped when she saw the screen door to our backyard. She stared. We could hear her breathing, deep and slow. We could not remember the last time we heard her breath, and we embraced its deliberate passage. We followed her gaze to the darkened remnants of our mango tree. The sickly sweet smell of ruptured fruit, littering the sparsely green ground, drifted in on the trades. We pushed the screen door open. "Do you want to go outside? Do you want to play? What do you want?"

She turned around, went back to her room, and stopped walking altogether.

Her silence infected our lives. Still afraid to voice our fears, words drifted through our minds: aberrant, unnatural, odd. We needed her to be more than a confirmation of our genius. So, we began to question our own desires as we observed her. It was as if a bubble had formed around her, pushing outward from her being, encroaching on our lives. Unknowingly, we welcomed its empty embrace.

In the night, an aroma floated through our house, and we followed its trail back to Tita's room. As she lay in her crib, we stepped closer to discover that the smell came from her little body. Immediately, we identified the scent of mango flowers. We picked her up, but touching her released a stronger fragrance as if we had rubbed our thumb against a tiny petal, bruising it. Her eyes were closed and she did not open them when we placed her back in her crib. We prayed.

Tita died the day our mango tree was born. It was immediate. One moment of careful consideration transformed into a release of pressure confined too long. Our mango tree sprung back to life the minute Tita took her last breath, spreading branches and flowering fruit, sprouting back into our existence.

Talking Story about Kilauea

'Ole – No Numbah

Pele had traveled across the islands, finding her final resting place here, on the Big Island. Living in Kona, she didn't really mean much to us because all the things she did happened on the other side of the island. She had power. We all knew the stories. It was her way to destroy and create, but she was just another god the ancient Hawaiians had worshipped.

We danced, sung, chanted about her, to her. She wasn't dead to us, not really. We draped ourselves in her stories. We respected the myths and legends. We knew she was both proud and jealous. She took her lovers at will and destroyed anything that stood in her way. It's not like we were afraid of her, but an earthquake here and there, and a part of you, deep down, started to believe. Believe that maybe what they said about her was true, was real. Nothing like feeling your house shake and your bed rattle to make you consider her wrath and her power. Of course, this was all buried underneath layers of belief, belief in men on the moon, belief in the glories of God, belief in cartoons every Saturday morning.

'Ekahi – Numbah One

The first time I saw lava with my own eyes, I think I was eight. We went to Hilo to see it and we had stopped at Ken's House of Pancakes to eat. From the parking lot, we could see a red glow over the slopes of the mountainside. I just couldn't imagine it was anything more than a big fire. I had seen a really big fire once when we went to visit my cousins down south in Pahala. They were burning the sugar cane for harvest. It was so haunas. I had to hold my nose closed and breathe through my mouth, but even that didn't stop me from smelling it. I hated it. It reminded me of when they burned the garbage at the dump. Even though it was miles from our house, the trade winds would blow it up the mountain. It never smelled like what a fire at the beach or in the grill smelled like. It didn't smell delicious. It didn't smell good. I had never understood why the sugar cane needed to be burned for them to pick the cane. We had some growing in our yard at home and we just cut it down with a sickle-shaped knife and sliced the outside off so we could eat the inside. Sugar cane reminded me a lot of bamboo, but where bamboo was empty, sugar cane was not. We would suck on the sweet stringy pieces for hours, trying to chew through them to get out all of the sweetness.

We stood out there, all of us, wrapped in jackets. The cool evening breeze coming off Hilo Bay made us shiver. I stared so long at that glow that my eyes watered. I wiped them on my aunty's sleeve as she held me, keeping me from running out into traffic, like I was a little baby. I could hear people around us talking about people losing their homes because the lava was heading right for them.

"Stop wiping your hanabata on my jacket, Hinalani, or else," her arms pinning me to her, so my head couldn't move.

"I neva do that. You stay lying aunty."

I thought she didn't like me very much because she was always holding me or pinching me or slapping my okole. I wasn't even kolohe, not like some of my other cousins. She was my aunty but she lived with us and she was younger than my two older brothers. I never really thought it was weird. It just was. There were families filled with siblings who were hanai, calabash, cousins. I had a friend whose sister was her mother but we didn't talk about it. So having an aunt who was my sister didn't seem that strange to me.

She played volleyball. She was really good at it. I'd watch her play when we were staying late after school. Sometimes she'd let me join in the circle when they'd practice. I'd try my best to keep the ball in the air, the other girls showing me how to hold my hands together, how to hit the ball just right, so it wouldn't hurt. I didn't feel like a little kid when she'd let me join them. My little hands and arms bumping the ball just as high and far as the others. We smiled and called out when the ball was ours. It sometimes felt like we'd play that way for hours. The ball staying always off the ground.

She was also a cheerleader. I liked seeing her wear her blue and white cheerleading outfit and carrying her pompoms. Her long brown hair made into two tight french braids, tied off with blue and white ribbons. She loved french braiding my hair. She'd pull my hair so tight, I could feel the skin of my eyelids and cheeks stretch. A few times, she'd use the rubber bands with the plastic marbles. She'd pull them so tight that they would slip out of her hands and snap hard against my head. I used to be their mascot but I wasn't good enough, at least that's what my mom said. I never yelled loud enough, even though I shouted as loud as I could. I never jumped high enough, even though I could do a toe-touch and land in a side split. I never said the cheers perfectly, even though my mother would make me repeat them over and over until I cried. I didn't like cheerleading after that.

"Hina, stop being kolohe."

"I not being kolohe. How come you think I stay being kolohe?"

"Because you keep moving and wiping your hanabatas on me. That's why."

"I not even. You stay lying."

"No make me tell your mada."

"Okay already, I going stop moving."

I was cold, so I leaned against her and stared at the glow of a fire I couldn't feel, her arms wrapped tightly around me.

'Elua – Numbah Two

One time I wen hear one story about how Pele wasn't even

Hawaiian. She wasn't even one original god. She wen come to Hawaii on a boat that wen look like one haole's boat. Not like the ones built by the Hawaiians. Some people wen say the standard for the god Lono wen look like the mast and sails of one haole ship. That's why we wen welcome Captain Cook when he wen land, cuz we thought he was Lono. Neva wen help he wen come during Makahiki. No wonder he wen stay so long. I would stay too if I wen land at the best party in the islands. Neva shoulda come back though.

Pele she get red hair. Garans she the goddess of fire and lava and volcanoes. Hawaiians they no have real red hair. We get brown hair that look ehu or can fade ehu in the sun but it no stay red kine hair like Ronald McDonald's. I no think Pele's hair stay Ronald red either but maybe more like the kine hair the Irish or Scottish get. I stay part Irish but my hair no turn ehu in the sun. I get one friend who stay Hawaiian but she stay pale white with strawberry blonde hair.

"How can you be Hawaiian? You look so haole."

"My granmada stay pure Hawaiian."

"Not even. You stay lying."

She even get green eyes. Neva seem fair she get one pure Hawaiian granmada and still look like one perfect haole. That's how I think Pele stay really look like but not the kine strawberry blonde but the kine hair that look like burning fire, all kine reds, oranges, and yellows.

I wen think maybe she was somebody who wen come to Hawaii, like one Viking. I wen learn in social studies that the Vikings wen discover America way before Columbus, so why den couldn't one woman with fire red hair land in Hawaii? I like think she was so beautiful that all the men wen want her so she wen stay and her affairs and fights wen become part of the myths of Hawaii.

'Ekolu – Numbah Three

We got up at four in the morning. Dad wanted us to be on the road before 4:30, so we could be at the volcano before the tourists.

He didn't want to make the offering with tour buses pulling up to the crater.

I asked him, as we piled into the Bronco, why we needed to do this every year, and he told me, "You know your grandfada was one kahuna, right Kalani?"

"Yeah, I stay know that."

"Well, wen he was alive, he had to make an offering to Pele every year. It was his kuleana."

"Why? He neva believe. We go church every Sunday."

"I know we all stay go church on Sundays. That no matter."

Sometimes he'd say things that I just couldn't understand. How can someone go to church and still give offerings?

We drove down to the edge of Haleamaumau Crater. The wind picked up dust and flew it into our faces as we all got out of the car. I didn't want to be there. I had slept the whole way, dreading having anyone see us there as my dad put on his special white tapa for the offering. He looked like he was going to a toga party like on Animal House. I wanted to laugh but I didn't want to get lickins. When he was dressed, I watched him pick up his offering and walk to the edge, placing the ti leaf wrapped rock on the ground before him as he started to chant. I never asked him what he said and he never told me but we all stood silent behind him.

I prayed for no one to see me there, standing by our Bronco, waiting for my toga-wrapped father to finish his prayer chant. I thought about the stories we would tell ourselves of human sacrifices. We'd laugh at virgins being thrown into volcanoes to appease some crazy, wrathful god. Pele didn't care if she got virgins. She'd probably want someone with experience, we'd laugh. Some gods, like Ku, preferred conquered warriors, and they'd be thrown into the shark-filled waters of Kawaihae. The idea of sacrifice to any god seemed ridiculous to me. As if throwing a helpless human, or even a criminal, into a caldera would ever stop it from erupting and destroying anything in its path. As I watched my father finish his chant, I wondered why we still offered anything to Pele or to any gods at all. I began to think that maybe going to church was just as strange as my father praying in his white robes at the edge of a sleeping caldera with the sun rising above him.

'Eha – Numbah Four

"Did you hear one guy almost fell out of one helicopter over in Volcano?"

"Not even! Serves him right. What do they think going happen if you fly a helicopter so close to Pele?"

"Stay crazy. I neva would even go in one helicopter in da first place."

"Even if was free?"

"Even."

"Shoots, I would go."

"You stay lying."

"No, garans, I would go."

"I like see da lava but I no stay crazy enough to fly in one helicopter, especially if da kine no moa doa."

"What? Neva have doa?"

"Nah neva have one. They wen hemo the doa special so tourists can feel da heat from the lava."

"Stupid haoles. But he neva fall out?"

"Nah. He neva. Good thing but I bet Pele stay hungry for moa haoles."

"Rogah that."

'Elima – Numbah Five

Today is volcano camp. She is excited to hang out with her friends, camping and talking story. Every year, the sixth graders hop on a bus and go to the other side of the island to spend a few days learning about the Volcanoes National Park. They meet at school early. She giggles with her friends as they climb into the bus.

"Look out. Ryan stay checking you out."

"No way!"

"You know he going try something tonight, I bet."

"You stay lying. He no like me li dat."

They decide to sing and play cards for the two-hour trip on Saddle Road. It's fun and bumpy, and they squeal as the bus bounces them in the air as they go over the little hills.

"Man, we going have so much fun."

"No kidding."

They arrive at the camp and it's a two-story dormitory. They are separated by girls and boys, each to a side of the building.

"Dinner is at eight. Come to the fire circle." Their teachers say. "We will have hot dogs, s'mores, and hot chocolate."

They are all happy to hear the news. They take their stuff to their rooms and laugh as they put on jackets and sweaters because it's colder than they are used to. They head out. The fire is big and they all sit on the stone bleachers, waiting for dinner. She looks up at the sky, the stars are so bright. She likes looking up at them. They were really lucky because they had special streetlights on the island so the telescopes could see the stars from Mauna Kea. She can see Venus. It is burning high above her.

She can see her breath and it makes her laugh. Her friend, Jen, looks up with her and also laughs when she sees her breath. It is so strange for them to feel so cold. They watch as everyone is given hot dogs and metal skewers. They are excited to roast marshmallows and drink hot chocolate. They push their skewers through their hot dogs, the red flesh giving away easily. They giggle as they huddle around the fire, talking story about the boys on the other side. They keep warm as they turn their skewers round and round. Soon they get bored and ask for hot dog buns and plates and the teachers pass them out. They put their burnt on the outside red hot dogs into cold buns and run to the table filled with condiments and chips to put ketchup and relish on them. They bite down and juices pop and flow in their mouths. They smile, happy and content in the moment.

The teachers pass around marshmallows and hot cups of cocoa and they all erupt in cheers. Their metal skewers piercing white puffs of sugar that dance in the flames. She sips her cocoa and trips over the foot of the friend in front of her, spilling her cocoa all over. Her friend screams as the hot liquid runs down her legs. She can see skin bubble but she thinks that can't really be happening. The teachers come running and she is scared she will be in trouble. They carry her friend into the dormitory and everyone starts talking about what happened. She feels bad and hopes her friend is okay. Later, she comes back, her clothes changed, but there are bandages on her leg. Her friend doesn't talk to her and she can't seem to say she is sorry. The joy of roasting marshmallows and making s'mores has left her. She doesn't even acknowledge Ryan when he sits next to her, his skewered marshmallow waving above the fire. That night after campfire songs, pajamas, pillow fights, and late night talk story, she buries her head under her blanket because the whole night her friend didn't speak to her and still hadn't let her say sorry. She tries not to cry because she doesn't want them to hear her and she falls asleep, the image of her friend's skin bubbling up huge and dark brown, like the burnt flesh of the roasted marshmallow on Ryan's skewer.

They hike across Kilauea Iki the next morning, waking up early while it's still dark. That's a really weird thing about coming to this side of the island. The sun actually rises from the ocean. All of her life, she has seen it rise over Mt. Hualalai. It makes her feel as if the sun is doing something wrong or she is doing something wrong by being somewhere she doesn't belong. When she looks at the sun, it doesn't look like her sun. The light, the clouds, they are different. She thinks maybe it will feel even stranger if she ever leaves the island.

Kilauea Iki is a crater. There are some bushes and a tree here and there but it's a flat ocean of lava rock, some smooth paho'eho'e, some sharp a'a. There is a simple trail that runs down almost the exact center. They walk in pairs with their trip buddies. She's lucky to be with her best friend, Jen. She feels like she is walking on the moon, all rocks and dust. She actually met two astronauts once and she got to wear a spacesuit. It was pretty cool. One of them, Onizuka, had grown up on the same mountain. She used to go to his family store all the time, especially after they picked coffee, so she was really sad when the space shuttle exploded with him onboard. They were all shocked at school because they couldn't believe it had happened. She remembers it vividly as they had played it over and over on the news, especially in Hawaii as he was one of their own. She remembers there was an actual teacher onboard too. She often wondered if her own teachers would have been brave enough to go into space. She had always wanted to go into space, to land on the moon, to travel to Mars, to visit the moons of Jupiter, to cross the interstellar divide to Alpha Centauri.

"You think we going get s'mores again tonight?"

"Of course! We stay camping! No can go camping without 'em!" She tries to sound happy about another cold campfire night. She hopes her friend will forgive her for spilling cocoa on her. She hadn't seen her since last night and she worries that she's too burnt to go hiking today. She imagines her trying to walk as the bandages rub against each other.

"Ryan was totally trying for score last night."

"Not even. Anyways I was too busy trying for stay warm."

"You coulda tried staying warm with Ryan." Jen teases. She rolls her eyes and then giggles, her friend's cocoa-burnt flesh briefly forgotten.

'Eono – Numbah Six

She watched the news. The flow had shifted and was heading towards the sea. She wondered if she should be concerned. It's been a long time since she paid much attention to what happened. Would lava heading to the sea make any difference in her life? Wasn't it in her nature to always flow to the sea. She'd been here so long now, living among them. Their lives so short. She sometimes missed the days when her life mattered to them. Her very existence, an essential part of theirs. She knows one day they will be gone and she will continue on always seeming to move from island to island.

She doesn't remember when she became aware. It must have been when the first people found her. They were so small compared to those who came later. Each successive wave of people, shaping her mind, her body, her power. Always changing to suit the need of the believers. Today, she can even reflect on her current incorporation. She assumes that is the way of things for her and the others. She has found that as time passes, she becomes less the creature of lust and destruction and more a creature of analysis and study. She watches them as they watch her. The ones who study her. Their instruments and probes always measuring her. She waits for the day when they too will be gone and wonders what will replace them.

'Ehiku – Numbah Seven

His mom once told him that people mailed back pounds of lava rocks every year. "Why they take 'em in the first place?" He asked, knowing the rules instinctively as all children of Hawaii did.

"Sometimes, people, they no believe that our 'aina is sacred. And wen they take home rocks for souvenirs, they get bachi, and they know they shouldn't have taken it." I nodded my head in agreement. We all knew that if you take the rocks, you have unbelievably bad luck until you sent the rocks back to Hawaii.

'Ewalu – Numbah Eight

If you walk without rhythm, you won't attract the worm. He thought a lot about this as he entered Thurston's Lave Tube. He could imagine a great worm had crawled through the lava rock, tunneling and carving out this almost perfect cylinder. He tried very hard to walk without rhythm, but have you ever noticed how impossible that is? To get to the tube you had to walk down staircases in the middle of a rainforest. He could imagine the Predator, camouflaged among the trees, hunting him. He'd rub himself with mud and take that alien out. The floor of the tube had puddles of water, and he could imagine Gollum, perched on a rock, asking him a riddle in the dark, his big fish-like eyes, glowing orbs. He'd put on his ring and run through the cold tunnel from Gollum and the orcs, his sword by his side. The tube was colder inside. He was surprised by that. He never really thought about how temperature would change inside rock. He was on an active volcano. It should be warm. He could imagine himself as Indiana Jones with rivers of lava beneath his feet, ready to devour him. He'd rescue the girl about to be burned alive as a sacrifice to Kali. The tunnel's surface wasn't exactly smooth and he put his hand against it. It chilled him. He shivered and he could imagine leaving the tube and entering an artic wasteland with his team of scientists. They'd fight the alien stalking them through their base as each of them was taken and replaced. He lifted his hand from the tunnel's side as he walked on. He saw the tube's opening up ahead and dodging more puddles without rhythm, he climbed the narrow stairs back into the sun.

'Eiwa – Numbah Nine

You always picked up the lady in white if you drive over Saddle Road. Everyone knew that. So why did my uncle just drive past her as we headed to the other side of the island?

"Uncle, how come you neva stop?"

"Why for I need stop?"

"Didn't you see that lady on the side of the road?"

"No, I neva. Why? You wen see one lady?"

"Yea, she was wearing one white mu'umu'u and she had long white hair. I thought you wen see her too."

"You stay lying. I neva see nobody on da road."

"Uncle why for I lie. I stay telling you da truth. Dea was one lady in white on da side of da road. You no think she going curse us for not picking her up?"

"Nah, I never see her. We going be okay. No worries."

But I was worried.

'Umi – Numbah Ten

There's a new island forming off the coast. The teacher says we can't see it because it's underwater, but it's definitely there. We dream of swimming down to it, seeing how the mountain forms, lava pouring out of its tops and sides. It won't reach the surface of the ocean for hundreds of thousands of years. We probably won't even be around anymore when it becomes an island with its own animals and plants. We think about the future of mankind when the teacher talks about the birth of Lo'ihi. With the possibility of nuclear war always lingering over us, it's hard to believe that any human would be alive to see that little island breach the surface. Will it be its own land or just another mountain of the Big Island? Do you think Pele will move there? We ask our teacher. She smiles. If any goddess would survive that long, it would definitely be her. We all smile and nod our heads, content in the lie that something of us will live on.

Ulu's Gift

A cool breeze danced across my skin as I sat on the lanai waiting for my sister to come home. I searched for her dark hair through the branches of the coffee trees, but I couldn't find her. Legs swinging, my bare feet bumping the railing, I thought about how she had promised to take me out to look for menehune tonight. I'd heard that menehune were like the dancing leprechaun on the Lucky Charms commercial. When I asked Ulu what she thought, she said leprechauns were silly because they were always trying to hide their pot of gold, but menehune were useful and hardworking because they built stuff we could use. I imagined a secret army, in one night, making stonewalls, fishponds, and taro patches.

I decided to walk through the coffee field, hoping to meet up with Ulu before she got home. The rows towered over me and I was glad it was still day time. I wasn't scared but you can never be too safe from the obake. I could see that the leafy branches were half full of red beans, and I knew we would have to start picking soon. I hated coffee picking season. You walk around all day with a basket strapped to your stomach and you have to pick only the red beans, because if you pick the green beans you get dirty lickins. If you talk too much or fight with your sister, you had to keep the sticky beans in your mouth, or else. I rather pick coffee than mac nuts. That's much worse. You have to bend over and run your hands through the fallen macadamia leaves searching for nuts. You can't use gloves because you might miss the nuts and those leaves are sharp and pointy.

I found Ulu reading under the breadfruit tree. She was always reading. She didn't really watch TV. She said you learned more from books. I didn't like learning and I sure didn't like reading. One time, I picked up one of her books, My Life in the Land of Milu, and started reading:

'I was six before I learned the meaning of bad and good, because at that time my father decided he preferred me over my other sisters and the attention was not unwanted. When no one else was home, he would pull me towards him and make me kneel, petting my hair and calling me a good girl. So it was here that I understood the meaning of good because I did as my father asked and did not yet know the meaning of bad.

My father was a fisherman. Well, that's what he thought of himself, but really he worked in a hotel kitchen at one of the resorts. He wasn't happy about waking up at three in the morning to cook breakfast and lunch for tourists, but you don't make money as a fisherman, at least that's what my mother said. My mother was a teller who handled money all day long and came home later than my father. This left plenty of opportunities for my father to spend time with me as all of my sisters were older and did not come home from school until much later.

In those days, my parents fought many battles and some of them were as follows: money wars, housework wars, marijuana wars, porn wars and cheating wars. Cheating wars were more common than any other war in our house. This was very bad luck for us because that meant we may have to a) watch my mother run around the house with a meat cleaver chasing my father, b) pack up the car with all of our belongings and sleep in a parking lot for the night, or c) get locked in my parents' bedroom as my mother cuts all her underwear into tiny little shreds. On any given night, it could be all three or any combination of the three. The first time I saw my mother chase my father with a meat cleaver I was four and I thought it was normal. My sisters would try to leave the house when this happened, but my mother always found a way to keep them with her.

When my mother thought my father was cheating, she would throw his clothes out of the closet, searching for the porn she knew would be hiding there. Whatever she found, she would show us what a disgusting man our father was and I would see naked people: men and women, women and women, sometimes there would be two men and one woman. My mother would take all these magazines outside and burn them in our fire pit and an eerie high-pitched shriek would travel up through the smoke. I always imagined it to be the ghosts of the people trapped in the magazines, caught forever, burning in the flames.

Since I was the youngest, no one paid much attention to me, so I would hide in the hallway closet. My friend Rose would join me. She never came when anyone else was there. I never minded. She was a good friend. Sometimes we would play hide and seek, but she would always win because I could never find her. Once, out of the corner of my eye, I saw her peeking out from the kitchen when I was alone with my father. She shook her head and popped back behind the wall before I could stop what I was doing. I was surprised, since she never showed herself to anyone but me.

Rose said she lived next door and that she was bored. So, she had decided to come over and play with me. I didn't mind. I didn't have anything else to do except watch TV and I wasn't always allowed to do that. She told me that there wasn't anyone at home most of the time. I asked her what her parents did, but she always wanted to play, instead of talking. She was good at keeping me company when I was lonely. I always wondered why she never came around when anyone else was home and I never saw her at school. What did she do all day long before I saw her? She would show up when I got home from school and leave when my sisters came home. She didn't like to come over on the weekends. She told me that she didn't like my family very much and that she preferred to play just with me. I never really asked her why she was always disappearing.

One weekend, because my father was a fisherman, we went camping. My mother hated to camp. She said it was dirty and she had better things to do then sit around in the shade waiting to cook food for everybody. I guess she didn't like swimming or laying in the sun. She said that all the spots on her face were from the sun when she was a child. So, instead of enjoying herself, she sat and grumbled.

The great thing about camping was the beach, because we got to stay in our bathing suits the whole time. We swam. We tanned. We ate. It usually was great as long as my parents didn't have any of their wars. At night, we would sit around the cooking fire and watch the flames jump and spark and the ashes float away. Sometimes on these camping trips, when my mother had been drinking, my father would spend time with me. This time was no different. He pulled me to the back of the tent when I saw my mother out of the corner of my eye. She saw what my father was doing and started to swear at me. She pulled me away by the strap of my bathing suit, tearing it. She screamed at me. Telling me I was a bad girl because I did as my father asked. And here I thought I had learned the meaning of bad. On and on my mother screamed as she dragged me across the sand by my bathing suit. No one stopped her and no one helped me, and I couldn't see my father. She stopped at the edge of the water still screaming about how disgusting I was and what a bad girl I was and how I didn't deserve the roof over my head that she provided. I cried, but she did not hear me.

Then, my mother tossed me into the sea.'

When I finished reading, I felt really sad and I wondered what kind of mother throws her daughter into the sea, and what kind of father does that kind stuff. Why would anybody want to read this? I just didn't get it.

After that, I stopped trying to read anything my sister had in her room. It just was a waste of time. Plus, I would much rather watch TV. You could see the whole world on the television, the jungles of Africa, the skyscrapers of New York, the North Pole, and outer space, too. There were no children being hurt or killed by their parents.

Ulu looked up at me as I walked out of the coffee field and smiled. I always thought it was funny to be named after a tree. She told me that the ulu tree was great. You could make poi, stew and even dessert from the fruit and bowls and utensils from the wood. I really didn't like ulu poi. It's yellow and smells like BO. I like the dark purple color and sour taste of taro poi. If you look at the taro plant, you can see that it looks like a person. The leaf looks like a big head, the stalk like a long neck and the taro root like a big rolly polly body. The ancient Hawaiians believed that humans were created from the taro plant and that the taro is our brother.

"So, we going go look for menehune tonight?"

"Yeah, yeah. We going stay at Aunty Hau's house cuz she not going bada us."

"Shoots. Wen we going?"

"Wen I pau read dis chapter."

"Watchu reading?"

"None of your beeswax!"

"No get all futless. I was just asking. You not still reading that Milu book."

"What Milu book?"

"You know the one with the girl getting thrown into the ocean by her mada?"

"Whatchu was doing reading my books? You know you not supposed to be in my room."

"I wasn't being ni'ele. I just wanted to see what was so great about reading, das all."

"Well, dat kine book not good for you. It's for adults."

"You not one adult."

"So, I can read like one adult. Anyway, I pau with dat book already."

"Oh yeah? What happened to the girl?"

"She wen go to the underworld and she had to work hard as a slave in the house of a ghost and her friend would visit her but wouldn't help her escape."

"What? That no make sense."

"That's why I told you not to read my books! They not for you. Just kule kule and let me pau reading this chapter."

So, I sat down next to her. I really didn't care what she was reading. She's just weird.

All I wanted to do was find some menehune. Ulu is the only person I know who can see menehune. Weird stuff is always happening to her, especially the last time we went camping. We were all sleeping, and all of a sudden, my dad woke me up. Before I could say anything, he shook his head and pointed at Ulu sleeping next to me. I could see that Ulu's hair was moving but there was no wind. It was so still I couldn't even hear the ocean. We just sat there watching as her long hair moved around her shoulders. I looked at my dad and he didn't seem scared. Then, the smell of maile leaf drifted over us and I got major chicken skin and all I wanted to do was hide under the blanket. I couldn't believe she hadn't woken up yet. I know I would definitely get up if someone was touching my hair. Then, the smell was gone and Ulu's hair just dropped back onto her shoulders. My dad walked over to her and woke her up. He asked if everything was okay. She told us she had the nicest dream. She was sitting in the rainforest reading when she met some girls. They told her how much they loved her hair and ran their fingers through it. Then, she watched them gather maile leaf and lehua blossoms to weave a lei po'o and they put it on her head. Ulu said she didn't mind and that it was very nice. They had to leave, but asked if they could visit again, and that's when daddy woke her up. Dad told her that every time we go camping, he saw her hair moving at night, but he always thought it was just the wind. This time there wasn't any kind of wind and Ulu's hair was still moving. Dad said he wasn't surprised because this stuff happened to his mom, too. I knew there was something different about grandma, but I never thought she was like Ulu.

"All pau. You ready?"

"Watchu think?"

"No act. I not going take you to find menehune if you keep it up."

"Sorrys. I just like go already."

"They no come out til night time, so stop being so kolohe."

I followed Ulu through the coffee fields. I just wanted to run, like running would make the sun go down any faster. Ulu told me that the ancient Hawaiians used to have men who ran around the island delivering messages for the ali'i. There were runners' trails all over. I imagined that I was running to save the kingdom from evil invaders.

As we walked to Aunty Hau's house, Ulu and I talked story about school. Ulu said her teacher Mr. Kimura was going let her tutor her classmates because she was such a good student. Sometimes Ulu can be high maka maka. Most of the time I don't mind, but when she starts bragging about it, I just want her to shut it. I guess it's because I'm not doing so well in school. It's just so boring. I don't mind ukulele class. That's fun, making your fingers dance like ukus over the strings. I'm getting pretty good, but you don't see me bragging about winning an award for best ukulele player in my class.

"How come you read so much?"

"I learn all kind stuff and I can travel all over."

"What? You just reading some words, you not going anywhere."

"You so lolo. Of course, I no go someplace for reals, but my mind can go anywhere the books take me. You know like that Milu book you read."

"I never like that book. It made me sad and I only read the first chapter. How come you like read that kind stuff? You want to see children get hurt and killed by their parents?"

"No, that's not why I read it. I read it because the girl goes to the underworld. She gets away from her bad parents and she lives a whole new life. She learns from all kinds of people. She'd never have done that if her mother hadn't thrown her in the ocean."

"I don't get it. So, she was killed and you okay with that?"

"I not okay with that, but she wasn't really happy, was she?"

"No, why didn't she tell somebody what was happening?"

"That's not really the story, is it?"

I thought about that as we got to Aunty Hau's house, she had just finished making dinner, my favorite, beef stew with rice. Aunty Hau was easy. She always asked how school was going and I would let Ulu do all the talking. They always liked Ulu. I think it's because she's so smart and she always listens to the adults. I mean really listens not just pretend listens when you just nod your head and say oh yeah now and then. Ulu says that's how you get them to do stuff for you. I tried listening to Aunty Hau, but after she talked about her sore back and how much she needed a massage from the tutu kahuna for the third time, I just couldn't. I kept staring at the taro on her neck, hoping that I'd never grow taro on my neck. After we pau eat, we watched the sunset from the lanai. I love watching the sunset. I always look for the green flash. Sometimes, I think I see the green flash because I've been staring at the sun for too long.

I strummed Aunty Hau's ukulele. It's the only time outside of school I get to play. My fingers danced over the strings, picking a C here and a G there. I really wanted an ukulele, but my parents said that it was useless and that I should learn to play the piano instead. Nobody cared if you played the ukulele. Ulu played the piano since she was four. My parents made me take lessons, but I hated the metronome. Every time I heard it tick tocking, I wanted to throw it at the teacher's head. Of course, that's not what good little girls do. I would never practice and my parents finally said it was a waste of money and stopped paying the piano teacher for my lessons, but Ulu, always being the good girl, still had lessons every week. I would tease her and say that she was a kiss ass, and she would say that I was so lolo and one hard head. I don't care what she says. I going buy my own ukulele when I get older and no one's going to tell me that I can't. I looked over at Ulu and saw that she was reading again. Always reading. Sometimes, she read so much I think her brain going get so big her head going pop! I started playing a song about centipedes, trying to get her to laugh, but she was so into her book, she didn't even look up.

We waited for the quiet snores from the living room. When the stars started to come out, Ulu got the flashlights we had brought from our house.

"You stay ready?"

"Yeah."

"You stay scared?"

"No way jose."

We walked across the road and into the rainforest. We really didn't need the flashlight, the moon was so bright and I wasn't scared. I didn't know where Ulu was taking me, but I was wondering if hunting for menehune was such a great idea. I started to imagine that the boogeyman was following me and I grabbed Ulu's hand. She just looked down at me and smiled.

"So, you no stay scared?" I let go and walked ahead of her. I didn't want her to know how scared I was getting.

"No worries. I no think you stay chicken."

"I no care if you think I stay chicken, cuz I'm not. Why I gotta be scared of some little menehunes? What they going do to me?"

"Kule kule. I think I stay hear something."

I wanted to tell her to kule kule, but that's when we heard the drums. I didn't really think it was anything, but Ulu got major chicken skin. I looked around and all I could see was the full moon shining through the trees. There wasn't a cloud in the sky. The drums got louder. I tried to figure out where the sound was coming from. I looked up at the moon and there was a huge white circle around it.

"You, stay close."

"Why come?"

"I think the Night Marchers stay coming."

"What? You stay joking."

"Kule kule."

"I no believe in the Night Marchers. What they going do?"

"If we stay out here, they going take us with them."

"What? Not even."

The only stories I'd heard were about the Night Marchers walking where nobody lived like on the lava flows down south, and if you happened to be in their way, they would carry you off with them. The drums started to get louder and I saw a row of fire coming down the mountain. Ulu started to pull me back to Aunty Hau's, but I couldn't move. I didn't want to go to the underworld. I didn't want to be the slave of some ghost. The sound kept getting louder. I think it was way too late to try and get back to the house, so she told me lay on the ground face down.

"No try look!"

As I tried to lay on the ground, making myself as flat as possible, I could hear water hitting the dirt and I remembered what you're supposed to do when the Night Marchers come. I knew I shouldn't laugh, but I couldn't help it. I started to giggle as I thought about how the same thing that protects you from the Night Marchers also helps when a wana needle gets stuck in your foot. Then, all of a sudden, I didn't feel like laughing anymore. Although I couldn't see what she was doing, I knew she was trying to save me. Then, she lay down next to me and we waited. I was so scared, but she just kept telling me to keep my eyes closed as the drums started to sound like they were ready to pound us into the ground. I could feel something walking very near us. I couldn't hear feet on the dirt or the leaves on the trees moving, but I knew something was there. I just kept my eyes closed and hoped that they wouldn't touch us. I really didn't want to die.

Finally, the drums started to get softer, but Ulu kept my head down and told me to wait. I listened because I still had chicken skin, and there was no way I wanted to become a Night Marcher. Ulu told me I could lift my head, but I didn't see anything except for this big wet circle around us. There were no footprints. You'd think they'd leave footprints. We stood up and I didn't care if there was pee on me and I hugged Ulu.

"You okay?"

I shook my head and I thought about that stupid book. I thought about that poor girl and how no one had really loved her, and I hugged Ulu again, really hard. I didn't think I wanted to look for menehune anymore, and we walked quickly to Aunty Hau's and we didn't look back.

Any Kine Boy

Kea wen almost try kill me again today. Sometimes, I stay think he neva mean it. Sometimes, I stay think he does. I was trying for ride the ten-speed dad wen pick up for me from his friend at the National Guard. It was cherry. Still good even though stay used. My first bike was used too. Dad wen buy 'em off one neighbor. I don't know how much it wen cost but mom probably wen think it was too expensive. That bike wasn't as cherry as this one. Kea was pedaling his brand new BMX hard down the hill, trying for race me. Lolo kid. I wen decide to slow down so he stay even with me but then I wen see him look at me and he wen smile. Then he wen pull his bike in front of me. I wen hit his front tire and wen fly over my handlebars and slam my head against the street. They neva take me hospital. I wen try for stand up but I wen palu. I neva eat pineapple. Why every time you stay throw up get pineapple? Kea was crying. Garans, he stay acting. The front wheel on my bike was all kapakahi. I neva even ride 'em for one day. No way they going try fix 'em. I going probably get dirty lickins for that.

My parents let Kea get away with choke kine stuff. One time, he wen want candy, so he wen open all the army C-ration cans in the closet for get the gum, candy and cakes inside. Wen my dad wen find out, he neva even get dirty lickins. I always get lickins for small kine stuff. No clean our room. Lickins. No cook the rice. Lickins. Watch

TV after school. Lickins. He stay eat mom's Oreos. He wen lie. I get lickins. He neva do his homework. I get lickins. He my kuleana they wen say. My kuleana? My okole. He neva listen to me. I try for tell them that but Kea just say he always listen to me. I cannot even give him cracks because he going cry and I going get dirty lickins for hitting him.

One time, we stay walking home from school. I just wanted for go home, do my homework, clean da house and watch He-Man. Kea was talking story. I wasn't listening. I was wishing I had the power of Grayskull and I was making sure the big black dog in the house down the street was in the backyard and not in the front. And real fast kine, I wen feel his shoulder hit my side just as one pickup truck came cruising past us. He wen try push me into the road and he just wen laugh.

"Why for you do that? I wen almost get all buss up."

"Cuz funny that's why."

"I going tell dad."

"So? I no care. He not going give me lickins anyway."

I wen walk behind him and I wen totally forget about the big black dog. He wen rush us. He was growling and barking. Luckily, he was on one chain. I just wanted for go home but Kea wen stop.

"Look at that stupid dog. You always stay scared of him."

He wen pick up one rock from the sidewalk and he wen throw it at the dog. It wen go flying and hit the dog on the head. The dog wen shut up but I wen grab Kea's arm and I wen start running. I neva like the neighbors know it was us. He was laughing and trying for keep up with me.

"Ho you wen see that stupid dog's face wen the rock wen hit him?"

"We going get dirty lickins if the neighbor find out was us."

"I not going get dirty lickins. They stay know you the one who stay scared of the dog. I just going tell 'em was you."

I neva like hassle with him because he stay right. They always believe him. One time, we wen go boogie boarding down White Sands. I was just riding the waves. I neva even cut him off and he wen try choke me with his boogie board leash wen I was trying for paddle out for catch some more. I wen tell on him because I wen almost drown and they neva believe me.

"Kea neva do that. He stay so small."

"I bet you wen just swim through his leash cuz you was daydreaming like you always stay doing."

"You should be watching your brother. If I catch you daydreaming out there, I am taking you to the car."

I wen just keep my mouth shut and watch him smile as we wen walk back to the water. My neck had one mean leash burn on it. I neva even like surf anymore but if I neva go out, he was going cry and tell on me.

He was sitting on his bed watching me trying not for palu. I wanted for sleep but dad wen tell me I couldn't yet. I wen au au earlier for clean the pineapple off me. I was sitting up in bed in my sleeping clothes. I couldn't see good and I wanted for close my eyes.

"Hey, no go sleep. You not supposed to."

"I not going sleep. Just go away. I no like talk story with you."

"Mom going give you dirty lickins wen she get home."

"She not going. I neva do nothing."

"She going send you back to your mada wen she find out you wen make your bike all hamajang." I wen try look over at him but my head wen start to pound.

"I neva even. You wen make my bike all kapakahi. Was cherry."

"Not even. Was old. Not cherry like my BMX. Now, your bike is all buss like you."

I stay tired of his hassles. What he wen say was true. Mom would probably give me dirty lickins and tell me she going send me back my mada. She neva going believe me. I neva even tell dad. Kea wen know I wouldn't tell on him. I neva see his bike but I bet he going tell 'em stay my fault if stay broken and I going get it for that too. I neva like go back to my mada. I wen neva live with her even though sometime she come by and take me go visit my other brothers who live around the island. I know she my mada but that's it. One time, Kea wanted for go too but mom told him no because she wasn't his mada and they wasn't his brothers. Kea wen call me adopted. It was the first time he wen ever do that. I wen get angry and I wen tell him at least I stay chosen. I think maybe that's wen he wen start making any kine to me. My head wen feel so heavy and light at the same time. I wen know I neva going say anything about Kea to our parents. He stay my little brother and he stay my kuleana.

Hard Skin

She rubs the raw meat against her wart and looks into the setting sun. Her grandmother says if she counts to ten, the wart will disappear. So, she stares as hard as she can, all the time counting and praying for her wart to be gone. Green and blue spots begin to appear and she blinks rapidly to shake them loose. It never crosses her mind to question the wisdom of staring into the sunset or of rubbing a piece of sirloin on her hand. She knows that this is the truth and that tomorrow, when she wakes up, she will no longer have this ugly wart on her finger. She imagines the wart sinking beneath her skin as the sun sinks beneath the water and wonders what happens to warts and where do they go. Not really wanting to know the answers, she lets those questions float away.

She stops rubbing, kneeling down in the dirt of her backyard. She is directly in line with the sunset between the tall and slender papaya trees her grandpa had planted when they had first moved to this house. She must continue to stare at the sun as she digs a small hole. Grandmother says she must bury the meat, and when she's done, she's to turn and walk back to the house without looking back or it won't work and she'll still have the wart in the morning. She doesn't want that to happen, so she digs diligently. The feel of the earth is soothing as her fingers pull out rocks, making room for her offering. As she walks back to the house, she wonders what would happen if she looks back. Would she turn to a pillar of salt like Lot's wife? Her mother is waiting at the screen door.

"Did you look back?"

"No."

"Good, good. Dust off your jeans and go wash your hands in the laundry room before you come in my house."

She walks around the yard to the laundry room, next to the garage, dusting herself off as she goes. She's afraid to look anywhere but in front of her. She remembers the first time she saw the wart. She was playing Chase Master with the other kids at school. She was It and she was running, pumping her arms, her legs crossing the distances between predator and prey. As she reached out her hand to touch the pony-tailed girl in front of her, she spotted the tiny, white bump on the forefinger of her right hand. She marveled at its sudden alien appearance. She tried to recall if she'd missed it while brushing her teeth that morning. She was so distracted that she failed to touch the pony-tailed girl, who was able to evade her and make it to Safe, a set of monkey bars at the far end of the playground. She saw that almost everyone had made it back, but she couldn't seem to concentrate on anything but the wart. She knew it was a wart. She'd read the fairytales of wart-nosed witches and she thought maybe she was destined to become one, but she didn't want to eat children or poison princesses. Should she go to the nurse's office? The bell rang and recess was over. Everybody laughed and told the pony-tailed girl they couldn't believe she hadn't been caught. Would anyone notice the fleshy growth on her finger? Would they make fun of her? She jabbed her hands into her pockets and thought of ways to hide it.

At first, she put a band aid on it, hoping everyone would think it was just a cut or a scratch, but band aids are expensive and she knows her mother will start to notice that they were running low. Then, it started to grow, and since she felt she could no longer use the family's supply of band aids, she began to draw on it, anything to hide its strangeness. The wart became the hub of petals, sprouting in a ring, an eye on the wings of a monarch butterfly in flight, or hidden at the center of an ornamental cross. At night, when her hands had been washed clean, she'd stare at it. At eye-level, it looked like the top of Mauna Loa, smooth with touches of crusted snow. She felt its hard, but pliant peak. Pushing on it didn't hurt. The only sensation she received was from her fingertips running across its summit. It was not smooth and it was not rough. She couldn't really describe what she felt. It was not like any other part of her body. It was and was not her flesh. In the mornings, as she daydreamed of far off lands, she would again hide it all under dancing fairies, bloated mushrooms, smiling cats.

Then, one day over a dinner of leftover spaghetti, her mother noticed a strange symbol on her daughter's hand, "What is that Lei?" She looked at where she had drawn an ankh after an inspirational section on Egyptian Mythology in class. She didn't think anything of it at the time. It was just another cool way to cover up her wart. Now she sensed that drawing symbols of other religions may not have been such a smart idea and she was suddenly afraid. Her mother got up from the table, walked over to her, and lifted up the offending hand, "Is that Satanic? That better not be a symbol of Satan on your body!" She pulled Lei from the table and dragged her to the kitchen sink. "Wash that off right now!" Quickly, Lei did as she was told. She didn't think it was a symbol of Satan but wasn't going to argue with her mother about it, especially not with her pinching her arm the way she did when she didn't want everyone to see how angry she was. "If I ever catch you drawing evil symbols on your body again, you are really going to get it!" As Lei was washing the black ink off her hand, her mother spotted it. "What the hell is that?"

She had a feeling her mother already knew what it was, so she wasn't sure if she should answer. "I think it's a wart."

"Let me see," she lifted her arm up to let her mother have a closer look.

"How long you've had it?"

"I don't know. A couple of months?"

"You must have done something. What did you do?" She pulled hard on Lei's arm. "You tell me, girl." Lei didn't think she had done anything to deserve this growing mound of foreign flesh on her finger, but what could she say to her mother? What could she do to quiet her anger?

"Maybe the obake touched me wen I didn't clean my room? Or, maybe I got it from that girl with the ukus and dirty feet?" Her mother laughed at this, and Lei could feel that the moment had passed and she was safe.

"Yeah, maybe the obake did touch you wen you didn't clean your room. How many times I told you not to hide stuff under the bed? You know the obake loves to live under messy beds." Lei nodded at her mother's wisdom. She would definitely clean under her bed. But in the back of her mind, she didn't think that the wart was caused by a messy bed.

As Lei continued to wash her hands at the laundry room sink, trying to remove the dirt from beneath her fingernails, she thought again of her mother's original theory of how the wart came to be. Unfortunately, the wart slowly grew, each day, conquering the smooth back of her finger, spreading towards each of her knuckles, and no matter how much she kept her room clean, it didn't stop. Drawings could no longer hide its growth and the kids began to tease her as kids are wont to do. "Pop it! It looks like a big zit! Did you uff a frog? You look like you going have a baby out your finger that thing's so big!" She didn't think their taunts were so great, which is probably why she wasn't hurt by them. She was sad because no one would eat lunch with her or play with her because they were afraid they were going to catch it. Who really wants to have warts all over their body? Sometimes, in frustration, she'd rush the worst kid, the one that teased her about uffing a frog and she'd hold her hand right next to his face and dare him to say it one more time. In those moments, she felt its power. She knew that the kids were afraid. She knew that they thought that warts were contagious, but until she'd stopped drawing on her hand, she'd played and eaten with all of these kids and not a single one had gotten a wart from her. She loved to see the fear in their eyes when she came near them. It didn't make up for being teased and laughed at, but it helped to ease the pain a little.

Once, at church, she learned about Job. She listened to the Sunday school teacher, a haole girl from Utah, talking about how

God wanted to prove to Satan that his servant, Job, a very wealthy man, would never renounce God, no matter what happened to him. Satan told him that the moment Job lost his money he would immediately stop loving him. God told Satan he could do whatever he wanted, so Satan had all of Job's animals stolen and his servants slaughtered. Then, he had all of Job's children killed. Did Job give up on God? No. Satan told God that if he hurt Job, Job would definitely curse him, and God said do what you want, so Satan covered Job in sores and Job cursed the day he was born, but did not curse God. Everyone blamed Job. They believed he was being punished for some kind of wickedness. Through it all, not once did Job curse God. As a reward for his unwavering faith, God gave him twice as much wealth and many sons and daughters.

Lei had never considered the possibility that God could actually let Satan test the faithfulness of his servants, hurting them or their families. That just didn't seem fair. No one said anything to her about her wart at church, even though it was on display for everyone to see as she picked up the sacrament of water and bread during her Ward's time in the chapel. Not even the other kids. She did wonder if her Sunday school teacher was trying to tell her something. She didn't really consider herself a servant of God and maybe this is why God was letting her be punished. She never really thought much about God.

She imagines he's a really tall haole with a long white beard, wearing really white robes, floating in the clouds above. Is she being taught a lesson? She's not sure what that lesson could be and she doesn't talk to anyone about it, especially her Sunday school teacher. Lei smiles at the end of the story as the class sings "Popcorn Popping on the Apricot Tree." It's a fun song, but Lei begins to wonder why they sing it. There are no apricot trees in Hawaii and what does popcorn have to do with God?

Lei loves to sing. It's one of the only reasons she doesn't mind church. She reads the hymnal as the Bishop drones on, trying to guess what songs are going to be sung next. They never sing in Hawaiian, but she doesn't mind. Most of the songs were originally in English, anyway. Her favorite is "How Great Thou Art." It reminds her of a love song. Not the kind of sappy love song on the radio like "Endless Love," but a true love song. Not that she knows what true love is, but she imagines it to be something pure and golden and light. She thinks about Job in this instance and realizes that love may not be what she imagines, but this thought is gone in an instant as the first notes of "How Great Thou Art" carries across the chapel from the organ's pipes, "O Lord my God, when I in awesome wonder, consider all the worlds Thy hands have made; I see the stars, I hear the rolling thunder, Thy power throughout the universe displayed." She notices that most people don't really know the melody of the first verse and the voices are subdued, but when her favorite part comes, she can feel the rising voices like the waves at high tide crashing against the walls and splashing back against her, "Then sings my soul, My Saviour God, to Thee, How great Thou art, How great Thou art. Then sings my soul, My Saviour God, to Thee, How great Thou art, How great Thou art!" As the words pour out of her, she feels something inside of her opening up and moving out of her, flowing with the notes into the wave of sound around her. As each wave pushes its way to the wall, another forms behind it, a continuous flow vibrating through her whole being and she can hear at the very top of all that sound, even higher notes reaching to the ceiling. She wonders if that's what God sounds like. At these moments, she forgets about the wart on her finger, the malicious teasing, the playground power struggles, the weird looks from her mother, and she swoops and dives in and out until the last powerful chord crescendos and all is silent. She sits but feels disconnected as her insides soar. Then the bishop drones on, firmly settling her back inside her body.

Drying her hands on her jeans, she remembers that feeling and wonders if she could feel like that all the time. She doesn't think that it's a good thing. If you feel like that all the time, how could you tell the difference between how you should feel versus how you do feel? She wishes that singing could remove her wart, but she knows that is foolish, as she's been singing every Sunday since she could remember and every Sunday since her wart came to be, yet nothing has changed. At least she doesn't think anything has changed. So, she decides that as beautiful as her singing is, this is neither the cause nor the solution to her problem. No matter how much she wishes it to be, she knows this to be the truth.

As she walks back to the kitchen's screen door, she recalls the luau they went to for her cousin's wedding. She wanted to hide her wart, but the band aids were too small now, and she couldn't draw on her hand. She asked her mother what she should do. "No worries. No one's going to notice." Except right off the bat, everyone started making fun of her. The aunties just laughed and told her she better clean herself better or it's going to spread all over her body and grow like taro along her arm and up to her neck. Lei didn't really believe them. She bathed twice a day. And, what did they know about bathing? She could see taro growing all over their necks, too. She didn't say anything to them. She knew better. The uncles just drank their beers and laughed along. The other kids called her hamajang girl, and told everyone to stay away from her before she bachi them and give them all warts. She sat in the corner near the stage and sang along to the band, playing "He Aloha Mele," a love song about stars and brown eyes, and wished she didn't have that stupid wart. Her grandmother saw her sitting by herself and called her over. Lei loved the smell of her grandmother. It was soft and sweet like gardenia after the rain.

"What's wrong?" She asked her wrinkled hands brushing Lei's hair away from her face.

"Nothing, I just want to sit by myself." She didn't really want to bother anyone with her problems.

"You know that's not true." Lei nodded but did not say anything. "Do you know what our ancestors called a wart?"

"No."

"'Ilikona, or hard skin. Do you know why you have an 'ilikona on your finger?"

Lei shook her head, "I don't know why. I thought it was because I didn't clean under my bed, or that I caught it from someone at school. Then, I thought maybe I was being punished for something bad I did, but I couldn't think of what I had done wrong. I just think it is because it is, you know what I mean?"

"Yes, I do."

"Really?"

"Sometimes, tita, our bodies show us what our minds cannot. Do you know what your body is trying to tell you?"

"That I have a big ugly wart?" Her eyes crinkled as her lips spread into a smile.

"You are so kolohe, sometimes. Yes, you have a big ugly wart, but why do you think you have a big ugly wart?" Lei wanted to tell her she had already thought about all of this, and she didn't think that she needed to do it all over again. "Yes, yes. You think you know everything. Your mind can play tricks on you. Just think about when you first saw your wart. What were you doing?"

She thought about the game of Chase Master she had been playing that day she saw the wart for the first time. She had been running behind the pony-tailed girl and she was thinking about how much fun it would be to pull on her hair rather than touching her shoulder, and the more she thought about that, the more she began to realize that the pony-tailed girl wasn't the only person she had really wanted to hurt. She had really wanted to slam that kid's face into the ground who kept teasing her about uffing the frog, and she really didn't have kind thoughts about her Sunday school teacher, either. And when she was singing in church, she really wanted to shove a hymnal into the bishop's mouth to shut him up, wishing that church was all about singing and less about preaching, She didn't think she had thought about anything when she was singing along to the band, but she realized, at that moment, she had been dreaming of all the ways she was going to get those other kids.

"I was playing." She said as these thoughts sped past.

"I see." And, maybe she did. "Let me tell you a story." And, Lei listened. "Once, there was a man, who was full of ideas of how people should be and how everyone would be happier if they just listened to what he had to say. Now, not everyone wanted to listen, but the man didn't care if they did. This bothered them, so they decided that maybe he had something to say after all. He told them that love is unconditional. Now, no one believed this. You can't get something for nothing, they said. And, he said that is not true. Love is easy. It's who you love that can be hard. If a man hurts you, do you love him? Of course not, they answered. And, he said that is not true. You must love that man even more because he does not understand that love is easy. Do you punish this man who hurt you? Of course you do, they answered. And, he said that is not true. You must not punish this man but love him for his flaws, and with your love, teach him to love. And they told him he was crazy. Why would we do that? He will never learn they told him. And, he said that is not true. He will learn that to hurt others is to hurt himself and to love others is to love himself. They did not believe him or understand. But he never gave up, and even on the day he died, he professed his love for all, never wavering as they nailed him to the cross on a lonely hill." Lei let the words wash over her, soothing that hidden spot she could now see.

"I see, Tutu." And, Lei learned how to get rid of the wart on her finger.

She enters the kitchen, walking past her mother, who thankfully says nothing. She closes her bedroom door and kneels beside her bed. She knows she should thank God for everything, and that she shouldn't ask for anything, but she does so anyway, "Dear Heavenly Father, please forgive me and please take my wart away." As her forehead presses hard into her clasped hands, she dreams of waking up free.

Ku's Aina

The kanakas from the fire department drove my Uncle Ku through town this morning. I could just imagine sirens wailing, him sitting high on top of the truck, two big blalahs, one on each side, drinking beer and waving to everybody on Ali'i Drive, his thin hair waving along with them. He loved riding on the truck. They had picked him up early and dressed him in his favorite aloha shirt before I had even gotten out of bed. When I went into the kitchen for some cereal, mom was crying at the table. I was afraid to say anything, since I never see her crying, not really. There are times when there's a sad movie on TV and I hear her on the couch behind me, but I don't think that this was the same kind of crying.

When I was younger, Uncle Ku told me I was named after him and that we had a long tradition of passing this name from one generation to the next. He said that our name had powerful mana and that we were the heart of the land. I always imagined that mana was a superpower that Hawaiians have like Superman's flying or The Flash's super speed. I wish I had superpowers. I would be the Super Kanak, able to eat twenty lau laus in one sitting. At Sunday school, I learned about how mana fell from heaven to feed these people who were wandering through the desert, but I don't think it was the same thing. How can mana be powerful and be food?

Last week we was up on the north side of the island. Uncle said we was paying respect to our amakua, the one we was named after.

I watched him wrap a rock in long green ti leaves. I saw his hands shake as he tied them. We placed it on the altar of the heiau. It looked like a really big lau lau ready to eat. I don't know what ancient heiaus looked like, but this one is in a large field of yellow grass growing along rock walls that are as tall as me. It's a huge rectangle and when you stand by the altar you can see the ocean. Uncle said that in the old days, our amakua would have preferred a human sacrifice. It reminded me of the movie Blue Lagoon, the part where they go to the other side of the island and they see a large black statue with an altar covered in blood. I felt weird about it, but I don't know why. He said that the heiau was built near the favorite hunting grounds of our amakua. He said that they used to throw enemy warriors and kapu breakers into the waters and all kinds of sharks would eat them. I don't think I'd liked to be eaten by a shark and I'm glad we don't make those kinds of offerings anymore. I wondered if the ali'i were ever sacrificed. When we got home, mom was mad and I thought I was going get it. He told her no worries, everything was okay, and that he wanted to ride on the fire truck around town.

Uncle always talks to me like one grownup. One day, I was offered to lick a plastic toy ring. I don't remember why. It was red and covered in Hawaiian chili pepper, but I didn't know it at the time. They told me to lick it, and like one dumb kid, I did. The burning was so bad that I ran all the way to my house screaming for help. Uncle was home. He was always home. He kept asking me what happened and all I could say was that my tongue was burning.

"What's wrong Ku Boy?"

"They made me eat chili pepper." At least that's what I was trying to say, but it really came out like "They may me ee ili peppah." I tried not to breathe as that seemed to make it burn even more. He just started laughing at me. I didn't think it was funny. Finally, he gave me a spoon full of sugar, not in the nice Mary Poppins way, and my mouth felt so much better. Then he gave me some juice to drink.

"So, what really happened?" He poured more juice into the cup.

"I was playing in the back and a couple of kids told me to lick this ring, and I did."

"Did they make you do it? Did they dare you?"

"No. I didn't even think about it."

"See that's your problem. You never think about what you doing." He gave me some bread to eat. "You remember that time you wanted some papaya in the tree and your friends told you to throw one rock at it? What did you do?"

"I threw one rock at the tree."

"You threw the biggest rock you could handle, didn't you?" I nodded, my eyes still watering from the chili peppers. "And what happened?"

"It hit the car windshield."

"Who's car windshield?"

"Yours," I answered, scared he was going finally give me lickins for it.

"And, what happened?" He poured me more juice.

"Everybody ran away and I got dirty lickins from mom."

"Did you get the papaya?"

"No."

"You missed right?"

"I didn't miss your windshield." He started laughing again.

"True, but how come you got in trouble?"

"Cuz, I broke your windshield?"

"No, because you never think before you act. If you had just thought about what you was doing, maybe you wouldn't have thrown that rock at the papaya, and maybe you wouldn't have broken my windshield and gotten dirty lickins from your mom."

"I guess so."

"You think you going learn your lesson this time?"

"Yeah."

But it wasn't the last time someone told me to do something and I got dirty lickins. We were doing laundry down at the Hele Mai Laundromat and I was really bored, so I started playing with the other kids on the outside patio. There was plenty cigarette butts on the ground and one of the kids picked one up and started to pretend to smoke. He looked really cool. I picked one up and pretended that I was smoking too. My mom caught me and made me eat fives butts off the ground and told me I was lucky we wasn't home or else she would have given me dirty lickins. I think I would rather have had dirty lickins. Mom told uncle when we got home, and he just shook his head as I sat next to him.

"What did I tell you about thinking before you act?"

"I know. I know."

"Then, how come you got busted pretending to smoke cigarettes? You know that your mom hates smoking."

"I know. I know. Sheesh."

"Don't you sheesh me! This is the last time I going tell you stop doing stupid shit!"

He was right. I sure didn't like that chili pepper or the cigarette butts or the dirty lickins. I just didn't know why I couldn't think stuff through.

When my dad found out that they took uncle out on the fire truck, he looked really pissed off. I thought he was going give me dirty lickins for sure, but I think he was more mad at mom because she called uncle's friends for come pick him up. Mom told dad that uncle had asked her to call his holoholo gang down at the firehouse to come get him. Dad started yelling at her, saying it's illegal and we going get arrested. She yelled right back at him. "Stay his last ride!" I don't know why dad was worried, uncle was friends with the police, they no mind. Then, we heard the sirens. They had brought uncle back. I saw him between his friends. His head was resting on a shoulder. It wasn't looking too good for the kanakas on the truck but they looked like they was crying. I looked over at my dad. I knew he was going let 'em have it, but he was crying, too.

My Kuleana

"Grandpa wea you stay?" I open the door to his room but he isn't there. Mom is going to give me dirty lickins if I don't find him quick. "Grandpa! Mom said you gotta come take a shower right now." I close the door and walk down the stairs to his garden. He's sitting on his stool. His left arm cradled on his lap. His right hand pulling weeds. He's not wearing a hat and I know I'm going to get yelled at because it's my job to make sure he's clothed and fed.

Every morning before school, I have to make his oatmeal for his breakfast and his soup for his lunch thermos. I have to walk them down to his room under the house. I have to open the door to the smell of shishi and something much stronger, something that pushes down on me. I have to place the tray of food on the table we got from the industrial area, a big wooden spool I imagine once held cable for an elevator. An elevator at one of the resorts in Waikoloa that goes to a suite that I will see when I am rich and famous one day. One day, when I don't have to do anything for anybody but myself. I don't know what will make me rich and famous but I know I will be and my house will be on Robin Leech's Lifestyles of the Rich and Famous. And everyone in my family will want to live with me and I will laugh at them and say no. It will just be me and my very handsome husband with green eyes and dark hair. In my dreams of being rich and famous, it's never anyone from Hawaii. Never John. It's always someone from the mainland. Some haole I've seen in movies or TV. I want a child with green eyes and dark hair, a child with red hair and green eyes, a child with blond hair and blue eyes, a child with blue eyes and dark hair. I know that if I find a handsome haole for each of my beautiful children, I will be so happy. Anytime I see a shooting star or blowout my candles, I always wish to be rich and famous, because I know that if I am rich and famous, I will have everything I have ever wanted. "Hey grandpa," I always yell, "your breakfast stay ready. I gotta go school. Make sure you take your medicine, okay? No make me watch you swallow 'em, or mom going be mad." I hate that I have to do this every morning.

I can hear a low grumble as he tries to stand up. I know he doesn't want to get up. I know he doesn't want to take a shower. He lurches up the stairs, past his room, and into our garden. He avoids the white sandstones my mother had my father place as a footpath. Their unevenness at war with his own. He walks past the mango tree. It isn't in bloom yet but I imagine green mangoes, sliced in shoyu and vinegar, or ripe and juicy as I bite through the skin, peeling it with my teeth as mango pulp slides down my chin. He hitches himself around the tangerine tree, branches scratching at his exposed and permanently dark arms.

He's angry. He doesn't want to shower naked in front of me, he gestures. I tell him he has to because she said I have to make sure he washes all of himself. I turn on the shower for him as he takes off his frayed shorts, held up with rope, and his worn t-shirt. He struggles pulling it over his closely shorn head with one arm. I'm adjusting the water temperature of our outdoor shower, because mom doesn't want him showering in the house as I see him. I help him pull the shirt over his head. He isn't grateful. His eyes are filled with spite. I get angry. I don't want to be here either. I don't want to be bathing my grandfather. Shaving his face. Making sure he washes his boto. I don't even want to look at his boto.

I lay his clothes on the bougainvillea bush that frames our yard. He enters the warm stream. I look at him. I make sure he washes himself or else I'll get it. "Grandpa no forget to wash everywhere. Mom going be mad if you don't clean yourself." I motion my hand towards the lower half of his body. He grunts, his anger matching mine. He turns around to face me, scrubbing his body, so I can witness him. Water hits me. I stare, not because I want to but because I have to. My mother's voice ringing in my ear. You make sure he wash himself good, Leilani, or else. You make sure he scrub his boto, too. Remembering this, I cringe. This isn't right. I don't want to watch him do anything in the shower but my fear of her fuels my irritation with him. "Grandpa, hurry up. I gotta do my homework. I like shave you already." He gestures that he is ready but I tell him to brush his teeth first. I watch him try to put toothpaste on his toothbrush. We both know he can't but he tries anyway. Finally, I just take the brush and tube from him and do it. I give it back to him without looking at him because I just can't take another stink eye.

He brushes his teeth. I don't have to watch him do this. I glance at the anthurium garden my mother planted under the eaves of the porch. Surrounded by crabgrass and rocks, their obake-shaped heads cluster around each other. I hated working in there. Pulling weeds, cutting anthuriums and watering – all for her garden. He coughs and spits, almost choking. I hit his back, trying to help him. He coughs harder. His spindly body shaking as he heaves. "Rinse your mouth grandpa, then I going shave you." He rinses and spits. I get the soap and make a lather, applying it to his damp face. I pick up the disposable razor as he stretches his face. I try to slowly glide it down his cheeks, not pushing too hard. I don't want to cut him. I work my way towards his mouth and he stretches even more. I run the blade over his upper lip and chin. His skin isn't taut enough and I pull it to get the razor closer. I become mesmerized by gray stubble and lined skin, soap pooling and dripping. I don't meet his eyes. I don't want to think about anything but the next section of his face. I rinse and shake the razor in the shower's stream. The stiff hairs cling, refusing to let go. "Okay, all pau now, grandpa. Make sure you wash your okole too." He growls as he turns into the stream again.

I get his towel off the bush. He takes it from me as I reach to turn off the shower. He tries to dry himself. His one hand wiping weakly over his chest and downward. I don't remember a time when he didn't have a stroke but I hear the stories of his drinking and fighting and fishing. He was a strong and scary man, but now all I see is my grandpa who can't even wipe himself dry. I help him because he's taking too long. I can feel his anger but I just want this to be over with. I dry one leg and then the other. I wipe his back side and dry his hair. I put the towel back on the bush, and I get his clean shorts and tell him to put his legs in. He leans his good arm on my bent shoulder as he lifts his legs one at a time into his shorts. I pull them up as he tries to help me with his good hand. I get a clean t-shirt and pull it over his head, first guiding his good arm, then his bad one. I pull it down. "Okay grandpa, I going get your dinner. Go back to your room." He puts his slippers on and stomps slowly off to his room under the house, trying to lift his bad leg as I watch him go. I gather his dirty clothes and put them in his basket in the laundry room before opening the screen door to the kitchen.

"Leilani, did grandpa clean himself good?"

"Yeah, mom, he did."

"You sure? I not going have to check him?"

"Yes, mom, I stay sure."

"Okay, go do your homework. I going tell you when his dinner stay ready."

I walk to my room down the hall. I want to close my door but I can't. I got so much homework. I open my math book, my hands tracing the scribbles and doodles on my brown paper bag book cover. I see Leilani loves John written over and over and wonder what John would think about me having to watch my grandfather shower and having to shave and wipe and dress him. I don't think he'd want to hold my hand or even kiss me behind the cafeteria. I imagine him pulling me along behind him as we sneak away during lunch recess. My hand hot in his. "You doing your homework Leilani? You better not be drawing on your notebook again. You know what your math teacher said about you always drawing on your notebook."

I remembered him taking my notebook in class and flipping through the pages, turning it over in his hands. "Leilani, you do know this is math class, right? Why are you drawing on your notebook?" I didn't say anything. I was so embarrassed that he was actually looking at my notebook. He could see all my crazy doodles of hearts, robots, stars, flowers along the edges of my polynomials and factorings. I could hear my classmates giggle and laugh.

"Ho, Leilani is going get it now."

"Better watch out Leilani! He going see the pictures of John."

I sank down as my teacher just kept flipping through my notebook. I prayed for the bell to ring. "Leilani, I am going to have to take your notebook. I think I will need to call your parents too." I really hate him.

When my mother got home from work that night, she told my dad to get the belt. "Leilani, you know how shame you made me? Your teacher wen call me at work. He wen tell me that you was being one bad student, always drawing in your notebook. Take your shorts off right now." I didn't want to but I knew it would be worse if I didn't. I started crying as I took off my shorts. "Don't you cry. This stay your fault. I going make you cry. Bend over the table right now." I hoped it was my father who would give me the belt. As I tried to stop from crying, fire erupted across my okole and I almost cried out loud but I stopped myself and sobbed. "You better not cry. If the neighbors hear you, you really going get it." Again, she hit me and it was hot and cold at the same time. My tears and hanabata ran down my face and into my open mouth as I tried to breath without screaming. I put my hand in my mouth as the next lash hit me. My cries passed through my fingers and she screamed for me to be quiet. "If I ever get one call from your teacher at work, the belt not going be the only thing you get." She hit me two more times, and I tried not to fall, my sobs shaking my whole body.

"I stay doing my homework mom."

"Okay, you better be. Your grandpa's dinner going be ready soon."

I work on some factoring as I wait for her to call me to the kitchen. I was so lucky John didn't know about my notebook. I would be so shame. I think about his soft brown lips as he leans down to kiss me.

"Leilani, come get your grandpa's dinner."

I close my notebook and get my grandpa's tray from the kitchen. I walk quickly down the cement stairs to his room. His door is open but he's not there. "Grandpa, you was supposed to wait for your dinner. Wea you stay?" I hold my breath as I put his tray down. I don't want to smell the food and his room. I walk down into the garden. I see him, again, pulling weeds. "Grandpa, you only going get dirty again. You know you not supposed to go into the garden after you pau shower. You know she going get mad at us." He just keeps pulling weeds, his head bent as he leans forward. "Grandpa, come eat. It's meatloaf and mashed potatoes. Stay ono, you know. Come eat before it gets cold." I hear him cough as he leans back. His darkened and crinkly skin moves across bones and saggy muscles. He pushes himself off his chair, lifting his shorts with the wrist of his bad arm, so they don't slide down his hips.

I turn around and wait for him at the door of his room. I watch him slowly come up the stairs. I have to make sure he eats all of his food. Sometimes, when I come home from school and bring his tray to the kitchen, there is still food on it. I know that if I tell mom that he hadn't finished his food, she'd yell at him, so I try to throw it away before she sees it. I don't know if he notices but I know that if I don't do it, he's not the only one who will get yelled at. He doesn't look at me as he comes in. He lowers himself onto his chair and prays. I can barely understand what he's saying. Sometimes he prays in Hawaiian. Sometimes he prays in English. I hear him say amene as he raises his head and grabs is spoon.

I don't want to watch him eat but I have to stay there until he is finished so I look out the door. My mother had some contractors put in a terraced garden right next to the house. The concrete was just wide enough for suntanning. When I wasn't busy with chores or homework, I would come lay out in the sun. It felt good to stretch out. The hot sun warming my skin. I'd dream of faraway places, faraway people, faraway boys. I dream of kissing John at the school dance. He pulls me close to him in the dark. His arms wrapped around me. Our bodies moving. I feel his breath on my neck. I hear a loud cough behind me. He's eating too fast again. I turn, walking towards him. I hit him on the back, hard. "Grandpa, I always tell you no eat fast. You gotta chew your food or you going choke." He keeps coughing, food and spit spraying from his mouth. I get his rag and try to wipe his face but he moves away.

"No," he growls.

I drop it on the table and keep hitting his back. Finally, he stops. "I told you. See what happens? Eat slow. We don't want mom coming down here." He picks up his rag and tries to clean himself. Pieces of meat and potatoes stick to his face. I want to help him but I know he'll just get mad. He picks up his spoon again. He's almost finished, and I can get back to my homework.

I look out the one window in his room. I feel the evening breeze washing some of the smell away from me. I can't see the ocean from here because his room isn't high enough but I can see the rows of papaya and banana trees. I can see the overgrown grassy bushes in the lots behind our house, where, every day, my grandfather slowly picks and pulls them down making more space for himself. My mother yells at him not to do it but he doesn't care. Every day, I notice that there is more garden and fewer bushes. Dirt stamped down by his lurching walk. Rocks lined up, making places for the things he wants to grow. I don't understand why he does it. I would rather watch TV all day then go in the sun and work in a garden.

"You almost pau?" He coughs a little and says yes. "You like me turn on the TV?" He doesn't answer me, so I just wait until he's finished. I watch as he shovels mashed potatoes into his mouth. I take his dishes when he's pau and walk back up the stairs. It's getting dark but I hurry because I am finally done. I put his dishes in the kitchen sink.

"You better wash them good," my mother tells me.

"Yes, mom." I wash them as I stare at the geckos hunting moths on the kitchen window. Their heavy bodies bending the screen inwards.

"Stop daydreaming Leilani or else." I finish the dishes and go to my room. "You better be doing your homework. No let me catch you reading."

"Yes, mom." I open my math notebook, my fingers tracing the hearts around my name and John's. I pick up my pencil and trace it over and over, making a space for myself.

Previously Published In:

"Uncle Willy's Harbor" first appeared in the *Notre Dame Review*, Issue No. 43, Winter, 2017.

"Dirty Lickins" first appeared in the *Jet Fuel Review*, Issue #10, Fall, 2015.

"Da Pier" first appeared in *The SFWP Quarterly*, Issue 21, Spring 2020.

"Pele's Daughter" first appeared in the *Guide to Kulchur Creative Journal*, Issue No. 5, 2015.

"Pele's Daughter" was reprinted in the *Notre Dame Review*, Web Issue No. 43, Winter/Spring, 2017.

"Opihi Tales" first appeared in *Souvenir Lit Journal*, Winter, 2016.

"Tita" first appeared in *Crack the Spine*, Issue 182, 2016.

"Talking Story about Kilauea" first appeared in *Pleiades*, Issue 38.1, Winter 2018.

"Ulu's Gift" first appeared in *Mud City Journal*, Issue 3, Fall/Winter 2016.

"Any Kine Boy" first appeared in *Rigorous*, Volume 4, Issue 2, May 2020.

"Hard Skin" first appeared in *Waccamaw, A Journal of Contemporary Literature*, Issue No 15, Fall, 2015.

"Ku's Aina" first appeared in *River River*, Issue 4, Fall, 2016.

"My Kuleana" first appeared in the *Baltimore Review*, Summer, 2016.

Author Biography

Melissa Llanes Brownlee is a Native Hawaiian writer, living in Japan. She received her Bachelor's in Creative Writing and Linguistics from Boise State University and her Master's in Fine Arts in Fiction from the University of Nevada, Las Vegas. Her work has appeared in print and online, including *Booth: A Journal*, *The Notre Dame Review*, *Pleiades*, *Baltimore Review*, *Jet Fuel Review*, *The Citron Review*, *Milk Candy Review*, *(mac)ro(mic)*, *Necessary Fiction*, *New Flash Fiction Review*, *trampset*, *Superstition Review*, *SmokeLong Quarterly*, and elsewhere. She was a finalist for the 2018 New American Fiction Prize and the 2019 Brighthorse Prize. She has received nominations for Best Small Fictions, The Pushcart Prize, and Best of the Net. She has been selected for Best Small Fictions 2021 and Best Microfiction 2022.

Printed in the USA
CPSIA information can be obtained
at www.ICGtesting.com
LVHW011054090824
787740LV00001B/46

What survivors are saying about
A Survivor's Secrets to Health & Happiness

A must read for ALL women and the men who love their women. Angi's book arrived amid great chaos in my life and was like gold to me! I was struggling with cancer, depressed over the break up of my marriage and unemployed. This book gave me the tools on how to take control, bring peace to live my life to my peak performance. — Susan V.

This book is wonderful whether someone has cancer or dealing with any health challenges. I found the chapter on rest/sleep particularly insightful. I used to work late or get up early to get everything done, but now set a curfew and schedule rest as part of my daily routine. Thank you, Angi for sharing your experience and wisdom. — Patsy D.

Survivors and families alike will find a wealth of lifestyle support in this manual and it should be on every bookshelf as a reference for a long, healthy and happy life. A stunningly helpful and caring book. — Sue T.

Other Titles by Angi Ma Wong

Baby Boomer's 4-Minute Bible

Been There, Done That: 16 Secrets of Success for Entrepreneurs

Feng Shui Art and Accessories

Feng Shui Desk for Success Kit

Feng Shui Dos and Taboos: A Guide to What to Place Where

Feng Shui Dos and Taboos

Feng Shui Dos and Taboos Day-by-Day Calendar (2003, 2004, 2005, 2006)

Feng Shui Dos and Taboos for Financial Success

Feng Shui Dos and Taboos for Health and Well-Being

Feng Shui Dos and Taboos for Love

Feng Shui Garden Design Kit

Feng Shui Home Design Kit

Lunar New Year Song CD

Practical Feng Shui Chart Kit

Target the U.S. Asian Market: A Practical Guide for Doing Business

Wind-Water Wheel: A Feng Shui Tool for Transforming Your Life

Women's 4-Minute Bible

Children

Night of the Red Moon

Who Ate My Socks?

Reggie the L.A. Gator

Reggie: My Story

Barack Obama: America's 44th President (Mom's Choice Award)

Barack Obama: History Maker (Mom's Choice Award, Pinnacle Award)

Editor

California Coastal Adventures / Bitter Roots: A Gum Saan Odyssey (Mom's Choice Award, Pinnacle Award) / *By the Grace of God* (Chinese) / *Of Rats, Sparrows and Flies* (Chinese)

Like this book and want to share it? Call 1-888-810-9891 or 310-541-8818 or email amawong@att.net regarding quantity/fundraising/corporate discounts.

A
Survivor's
Secrets
to Health &
Happiness

by Angi Ma Wong

Graphic design: Christine Barnicki
Editor: Janet Ring

For information and author events call 1-888-810-9891 or 310-541-8818.

ACKNOWLEDGMENTS: My thanks and gratitude go to my husband Norman and Mom Lillian, Jason, Wendy, Jamie, Steve, Bill and Bob; to my brothers and sisters: Andrew Ma, James and Dora Hsu, Amy and Sam Wei, Nancy Tsui, Dixon and Eileen Hsu, Franklin and Jean Woo; to my Aunties Loretta, Laura, Shirley and Gertrude; and my treasured friends: Lilian Wu, Christine Barnicki, Sylvia Benko, Patsy Dea, Tobie Gurewitz, Michael Josephson, Echo Lee, Bobbi Leung, Vicki Radel, Betty Rombro, Gary Smolker, Suzanne Somers, Deanna Ssutu, Gina Sweeney, Yvette Trinh, Sue Tyree, Susan Vose and to Drs. John Link, Hugo Hool, Thyra Endicott, Maoshing Ni, Zhang Shao Bing and caring staffs at Torrance Memorial Medical Center, Cancer Care Associates and Rising Star Medical Center.

IN LOVING MEMORY OF

my dad, Shiu Tong Ma, who modeled
a love for learning and extraordinary human relations

my mom, Renee Cheng Ma,
from whom I inherited a passion for art, beauty and nature

and my Ma and Cheng grandparents
who gave me the gift of history, culture and community service

To all whose lives have been touched by cancer,
and in memory of those we have cherished and lost,
especially those in my Rotary family

Author's Note

"Wow! You look fantastic."

"Where do you get your energy?"

"Each time I see you, you look younger."

"How did you do it?"

This book is for my family, friends and acquaintances who wanted to know the secrets as to how I had lost and kept weight off, stayed grounded, optimistic and upbeat through my cancer treatments and clinical trials, and at the same time, have enjoyed peace of mind, body and spirit.

Having survived waking up in a burning bed, escaping a sinking boat, three rear-end car accidents and cancer three times, you might call me lucky. I consider myself truly blessed.

All of us are survivors, whether of illness, separation or divorce, disease, or just life in general. *A Survivor's Secrets to Health and Happiness* has evolved from personal research, my own experiences, information and files gathered through the years to remember and share.

The tips that follow for healthy living are loosely arranged to take you through your day, from the time you get up in the morning to when you retire for the night. The philosophy about happiness has evolved from age and experience. Being a lover of words, I have freely included quotes from many different sources and from people who articulated ideas and thoughts well.

Please understand that I do not profess to be a medical professional, so it is important for all who read my words to seek the advice and guidance of your own trusted medical professional before you embark on any of the prevention and nutritional strategies you read about either here or from any other resource.

While these worked for me personally at various times and sometimes concurrently, do recognize that each of you is a unique human being. What is or was effective and safe for one person, even within your own family, may not be for another.

Furthermore, a treatment or something that was effective for you years ago may not work later in your life. It is the way of nature for us each to stretch out and continue to grow and change — physically, intellectually, emotionally, sexually and spiritually, and in all other ways that we are meant to change. Exercise your personal power through knowledge and free choice by doing what's best for yourself within your beliefs and faith. Let them guide you to doing what feels right and comfortable for you.

⊛ ⊛ ⊛ ⊛

If I hadn't been a good Chinese daughter and listened to my mother, I never would have discovered that I had cancer. After my folks back East received the pictures of my February birthday dinner in 1989, Mom called.

"How come you're so fat?" she asked with her typical candor.

If my own mother considered me to be overweight, it was time to do something about it. While nursing my youngest child, I was constantly hungry and thirsty and ate a lot, but my metabolism was active and there was no worry about gaining weight. Unfortunately, I didn't change my habits after Steve was weaned and the pounds remained through the years.

After hearing Mom's candid remark, I resolved to change my ways and through sheer will power, put myself on the Smaller Plate, Smaller Portion (SPSP) diet. My fat, salt and sugar intake were reduced and five light meals a day replaced three larger ones. A year later, I had lost 15 pounds and happily kept it off.

One spring night while soaping in the shower, I discovered an unfamiliar lump in my right breast. Not finding anything similar on the left side, I immediately made an appointment for my first mammogram on the next day. Within days of subsequent lab work, five very uncomfortable needle biopsies, and a consultation with a plastic surgeon regarding reconstruction, I got the news that I had a tumor. It was a bit overwhelming, but not frightening, and I felt I could deal with having a lumpectomy. With the love and support of my family and friends, my spirits and hope for survival remained high and within a month, the tumor was removed.

If I hadn't taken the advice of a friend, I would not be alive today. It was Tobie who suggested that I get a second opinion after my surgery, and I agreed that it was a reasonable and prudent thing to do. My pathology slides were delivered to the lab of the oncologist she'd referred and the results came back within days.

The pathology department of the hospital at which I had my lumpectomy had missed something critical. The oncologist's lab found that 10 per cent of one of 19 removed lymph nodes had cancer cells present. Now I was facing both radiation and chemotherapy and by mid July I began the treatments, completing them by early December. My hair thinned but did not fall out. The nausea occurred only during the first few days of my last three treatments and on the whole, I weathered the summer pretty well.

But ten days after my last chemo, my family and I went on a multi-generational, three-week trip to China, Hong Kong and Taiwan. Truthfully, it was not a good time emotionally, psychologically or physically for me as I didn't care to or feel well enough to travel when my immune system was at its lowest. But the journey had been planned for over a year and we were committed to going.

My instincts were right. Two days after our return from that whirlwind trip abroad, I plunged into a depression caused by a hormonal imbalance brought about by the chemotherapy.

During the following months of rest, recuperation, therapy and a leave of absence from my position as a public relations professional with the Los Angeles Unified School District, the words of author H. Jackson Brown described my mindset: "When you look back on your life, you will regret the things you haven't done, more than those you have."

Throughout my adult life, I knew in my heart there was another world beyond academia, and my cancer experience drove home the point that life was too precious and short to waste on not actuating many of my dreams. A life-long reader and writer who envied her husband's business trips to all corners of the country and the world, I wanted to write a book and have a business of my own, although doing what, I had not a clue.

On a beautiful morning while sitting under blossoming fruit trees next to my *Koi* fish pond and pondering options for redirecting my life, I experienced an epiphany. I actually felt God's grace flowing through me like an infusion as His purpose for my life became crystal clear. The moment was exactly as the cartoons show it — a light bulb going on in my head or a zigzagged lightning bolt flashing.

My love for and appreciation of my Chinese heritage and culture, learning, reading and writing came through my parents. With my upbringing in four countries as a diplomat's daughter, a change from my architecture major to English and history, and a passion instilled by my grandparents for helping others, I knew exactly what I wanted and had to do to serve others: bridge cultures for better business between Asians and non-Asians.

With no business or accounting experience and nothing but a vision, passion and mission that spawned a no-can-fail attitude, I coined the moniker "intercultural consultant" and took the first step on a thousand-mile journey. It was on St. Patrick's Day 1989 that I applied for a business license and wrote a check to have stationery and cards printed. I then studied everything about business startups that I could get my hands on and was on my way to meet my destiny as an entrepreneur and consultant.

If I hadn't been a good Chinese wife and listened to my husband in 2004, I would not have made the appointment for a routine physical exam, which included a mammogram that revealed a new, small mass inside my right breast. A mastectomy was followed by chemotherapy and daily dosages of Arimedex, and I began to see a doctor of traditional Chinese medicine (TCM) to aid my body in detoxification and healing.

January of 2007 arrived. For three weeks, California experienced rare, colder-than-normal temperatures that hovered near or below freezing for the first time in a century. The weather killed trees, fruits and vegetables statewide, caused water to freeze in and break pipes, and generally raised havoc everywhere.

During one of my daily 2.5-mile morning walks, I stepped onto what I thought was just a dark ribbon of sprinkler water running across the road. But it had frozen, becoming black ice, causing my foot to slip and down I went onto my left hip. Throughout the rest of the year, acupuncture treatments, massage and physical therapy filled my calendar as I struggled to manage the pain for what I thought was a bruised hip. But one morning a year later, I woke up in agony, unable even to swing my legs sideways to get out of bed.

An x-ray was followed a few days later with a chilling phone message left on my voicemail informing me what the radiologist had found.

"You have bone cancer."

The news was devastating and after hearing it, my husband and I could only hold onto each other and cry together. During the appointment with the oncologist we were told the cancer which had originated in my breast, had reached the fourth stage, spreading to other areas of my body.

It was a frightening time for all in our family, but when I finally calmed down again, I realized that the message represented another opportunity in life. It was a third wake-up call sent to me from a higher power. It forced me to once again, take a hard look at my diet and lifestyle, and find room and motivation for improvement and change. I have accepted that I have metastasized breast cancer (MCB) but have also resolved to do whatever is necessary to help my body heal, fight and extend my life.

Things had to and did change. Two years and a second radiation and third chemotherapy treatment later, I am thinner, healthier, and under the care of a traditional Chinese doctor. No longer am I conflicted about using complementary treatment, by combining Chinese nutritional habits for prevention and Western medical science and technology. Radiation and chemotherapy have helped me again, as has the vast body of knowledge that is traditional Chinese medicine (TCM). To me, it is the best of both worlds.

I conscientiously slowed down the pace of my life and delight in an increase in a feeling of serenity of mind and spirit, achieved through meditation, visualization and creativity and taking my morning walks surrounded by nature. Meanwhile, the vigilance continues related to on-going monitoring of my health for any new activity, osteoporosis and other considerations following chemo.

Now I am convinced that we already have at least one cure for cancer, and that is prevention. It is the theme of this book. Moreover, I deeply acknowledge, appreciate and thank the countless dedicated medical and research professionals, from every cultural heritage, alternative, complementary and traditional practitioners alike who have shared their knowledge through the ages and contributed to the longevity and quality of life of so many of us survivors.

My support goes to patient support organizations as well as cancer research that focus on predictive medicine so that science can eventually provide us with sophisticated genetic-screening tools and new treatments for those who are at high risk.

It is neither by accident or coincidence that there are 55 sections that comprise *A Survivor's Secrets to Health and Happiness.* In Chinese numerology and feng shui, five is the number of change, motion, excitement, movement, activity and transformation.

When the two digits are added together, the total is 10 and, adding 1+0, the base number is 1. One is the number for independence, willingness to take risks, sowing the seeds, starting new ventures, learning from experience, rather than others, progress and finally, individual creative pursuits.

While Buddha achieved enlightenment while sitting under a bodhi tree, by God's grace I discovered my purpose in life twenty-one years ago during a moment of transformation and light while sitting under an avocado tree (I live in California) next to my koi pond. My mission became and is clear: to acquire as much knowledge as possible to share, and to spread a message of faith, gratitude and hope as long as I can, to as many as I can.

Best wishes for your journey to beauty, healthy living and happiness for the rest of your life.

—Angi Ma Wong

Table of Contents

Author's Note

Table of Contents

Secrets to Health

1. Wisdom from an ancient philosopher 1
2. Get (back) in touch with nature 3
3. Old is new again 6
4. Your first drink of the day 9
5. The mother-of-the-bride's dress 12
6. Examining a food label 14
7. Check your information sources 18
8. Country diets versus city diets 22
9. Develop sound eating habits 25
10. Timing is everything 27
11. When to eat what at each meal 29
12. Eat multiple meals a day 30
13. Keep a good alkaline-acid balance in your diet 32
14. Get into the SPSP habit 35
15. Limit one protein per meal 37
16. Combine foods properly 39
17. Make your own soups, teas, and smoothies 41
18. Drink hot liquids during a meal 44
19. How to eat your meals 46
20. Bring color to your food 49
21. Eat seasonal foods 54
22. Watch what you put onto your skin 58

23. Remove toxins from your environment 61
24. Use natural cleaning products 63
25. Keep the air clean inside your home. 66
26. Keep your home and work space germ-free 68
27. Personal health habits in public places. 71
28. Staying healthy while traveling 75
29. Get rid of poisonous people in your life 77
30. Don't let "dirty" electricity ruin your health 79
31. Get a good night's rest 83
32. And for our planet 86

Secrets to Happiness

33. Be true to yourself 91
34. Love what you do 94
35. Your purpose in life 101
36. For everything, there is 112
37. Missing the gold 115
38. Ways to be rich 119
39. When you're feeling down 123
40. How to be happy 127
41. Keep score of your successes 131
42. How to choose a mate, friend or partner 134
43. Be kind to yourself 136
44. Response-ability 144
45. Don't put your dreams or life on hold 147
46. How to make smart decisions 154
47. That I may serve 156
48. Fight fear 160

49. Riches that cannot be stolen 168

50. Enjoy the peaks and the valleys 172

51. How to be remembered 174

52. How to measure your life 178

53. Choose your battles 180

54. Love is 184

55. Last words from a saint 187

Recommended reading 189

Resources 191

Index 193

Secrets
to Health

If you aren't getting the answers, you aren't asking the right questions. —Enez Johnson

1 Wisdom from an ancient philosopher

Those of you who are familiar with my work have seen one of my favorite quotes by Confucius in my other publications. I always thought it would be the ideal saying to put at the main entrance of every school so all who entered, both children and adults alike, could read and remember its message in their hearts.

If there is light in the soul, there is beauty in the person
If there is beauty in the person, there is harmony at home
If there is harmony at home, there is order in the country
If there is order in the country, there is peace in the world.
—Confucius

I bring it up here because I believe that it is the heart of this book about health and happiness. For your mental and physical health, seek the light that is SUNlight, which the body converts to Vitamin D when it hits our skin.

As we age, we tend to lose the body fat that keeps us warm, so we put on hats and long sleeves, and stay indoors, thus depriving ourselves of vital Vitamin D which gives us energy, boosts our immune systems, keeps our moods in balance, and enhances our bone health. Even younger folks aren't getting enough of this essential vitamin because they mostly work indoors and use sunscreen when outdoors.

People who have the lowest levels of Vitamin D are 40% more likely to catch colds and flu. Those who take daily supplements of at least 800 to 1200 IU of Vitamin D a day lower the number of colds or flu they experienced.

Unfortunately, widespread avoidance of the sun due to fear of skin cancer, which occurs from over-exposure, has resulted in a decrease of Vitamin D in our average blood levels, according to a report in the *Archives of Internal Medicine,* which was featured in the 2009 September/October issue of *AARP* magazine. In the same article, Vitamin D's benefits included a reduction in the risk of cancer (at least six different types), heart disease (especially men), hip fracture, tooth loss and an increase in muscle strength.

So get outside and soak in the sun! Better yet, walk for at least a half hour daily, either in ten-minute increments or all thirty minutes at once, but however you do it, try to expose your bare skin to at least 10 to 20 minutes of sunshine daily if you can. Both the oxygen that you inhale and the Vitamin D that your body makes when sunlight hits your body's largest organ (the skin) are powerful allies on your path to better health.

2

Get (back) in touch with nature

In the manic hustle and bustle of 21st-century life in which we are surrounded by science, technology, computers, mobile and cell devices and electronic communications, exercise and a routine of being outdoors energize me every morning. It gives me the feeling of being grounded each day and prepares me mentally and physically for the day ahead. Combining your exercise with communing with nature is a great way to reap the rewards of both.

My daily walk is something that I am religious about. It began fifteen years ago after I took a free test at a Rotary-sponsored health fair and discovered that my cholesterol levels were higher than normal. The discovery impelled me to launch a daily routine that now starts my day. Being a morning person, I find that getting up and out right away best fits my natural body clock and lifestyle before my day becomes too busy. An added benefit is that the exercise clears my mind and generates new energy as well as stimulates creative thoughts and ideas, so I carry a pen and pad in my pocket to jot them down.

The sun shines not on us, but in us. —John Muir

Only you can choose the most convenient time and that is the one decision key to adhering to any exercise program. Whether you're an early bird or a night owl, get out and moving and back to nature by at least walking or biking at least half an hour daily, five days a week.

If you can't fit in a solid half hour, break it into three 10-minute workouts. Step out of your office and walk outside, around your building, away from your desk and the computer for 10 minutes. Hold your head and shoulders straight with your tummy tucked in and swing your arms as you breathe deeply from your diaphragm.

Women over 50 who either ride their bicycles or walk moderately 45 minutes a day for five or more days a week only contract colds 30% of the time, compared to the 50% of women who exercise only by stretching once a week. Initially it takes exercising seven days a week to lose weight and five days a week to maintain those lost pounds.

You'll be increasing the oxygen and blood flowing throughout your body, speeding up your food absorption, and getting nutrients out to your cells, strengthening your heart and many other muscles, preventing a stroke or heart attack and decreasing stress hormones.

The best thing about walking is that it's free, except for an investment in a comfortable pair of walking shoes. Two pairs are better so that they can be worn alternately, allowing each to dry out. You don't need to drive to and from a gym or health club, pay membership fees or keep up with or spend on the latest in exercise fashions.

You don't have to share equipment handled and touched by countless other people who have left behind their germs and sweat. You won't expose yourself to showers, floors, lockers and other facilities shared by who knows how many strangers.

Moreover, there is an entire branch of traditional Chinese medicine dedicated to reflexology, based on the belief that all of our body's organs and functions are activated through the acupressure points located on the bottoms of our feet. When we walk, we are literally and actively contributing to our own good health and well-being.

Imagine that with every breath and step you take, your immune system is getting a boost, not to mention your overall health. Don't be surprised to find your cholesterol level and blood pressure lowered, your diabetes and weight tamed, your emotions in better control and your feeling of general well-being enhanced immensely.

If walking doesn't appeal to you, swim, bicycle, shoot hoops with your kids, push the old-fashioned lawn mower across your yard or the mop and vacuum inside your home, garden, dance, even wash windows. All of these can give your body the workout it needs to keep in shape as you stretch, reach and pull your muscles. Whatever activity you choose, keep active to burn up the calories.

Remember to warm up before and cool down after you exercise. Eat a snack that has both a carbohydrate and a protein within 15 minutes after working out so your body can transform your food into muscle-healing glycogen.

Your body, mind and spirit will all thank you!

NATURE IS PAINTING FOR US, DAY AFTER DAY,
PICTURES OF INFINITE BEAUTY
IF ONLY WE HAVE THE EYES TO SEE THEM.
—JOHN RUSKIN

3 Old is new again

I grew up with and am a passionate believer in the philosophy that is the foundation of traditional Chinese medicine (TCM) to prevent illness and disease naturally. It works through following a good diet that boosts my body's regenerative and recuperation powers from inside out, coupled with exercise and a balanced lifestyle. TCM is based on the profound belief in the mind-body-spirit connection that has been known and practiced in China for thousands of years, long before Western medicine developed.

The major difference is that TCM has always focused on treating the whole person, connecting the mind, body and spirit, and emphasized *preventing* illness and disease in the first place, not just curing the symptoms as does Western medicine. The three core tenets of TCM (and feng shui, acupuncture, acupressure, reflexology, meditation, martial arts, tai chi, chi gong, herbal and folk cures) are: the flow of vital energy (chi), the five elements (wood, fire, earth, metal, water), and the balance between yin (female, nurturing, dark, quiet) and yang (male, aggressive, light, active). To the Chinese way of thinking, culture and life, these three integral components determine the state of our health, well-being, relationships and ultimately, our lives and longevity. Many of our health challenges today originate from our lifestyles, diets or emotions.

Because the basic philosophy of TCM is vastly different from Western traditional medicine's methods of curing sickness and disease, it has taken over a generation for it to be accepted in the United States by health professionals and mainstream America. And yet for thousands of years, Chinese traditional medicine has been well documented and practiced throughout the history of the world's oldest continuous civilization.

It is holistic, natural and integrated, utilizing what is provided to us in the form of organic material such as plants, flowers, trees, roots, vegetables, fruits, herbs, spices and even animals. On the other hand, most Western medicines are synthetic, developed by pharmaceutical companies and are mostly untested as to their longtime effects on humans and their environment.

Chinese tradition teaches us to eat appropriately to maintain balance in our lives and to prevent disease and illness in our bodies, spirits and minds. Even our meals are cooked to include the five flavors: sweet, salty, bitter, sour and pungent, and foods are designated as being either yin or yang and having either cold or hot energy.

Each of those same elements is associated with an emotion, a major organ or system within our bodies, a taste, a compass direction, a number, an animal symbol, a color and many aspects of our lives.

Heart problems? Bring more joy and laughter into your life. Liver or vision problems? Manage your anger and frustration. Have trouble breathing or something wrong with your respiratory system or lungs? Get grief counseling right away. Stomach, weight or digestive illness? Take measures to stop worry and stress, which research has shown causes you to overeat, neglect exercise and sound eating habits and gain weight. Kidneys or hearing malfunctioning? Face your fears.

We meditate and savor quiet time and serenity to bring peace to our minds, bodies and spirits. We balance life with joy and activity, working hard and exercising. We nourish and enrich ourselves with knowledge, satisfying and loving, familial relationships and strong faith systems. We accept that life is a integral part of a grand universe as well as nature, both of which move in cycles of birth and death, to repeat over and over through time.

Thanks to modern technology, the Internet and the old standby, books and libraries, information is readily available to all of us. We have free choice to empower ourselves and take charge of our health.

Your first drink of the day

Water is essential to all life on, and the life *of* our planet. It is probably the most precious resource that we have. Every creature or plant that has ever existed here required water, either to drink it or live in it. Wars have been waged and lives lost in both the animal and plant kingdoms to obtain water, its access or its source.

We humans can live without food for seven days, but would perish if we did without this elixir of life for three days. It doesn't take much imagination to understand that without good old H_2O, there would be no life on our planet and it would be as barren as the moon.

Here's how critical water is to the proper functioning of our bodies. It makes up 83% of our blood, 75% of our brain and muscles and 22% of our bones. Water is the conduit that removes waste, transports and aids in the absorption of oxygen and nutrients from our food to our bodies, prepares oxygen so we can breathe it, protects our organs and joints, and keeps our bodies at an even temperature.

Both my Uncle Arthur and his wife, Edna, who were both physicians, gave me the following advice.

Take your first drink after you wake up in the morning upon arising from a good night's sleep. The first thing that should enter your system is warm, filtered water within the hour. This habit is practiced by many people in Asia, especially in Japan, to aid in food absorption, to get their bodies' "plumbing" activated by stimulating their intestines and to help flush out the waste produced in their bodies while they were sleeping.

Drink between two to four glasses of warm water on an empty stomach first thing in the morning, and then brush your teeth, clean your mouth and do not take any food or water for 45 minutes.

I find that break to be the ideal time to go on my morning walk and return home in time to eat my breakfast within the hour of my rising. That water will hydrate your body and keep your kidneys and liver in good working order, as well as keep your skin clear and your mind and spirit soothed as you commune with nature.

Invest in a water filter for your kitchen faucet, either under the sink or a removable one on a pitcher. Filtering your water removes the carcinogens before you drink it. You can add freshly squeezed lemon juice to help maintain your pH balance at the beginning of the day. You can also drink a cinnamon (1 teaspoon)-honey (1 tablespoon)-apple cider vinegar (2 tablespoons) mixture that is dissolved in warm water, or sip a cup of non-caffeinated herbal or green tea before breakfast. You can have any of these drinks as it is gentle on your stomach, natural and healthy during your day as well.

While you may not think of yourself as a plant, here's a daily human "irrigation schedule" to maintain for good health:

🌀 Two glasses of water upon rising for your internal organs
🌀 One glass of water a half hour before meals to aid digestion and help weight loss by feeling full

☙ One glass of water before your bath or shower to lower your blood pressure

☙ One glass of water before retiring for the night to help your blood circulation, which helps to avoid heart attacks or strokes

WATER IS PRICELESS. USE IT WISELY AND PRUDENTLY, TREATING IT AS THE TREASURE IT IS TO BOTH YOURSELF AND THE PLANET.

5 The mother-of-the-bride's dress

Our older daughter, Wendy, was getting married, and our family was caught in the frenzy of pre-nuptial preparations for the Chinese-Filipino-Catholic-Navy wedding to be held on the first Friday of March 2007. Wendy had decided that she would like her bridesmaids to wear the traditional, form-fitting, ankle-length Chinese cheongsam with its distinctive high Mandarin collar and slits up the sides of the dress.

Together Wendy and I found the elegant, peach-colored raw Thai silk fabric and delivered it to the custom dressmaker who specialized in making the dresses for Chinatown beauty pageant contestants and brides-to-be.

My cheongsam would be in a complementary raspberry hue in the same style. As the mother of the bride, I decided that I wanted to rid myself of my slightly protruding tummy and slim down to be svelter on my daughter's big day. My oldest son Jason suggested that I go on the "no-white" diet, which sounded easy enough.

"Eliminate all the whites," he told me, "white sugar, white flour, white bread and white rice." "White" meant that sugar, flour, bread and rice that is labeled "enriched" has been bleached, scrubbed, or generally processed or altered in some way so that the nutritional value has been removed.

So I stopped eating white rice, which wasn't a big sacrifice because I'm not a big carbohydrate consumer anyway. I tried to substitute brown rice and wild rice, which my husband didn't like, and discovered other wonderful grains such as quinoa, couscous, faro and amaranth, which are nutritious substitutes for rice.

Reading each label of every packaged food I bought became a new habit and, more often than not, I rejected many because of their high sodium or sugar content. Honey, maple syrup, or stevia-sweetened old-fashioned oatmeal in the mornings. Occasionally, whole wheat bread became French toast made with egg whites, or was toasted and spread with sunflower or almond butter, and then sandwiched with banana or apple slices.

I learned that grape seed, sesame, red palm, flaxseed and olive oils should be staples in our kitchens, along with rice vinegar, turmeric, cinnamon and sea salt. Red palm oil was the best for deep-frying and sesame oil the best for stir-frying, because they have a higher burn temperature than olive oil. Fish and krill oil supplements are highly beneficial to our health.

My only regret was that I didn't start on the no-whites effort early enough, as in *before* the holidays, instead of waiting until only a month before the wedding. Alas, this mother-of-the-bride definitely looked well-fed and pleasantly plump in the wedding pictures.

But voila! Within a month after the big day, the mirror showed results — I had dropped fifteen pounds.

A Chinese proverb says: "Evil enters the body through the mouth," which is another way of saying "You are what you eat." Likewise, good health and illness prevention enters the body through the food you allow into your body.

6 Examining a food label

In January 2009, Dr. Mehmet Oz was a guest on the Oprah Winfrey show and revealed five ingredients we should watch out for in packaged foods. While I did not see the show, the information was shared with me by a receptionist at my oncologist's office and I added it to a little card I carry in my wallet.

Don't purchase or eat any product that has any of the following words listed *among the first five* ingredients on a food label:

1. Sugar
2. High-fructose corn syrup
3. Enriched wheat flour
4. Saturated fat (animal fat)
5. Hydrogenated oil

I call these the Fatal Five as they are among the unhealthiest components found in our food today.

Federal law requires that ingredients on every food label must be listed in order by the amount used to make whatever is in a processed food. Quite simply, it means that when you see sugar listed first after the word "Ingredients" on a package, there is more sugar than anything else in the food inside, followed by the second ingredient, then the third.

If you see "enriched wheat flour" listed first among the ingredients on the wrapping on a loaf of bread, don't be fooled or misled as many of us (me included) have been. The word "enriched" means that the wheat flour has been processed, i.e., bleached, or has additives of some sort included. It does *not* mean nutritious ingredients have been added to the wheat flour, the main ingredient used to make that bread.

More often than not, other common descriptions, such as those listed below, can be very misleading.

- Good source of whole grains
- Organic
- Sugar-free
- High fiber

For an experiment, go to the bread section of your grocer or a health food store. Pick up several similar types of bread from different companies, for example, compare five or six different loaves of "wheat bread," "multi-grain bread" or whatever kind you enjoy or usually purchase.

Read and compare the labels and make note of the order in which the ingredients are listed, remembering that the quantity of any ingredient puts it closer to the head of the list. A simple comparison will reveal how much sugar, sugar substitutes and other artificial sweeteners, preservatives, salt and other "things" are included.

Check *everything* on labels, including the number of calories, amount of sodium and other nutrients on any packaged food you buy. This custom will also help you to identify anything to which you may be allergic, such as milk, soy, eggs, peanuts, wheat, fish, coconut and shellfish.

Have you ever noticed how many grams of sodium can be found in the following items: a can of V-8 juice (which you can duplicate by substituting a can of tomato juice and adding hot sauce, celery juice or stalk and pepper to taste) or soup, a tub of cottage cheese, a package of chips, a box of baking mix, an envelope of miso soup or other processed food? At the cost of 150,000 deaths and $24 billion a year in the United States, salt consumption has resulted in an alarming increase in strokes, heart disease and hypertension.

If we are to keep to a healthy 2000-calorie-a-day diet, but we're not careful, we can consume between 400 and 1500 mg of sodium and one to three days' amount of saturated fat, by eating a box of popcorn from the movie concession stand, according to WebMD.com.

Don't overlook the amount of the different kinds of fat, such as artery-clogging saturated fat, trans fat, and cholesterol. These bad fats are found in red meat; whole-milk dairy products such as ice cream, butter, cheese and sour cream; creamy sauces and dressings; anything fried; palm and palm kernel oil, cocoa butter, peanut and coconut oil (although great for moisturizing your skin) and lard.

Good fats are monounsaturated, such as olive, canola, argan and grape seed oils, and unlike saturated fats, do not become solid at room temperature. Take another look at the small print of the ingredients in that protein powder or bar that you eat and you may be shocked. By the way, if you are paying more for more protein in a protein drink, shake or food, think again. Your body can only process 5 to 9 grams of protein an hour so if that canned or bottled shake you buy and drink has 43 grams listed, 34 of those grams and your money literally goes down the toilet as it is eliminated from your body.

Developing a habit of religiously reading food labels is one of the best things you can immediately begin doing for yourself and your family. You will save money and time on doctors, tests, lab work and hospital bills later as you prevent health problems.

Good nutrition and health starts at the grocery store before you bring food into your home and launches you onto a lifelong path to looking and feeling great, enjoying good health and longevity.

7 Check your information sources

Three years ago and even recently this year while I was working on the manuscript of this book, friends and relative sent me the same email entitled "Cancer Update from John Hopkins." I printed and added it to my growing note file. Basically, the report detailed eating a healthy, common-sense diet that included multiple servings of fruits and vegetables daily, with seeds, nuts and other sources of protein, and most importantly, removing all meat from one's diet: beef, pork, lamb, veal, venison, and only eating organic chicken and sustainable, deep water fish.

When we consume any of these meats, we are also ingesting all the chemicals, pesticides and other ingredients that have been added to their food. It is well documented that many different kinds of hormones are fed to dairy cows to increase their milk production. The beef we eat come mostly from those cows and the hormones are absorbed into our bodies. Look into getting your protein instead from organic meats identified as free range or grass-fed and other sources.

One particular sentence in the Hopkins report jumped out at me because I had not heard it before. The report stated that eating red meat caused sugar cravings and sugar feeds cancer growth. I thought about a typical American meal, with lots of animal meat and starches, followed by a sweet, sugary dessert. But since then, the fact that eating refined sugar contributes to cancer growth has shown up in many articles and media features. Images accompanying reports about rising obesity across our country also showed overweight people whose diets consisted of meat and potatoes, followed by huge desserts.

I believed this to be great information, so I tested the theory and eliminated red meat and dairy from my diet. Amazingly, my sweet tooth disappeared, along with my love of ice cream, which was quite remarkable for me for while living at home, I often shared a dish of ice cream with my dad late at night.

But still, as any author, I felt impelled to examine the source of this information originating from an email, looking and sounding so official, and was astonished at what I found. The "update" was debunked as an email hoax by the Sidney Kimmel Comprehensive Cancer Center at Johns Hopkins University.

In November 2007, the World Cancer Research Fund — American Institute for Cancer Research, was attended by experts from the university and the following eight guidelines appeared in its report "Food, Nutrition, Physical Activity and the Prevention of Cancer: A Global Perspective."

a.   Be as lean as possible without becoming underweight.

b.   Be physically active for at least 30 minutes every day.

c.   Avoid sugary drinks. Limit consumption of energy-dense foods, particularly processed foods high in added sugar, or low in fiber or high in fat.

d.   Eat more of a variety of vegetables, fruits, whole grains and legumes such as beans.

e.   Limit consumption of red meats (such as beef, pork and lamb) and avoid processed meats (sausage, ham, jerky and so on.)

f. If consumed at all, limit alcoholic drinks to two a day for men and one for women.

g. Limit consumption of salty foods and foods processed with salt (sodium).

h. Don't use supplements to protect against cancer.

While much of the phony email gave common sense advice and it was discredited as a hoax, just receiving it led me to further investigation as well as eliminating red meat and sugar from my diet. I was fortunate that while the report was not generated by the university, the guidelines were still sound and useful in effecting my weight loss.

But be forewarned. There is an incredible amount of information on the Internet. However, there are no regulations, censors or entities that oversee its content. As the ultimate manifestation of the freedom of speech, the potential for scams, fraud, theft and other criminal activities is great. You cannot know who has posted anything that you hear or see on this medium.

It doesn't take much for dishonest, evil, mean-spirited, cruel, unscrupulous or heartless people to prey on others. Anyone can fabricate, write, cut and paste, alter, steal and post any word or image and send it throughout the world in minutes. The marvelous, convenient technology of the Internet then becomes a sticky web that entraps the naïve, innocent, gullible and weak.

There are countless publications, Internet postings and also a lot of excellent information available covering men's and women's health and well-being. Those that have stood the test of time, such as *Prevention* magazine, which has been around for 60 years and read by over 10.5 million in the U.S. alone, are trusted and authoritative sources. Are you surprised to learn that the American Association of Retired People (AARP) bulletin and magazine are the two magazines in the United States with the largest circulation, both with over 24 million each? Cross-check information and rely on dependable sources and publications that have established their credibility over time — *Reader's Digest, Woman's Day, Family Circle* and others.

The old sayings, "If it sounds too good to be true, it probably is" and "Don't believe everything you hear or read" are still worth remembering.

8 Country diets versus city diets

The story about Professor Janet Plant also came to me through an email. She is a scientist from the United Kingdom who was treated five times for cancer with radiotherapy and chemotherapy.

During a trip, her husband's well-meaning Chinese friends had given to him herbal suppositories in addition to cards and messages, to take back to Plant as cures for her breast cancer. The Plants, who are both scientists, got into a discussion and were curious as to why women in China had practically non-existent incidences of cancer.

The proverbial light bulb went off when both Dr. Plant and her husband realized at about the same time, that Chinese women did not consume dairy products. The Chinese diet in the 1980s showed only 14% of the caloric intake was from fat, while the Western diet indicated 34% was from fat. The Chinese diet did not include, cow's milk, cheese, ice cream or yogurt, nor were any of these fed to their babies.

Statistics indicated that Chinese women in general only got cancer at the rate of 1 in 10,000, in Hong Kong, it was 1 in 34, and in the United Kingdom, the ratio was 1 in 12. Even in the aftermath of the atomic attacks on Hiroshima and Nagasaki, the incidence was still only half that of Western women living in industrial cities.

When I read Dr. Plant's article, I remembered something that had happened to me over 20 years ago when I had my first cancer experience. My oncologist at the time said he could only think of one reason why I was the first and only one of four sisters to get cancer, with no history of it in my parents or my family. He speculated that it was because I had been adopted at six months old into the Ma family and had spent my childhood growing up in New Zealand.

When I heard him say that, it made perfect sense. During my childhood, I grew up eating lots of red meat in the form of lamb and drank milk that was delivered to our home in bottles with an inch of cream at the top. Moreover, I had reached puberty in Taiwan early at the age of eleven and breast fed my children, two other conditions that put me on the high-risk category to get breast cancer. On the other hand, my three sisters had grown up in China and Taiwan where eating beef, cheese and yogurt and drinking milk were not common in their Chinese diets.

The Japanese-American radiologist at St. John's Medical Center in Santa Monica gave me some alarming statistics when my first tumor was discovered in 1989. Japanese women only developed breast cancer at the rate of 1 in 4,000 and American women were getting it at the rate of 1 in 11.

But the ratio for fourth-generation American women of Japanese descent was 1 in 8. His opinion was that lifestyle and diet were the culprits. (Unfortunately, today's breast cancer rate among non-Asian women in the United States has caught up to 1 in 8.)

In Hong Kong, a British colony for ninety-nine years, the breast cancer rate among women is 1 in 34, especially among the more affluent. That figure is traced to eating a primarily Western diet richer in fats, red meat and dairy products, in sharp contrast to the far healthier diets of Chinese women.

The latter's meals remain predominantly comprised of vegetables, fish, chicken, rice, soups, and some pork, typically the traditional foods of southern Chinese provinces. Moreover, most of the women in China still worked in rural areas outdoors in contrast to the Hong Kong residents who lived in and worked in high-density factories and office buildings in Hong Kong and Kowloon's countless high rises.

Dr. Plant eliminated beef and dairy products from her diet and monitored her tumor, which began to shrink within a very short time.

9 Develop sound eating habits

Food is an important component of any culture and many of our habits stem from our ethnic or geographic origins. Sources of water, protein, fruits and vegetables, grains, nuts and seeds, oils, and cooking methods, availability and accessibility of food and drink, and even economic factors influence what, how, why and when you eat and drink.

There is truth in the old saying "You are what you eat." Good nutritional and eating habits are formed during your childhood and often stay with you throughout your life. If you ate a lot of junk food, sugar, desserts, salt, red meat or basically anything often, it became a part of your diet.

Unfortunately, almost every food that you purchase that comes in a can, box or bag has been processed in some way and has additives, generally in the form of salt, sugar or preservatives. With the decrease in daily physical activity combined with the increase in the use of technology, tools, games and equipment in first and second-world countries, it comes as no surprise that both childhood and adult obesity has become a global health crisis. On one end of the spectrum are countries that cannot feed their populations who are starving to death. On the other hand, in industrialized nations, obesity from eating too much unhealthy foods manifests itself as heart disease, stroke, diabetes, cancer, high cholesterol and blood pressure.

Research has shown that cancer is the scourge of modern civilization, found almost exclusively in the world's metropolitan areas of its industrialized nations, but rarely in primarily agricultural regions and countries. As a matter of fact, a preponderance of the longest-living people in the world is primarily found in rural or remote areas.

Consider how often you do the following:

- Consume barbecued, grilled or fried foods
- Drink ice water or cold drinks filled with ice
- Eat raw vegetables or at salad bars
- Experience food allergies, headache, burping, heartburn, bloating, passing gas, loose stools or a stomachache after a meal
- Drink more than two glasses of alcohol a day

These dietary habits strain your stomach, digestive system and liver's ability to digest all food properly. Even vitamins, supplements and medications need to be broken down efficiently to be absorbed into and benefit your body. Do not disregard the possibility that some of the herbal, protein, vitamin or other supplements you are taking may actually be accelerating cancer growth in your body.

Your body's normal temperature is 98.6 degrees and drinking or eating cold foods causes a "shock " to your digestive system. Discomfort such as those mentioned above can be avoided by eating cooked foods, i.e. stir-fried or steamed to retain their nutrients, avoiding cold foods and icy cold drinks.

The more natural your food is, the more it benefits your health.

10 Timing is everything

After my second cancer experience in 2004, sixteen years after the first, I was under the care of a new oncologist. I had completed my chemotherapy, had surgery, lost my hair and was feeling pretty low. Concurrently, I was busy preparing our family home of eighteen years to put on sale. It was a hectic and anxious time, but we were able to sell our house and at the same time, find our first home to enjoy as empty-nesters.

Every three months I would dutifully keep my appointment with my oncologist and it was uplifting to hear from him that I was doing well. He asked me if I had any concerns.

"I want to lose some weight," I told him. "Getting rid of those last 20 pounds would be wonderful."

"At what time do you eat dinner?" was his next question.

"About 8 to 8:30 p.m. every night," I answered, going on to explain that I habitually waited to share the evening meal with my husband.

"Just eat an hour earlier," he advised and further explained that eating an earlier dinner would give my body time to burn off calories with regular activity before I retired for the night. Before 7 p.m. was good, but before 6 p.m. was even better, I learned.

It wasn't too difficult to shift my nightly eating custom, nor convince my husband that I would be starting and finishing my evening meals before 7 p.m. without him. There was no more snacking or waiting in hunger for him to arrive home later from his own activities, many of which were conducted more than a forty-five minute drive away.

This one small change worked! I saw the pounds start to drop off.

11

When to eat what at each meal

I don't remember where I picked up this tip, but after some thought about our digestive systems, it was another strategy that really made a lot of sense. At meals, eat the protein first, then the vegetables. This practice is more natural and in tune with how your body digests your food.

You should eat protein at the beginning of your meal because it takes about twenty-four hours to digest in your body. Following it up with your vegetables, which have all-important fiber helps your body process food along your interior plumbing more efficiently.

The French got it right by eating their salad at the end of a meal, while the Chinese traditionally serve hot soups or fresh fruit for dessert instead of cakes, ice cream, pies and other sweets loaded with carbohydrates, sugar and calories.

A good analogy is how you use hot soapy water to wash your dishes to cut and remove the grease on your dinnerware, cooking and eating utensils, getting everything squeaky clean. Drinking hot liquids, including water and tea, assist your body in breaking down the fats you have consumed, and move them out of your body, much like how hot, soapy water cleans your dishes.

12 Eat multiple meals a day

Another strategy that worked for me twenty years ago after my mom made that comment about my weight was to nibble all day, instead of eating three large meals. By not going for more than four hours in between eating *something* and eating small meals throughout the day, I didn't feel starved.

Every few hours, I'd munch on nutrient-rich, detoxifying and alkalizing foods, which almost always included a protein. These included the following:

- unsalted nuts, seeds, popcorn or trail mix
- low-fat string cheese, cottage cheese or hard cubes or wedges
- apples or other juicy fruits, nori seaweed snacks
- a protein drink or smoothie
- non-fat yogurt
- soup
- mashed canned sardines, chicken or peanut butter spread on whole wheat crackers
- three-bean or grain salad (e.g., made with quinoa, couscous or amaranth)
- vegetables such as carrot, celery, cauliflower and broccoli and other vegetables that are usually found in a relish tray
- pickled herring, oysters or clams or salmon and tuna salads

If you prefer or can't break the three-large-meals-a-day habit, you still can eat any of the aforementioned mini-meals as snacks. Throughout the day, keep drinking water, following each drink with a pinch of sea salt. Drinking at least 16 ounces of water before any of the three major meals will help you to feel full before you even begin eating, as well as stimulate your metabolism by 25%. The more water you drink during the day, the less you will crave sodas and other sweetened drinks.

The important point to remember is not to go for long periods of time without food, which results in becoming hungry at mid-morning as well as mid-afternoon, causing your blood sugar level to drop and setting off cravings. Be sure to get proteins, both simple and complex carbohydrates and water-rich fruits and vegetables during the day.

Over millions of years, your body has evolved to react to food deprivation by sending signals to your brain that it is starving. It is at these times that you may crave and then binge on salt-laden or sugar-filled snacks or what we know as junk food.

Even worse is if you wait too long to have dinner and end up over-eating to satisfy your hunger and then go to bed on a full stomach. Your digestive system is left overworking to break down your meal for absorption, which disturbs your rest and converts the starches to sugar during the night.

If you are undergoing treatments or taking medication that brings on nausea, here's something I learned during my pregnancies and later as a chemo patient. Eat all your meals "dry," which means not to drink any liquids *during* your meals. But after an hour, you may eat fruit and drink lots of liquids, such as water flavored with lemon or lime juice or soups and broths, but avoid caffeinated drinks.

13 Keep a good alkaline-acid balance in your diet

It all started millions of years ago when *homo sapiens* came onto the scene in prehistoric times and humans originally ate an exclusively vegetarian diet. Then in the last few centuries after the Industrial Revolution, meat and poultry production became industrialized, computerized, processed and more recently, genetically altered.

Antibiotics, hormones, chemicals and other additives were introduced into the diets of animals raised for food and these eventually made their way up to the top of the food chain and into our bodies.

Enter pH (Potential for Hydrogen) and the magic number of 7.0, which represents liquids, such as water and human blood, as being neutral. If there are more hydrogen (the H in the H_2O of water) ions in a liquid such as our blood, the more acidic it is. Any pH reading below 7.0 is considered acidic and above 7.0 is deemed alkaline. Our bodies work hard to neutralize acids that accumulate in our bodies' fluids and to keep our blood at an alkaline level of 7.3 or 7.4.

We must do our part in assisting our bodies in maintaining an optimum acid-alkaline balance to remain healthy, but unfortunately the modern diet in Western countries contributes to a serious imbalance in our pH levels. Research indicate this imbalance influences our immune and digestive systems, our joints, bone strength, hormones and the functioning of our vital organs, and contributes to an explosion of health problems, illnesses and diseases.

Consuming meat, all foods that have been processed, preserved, refined or packaged such as white flour, sugar, bread, rice, artificial sweeteners, pasteurized foods such as cheese or milk, alcohol, and caffeine (in coffee and soft drinks) all tip the pH balance toward a highly acidic state internally. Even eating fruit with your meal, instead of separately, can cause an acidic condition over time. Start eliminating or reducing your consumption of these foods.

To correct your pH imbalance, be sure that fresh and sea vegetables, whole grains such as millet, barley and oats, fruits and other alkaline-forming foods comprise at least 70%–80% of your diet. Chlorophyll, which is found in great abundance in green vegetables such as broccoli, asparagus, Brussels sprouts and mustard greens, is a powerful antioxidant and boosts the efficiency of the liver, the body's major detoxifier, to remove accumulated pollutants and other wastes.

Our modern day diets are very acidic, which overtaxes our bodies and can cause many health problems. If you remember your basic lessons about acid and alkaline balance (pH), you will also recall that an imbalance of either one results in disease and illness.

When we combine eating fruits, such as for a snack, with proteins and starches, the fruits start to ferment the other foods, which then become acidic. But just by eating fruits together and on an empty stomach, they convert to healthy alkaline to help balance your body's pH levels. Another good time to consume fruits is before a meal. For example, if you order a lunch or dinner at a restaurant and you have a choice between French fries or a fruit salad, choose the salad and eat it first.

Mid-morning and mid-afternoon are the most ideal times to eat fruit as your breakfast and lunch have pretty much left your stomach, which is empty again. Fresh fruits, which provide fiber, and freshly squeezed juices are more beneficial to your health than those that are canned. Check the labels on canned juices and you will discover how much not-so-hidden sugar is in them.

14 Get into the SPSP habit

At the same time I was nibbling throughout the day, staving off hunger, I also put myself on the SPSP diet. SPSP stands for Smaller Portion, Smaller Plate. In the West, we tend to eat our food served from large-sized plates and fill the plate up.

Meanwhile, the food industry has been steadily increasing the sizes of meals for many years and unconsciously, also our caloric intake, resulting in the alarming explosion of obesity, both in children and adults.

If your parents were like mine, survivors of the Depression era, they urged us to clean up our plates so as not to waste food. Remember being told, "Think of the starving children in _____ (fill in the country, usually China)." So being obedient children, we listened and obeyed.

Consider a new way of eating your meals by using smaller plates, such as salad size, especially in the evening. You can still fill up your plate so you don't feel deprived, but common sense says that you will only be consuming less.

> If you wish to grown thinner, diminish your dinner,
> And take to light claret, instead of pale ale. —H.S. Leigh

If you shove your food into your mouth, wolfing it down and barely chewing each bite, you will have consumed a larger quantity in the first twenty minutes than if you had eaten more slowly and enjoyed your meal. It takes that amount of time for the stomach to relay the message to your brain that it is full. Everything you eat afterward is over-eating.

Take your time to eat slowly and chew your food thoroughly (33 chews to each bite) and put down your fork in between bites. Relax and savor the flavors. Let your 10,000 taste buds do their work so you can truly appreciate your meals.

If you have difficulty slowing your pace, try eating spicy food, which forces you to take smaller bites, breathe or drink water. By the way, eating heavily seasoned foods speeds up your metabolism.

You'll be doing your stomach a big favor by helping it to break down what you eat so that your body can use it for absorption, healing, energy, regeneration and growth. Twenty minutes into the meal, you will begin to feel full. That's your signal to stop eating.

You might even like to try out the theory that using blue-colored plates makes your food appear less appetizing and cause you to eat less!

15

Limit one protein per meal

Your stomach works hard to digest what you eat and even harder if you are putting different kinds of proteins into your body, so it's best not to combine beef, pork, shellfish, fish, chicken, duck, lamb and veal. What kind of meal has so many types of proteins, you may ask?

If you've ever attended a Chinese banquet or overindulged at an all-you-can-eat buffet, you've experienced a cornucopia at its best, or shall I say, its worst. Even the "turf and surf" combo or the sampler at your favorite restaurant or barbecue house will tempt you.

When your digestive system is severely taxed by the introduction of such a variety of proteins, it does not work as effectively or efficiently. It also takes longer to break the food down and get it into your body.

Imagine that the undigested food remains in your digestive tract longer, and unless you have followed up all those proteins with lots of fiber-rich vegetables, things get pretty sluggish inside. Undigested food may even stay in your body longer, and may even start fermenting. Pretty nasty, eh?

By choosing to eat one type of protein, you are being kind to your stomach. If you feel like having chicken, have a chicken-based soup and a chicken entrée. If you choose a seafood, select an appetizer with a complementary ingredient or broth.

If you can't give up your red meat habit, at least do the following: reduce the amount; trim off the visible fat as well as the skin from poultry; avoid any meat that is burnt, charbroiled, barbecued or processed, such as salami, sausage, hot dogs and so on, choose leaner cuts, and reduce the frequency as well as the quantity to a total daily amount that is no larger than the size of your palm.

Other sources of protein are edamame, chickpeas and all kinds of other beans, walnuts, pine nuts, chestnuts, pumpkin seeds, black beans, pistachios, pecans and non-fat-dairy products from grass-fed (not corn-fed) cows, i.e., Swiss cheese. Tofu, tempeh and other soy products can also be protein sources, but some people have cancers that thrive on soy, and therefore cannot consume these foods.

By the way, waste by-products should be moved out of your body within 16 to 24 hours. As mentioned earlier, eating your veggies at the end of the meal keeps your internal plumbing working effectively to do just that.

If the food remains in your body, toxins will accumulate, clogging up your body chemistry and accelerating aging. Unfortunately, it takes four days for body waste to be eliminated from the average American, a direct result from our unbalanced, acidic diets.

By eating slowly you assist your body as it digests food to refuel, rebuild and recharge. Chewing and eating at a slower pace gives you time to relax, feel full delight in the nuances of diverse flavors and increase the pleasure of individual foods as well as the whole meal. By following up your protein with those healthy, fiber-rich dark green and other colorful vegetables that boost the digestion and absorption in your body, you'll also be healthier.

16 Combine foods properly

Learn to combine your foods properly for maximum digestion and improved nutrition. Eat protein with green and low-starch vegetables or low starches with vegetables only, with no animal protein. So you can eat your chicken or fish with all the veggies you like or have the bread, pasta, rice or potatoes you love with vegetables or salad at any meal.

You need carbohydrates as brain and body fuel to generate energy and a clear mind and keep you psychologically on an even keel. You can actually double the amount of carbohydrates you eat and still lose weight, but pay attention to the kinds and quantities of starches that you consume.

Simple carbohydrates such as most fruits, winter squash, corn, rice, instant oatmeal, grains and breads and low-fat milk, when eaten alone or in large quantities, quickly become glucose. But combined with complex starches (lemons, cauliflower, berries, artichokes, beans, cucumbers, bell peppers, summer squash, grapefruit, legumes, broccoli, limes, mushrooms, tomatoes, and green, leafy veggies) eaten together with proteins such as chicken, fish and steak, on the other hand, can help your body's blood sugar levels stay balanced.

Try to get into the habit of not consuming starches during your evening meal as these all convert to sugar in your body and are then stored as fat. If you do have a starch-heavy meal, engage in a brisk walk or exercise afterwards to rev up your metabolism. Your liver can't handle all the accumulated body fat, especially when it is combined with the environmental toxins and pollutants that we are exposed to.

It's easy to remember. The familiar expression "meat (protein) and potatoes (starch)" is the worst combination, especially if your potatoes are covered in butter, cheese and sour cream. Have your spuds plain or lightly seasoned with a non-salt herb and garlic sprinkle, or use non-fat plain yogurt instead of sour cream. Try cutting down on potatoes by having healthy baked yams or sweet potatoes, skipping the butter, brown sugar and marshmallows. Drizzle them with honey and top with chopped walnuts or pecans instead.

Keep portions of simple and complex carbohydrates and protein equal in size and get into the habit of only eating half of an obviously oversized restaurant portion when dining out, or stop eating when you are 70% full. You'll see the benefits of your self control in a decrease in weight and waist size and an increase in energy, stamina and a feeling of all-around well-being.

17 Make your own soups, teas and smoothies

While you can pay good money at a popular juice bar for a protein shake or smoothie, most likely you probably already have all the ingredients in your own kitchen to make your own. Keep in mind that some of the best and healthiest foods for you are often the cheapest and easiest to find and buy.

They are also the most powerful in fighting illness and disease and promoting healing. Garlic and honey are two examples of these foods. Likewise, apple cider vinegar and cinnamon are found in almost every kitchen as are other herbs and spices.

A good blender or juicer is a worthwhile investment to create your own immunity-building drinks, smoothies, soups and teas at home, and a slow cooker is a godsend for making a nutritious soup or stew to have waiting for you at the end of your day.

While we are accustomed to drinking ice-cold liquids, they are a shock to your system, so decrease the amount of ice you add to the smoothies. Substitute low-fat or non-fat yogurt as a thickener instead of whole milk or cream. There is a wealth of information available about how to make or combine your ingredients, but here are just a few to try:

- Carrot, ginger, apple
- Apple, cucumber, celery

- Apple, carrot, tomato
- Bitter melon, apple, milk (soy, dairy, nut, rice or low-fat)
- Orange, ginger, cucumber
- Pineapple, apple, watermelon
- Banana, pear
- Cucumber, kiwi, apple
- Carrot, apple, mango, pear
- Honeydew melon, grape, watermelon, milk
- Banana, pineapple, milk
- Papaya, pineapple, milk

These combinations make terrific, nutrient-rich mini-meals or in-between meal snacks during the day. You can pack home-made soups into a wide-mouth thermos and take them to work with you. When you are preparing meals, put aside the vegetables and fruits to slice and dice to create your soups and smoothies, saving money and calories at the same time.

An added benefit is that you don't waste anything left in the juicer or blender. The pulp can be tossed into soups as a thickener or can also be saved in a jar and do double duty for your skin toner, astringent or mask for your face.

Involve all members of your family in budgeting, planning and shopping for and preparing nutritious meals and snacks for the whole family. In the 21st century with one or two working parents being the norm, the notion that only the adults cook for the entire family has gone by the wayside. After all, you are already providing the income to pay for the food.

Challenge children to explore and find new menus to try and assign them to prepare the family meal at least once a week.

Encourage experimentation with different herbs, spices, vegetables and fruits. At home, try to duplicate your and their favorite ethnic meals. What a wonderful gift to give to your children by teaching them how to plan and cook for themselves and others after they leave home.

18

Drink hot liquids during a meal

In the 1860s, the Chinese railroad workers ate vegetables grown and brought in from California's central valley, as well as dried squid, shellfish and fish from the Monterey Bay coast, and poultry and pigs that were raised in their camps as fresh protein sources. Most importantly, they boiled their water from melted snow to make tea, killing all bacteria so they rarely became ill.

Meanwhile, the Western railroad workers were getting dysentery and other nasty digestive disorders as they waited for their meat to be hauled for several weeks up into the Sierra Nevada mountains in supply wagons, long before ice, ice boxes and refrigeration were invented. Their water was transported up into the mountains sloshing around in huge wooden barrels.

Think about how many overweight Chinese, Japanese, Korean and Vietnamese people you see when you travel to their home countries or among Americans of Asian heritage or new Asian immigrants to the United States. The practice of drinking hot tea and soup with meals is an excellent practice. These hot liquids help to speed up metabolism and move food through the digestive system.

In contrast, if you drink ice cold water with your meal, your food congeals and digestion becomes sluggish, turning the food into fat, which lines the intestines and slows down absorption.

Just as we use hot water to cut grease more effectively than cold water when washing our dishes, hot drinks such as water, tea, soups and even those hot red or green bean dessert soups at the end of a Chinese meal aid the enzymes and digestive juices in your system to break down and move food more quickly through your body.

Even on sweltering days, many Asians drink hot water or tea in order to perspire, which in turn cools as well as removes toxins from their bodies.

19

How to eat your meals

In the morning, eat like the emperor; at midday,
eat like a merchant; in the evening, eat like a beggar.
—Chinese proverb

The largest meal of our day should be our breakfast. It also happens to be the most essential. "Breakfast" comes from the words "break the fast," the long period of time between our evening meal and that which begins the next day. While we sleep, our bodies are digesting our food and converting it into the energy we need for the next day. Healing, resting, growing, preparing to eliminate waste and generally recharging our human batteries, emotionally, physically, and psychologically all take place as we rest.

Cook old-fashioned style oatmeal or make your own granola, and sprinkle it with cinnamon and healthy nuts such as pistachio, Brazil nuts, almonds and walnuts. Another option is to spread almond or sunflower seed butter on whole-grain toast or a muffin. You can create your own healthy protein shake or smoothie with good things added including oat bran, flax seed that you've ground yourself, or wheat germ. Sweeten with honey that is raw, uncooked and unfiltered or use other excellent alternative sweeteners such as stevia, blackstrap molasses or maple syrup.

Maple syrup is an excellent source of the minerals manganese and zinc, which activates the immune system and shortens the length of a cold, according to Detroit's Wayne State University's study reported in the August 2000 *Annals of Internal Medicine.*

On the other hand, the popular sweetener made from the Mexican agave succulent, while lower on the glycemic index, should be used sparingly as it has 20 more calories than table sugar and fewer antioxidants.

Low or non-fat milk products from grass, not corn-fed beef and dairy have the following benefits: four times higher Vitamin E levels, more antioxidant beta carotene, less saturated fat, less Omega 6 and more Omega 3 fatty acids, and less chance for products from sick animals. Also switch to using more egg whites, which, without the yolks, help to lower your cholesterol level.

Be sure to drink warm liquids first and then eat your fruits, followed by proteins and finally your starches. This sequence aids your body's natural digestive processes and jump-starts it for the day.

Research has shown that children who eat breakfast regularly are less subject to obesity in their adulthood, are more mentally alert during their school day and are in general, more healthy mentally and physically.

Your midday meal should be smaller in its portions. You might want to avoid eating pasta, noodles, rice, potatoes or other simple carbohydrates as they tend to make you drowsy in the afternoon.

The protein-vegetable combination is ideal in the middle of the day as it will take longer to digest and will keep you feeling fuller longer. Have a salad, a veggie sandwich or, if you do have protein, such as chicken, tuna, turkey, tofu and so on, combine it with green vegetables. Doing so improves your metabolism to move food though your body more efficiently. At mid-afternoon, have fruit or another healthy snack to tide you over until the next meal.

For your last meal of the day, help your body to wind down and decompress from the many activities that required your attention, and give your digestive system a rest during the night. Choose soup and a salad or some other small, light and nutritious meal utilizing good food combinations, which is most beneficial for you at the end of your day.

A large, late meal may cause heartburn, indigestion or insomnia, disturb your sleep or even give you nightmares. Meats will remain in your body, taking up to 24 hours to digest and even fermenting in your digestive system, with starches converting into glucose and then fat during the night. To help digestion and speed up metabolism after a meal that is starch-heavy, get physically active afterwards by dancing or taking a walk.

20 Bring color to your food

For years I've had a framed poster in my kitchen that is not only colorful and artistic, but a wonderful and valuable reminder of the importance of including fruits, vegetables and legumes in our family's diet. This simple but delightful print was produced by the American Cancer Society and is a grid, completely filled with photographs of natural, cancer-fighting foods.

Think salads with extra goodies such as seeds and nuts, cubed tofu and cooked amaranth or quinoa tossed in to add variety and vitamins.

Here's a list of many of the foods included, with their vitamin and mineral-rich properties and the best ways to cook the superstars:

- Acorn or spaghetti squash
- Almonds (Vitamin E)
- Apples*+
- Apricots
- Artichokes+
- Asparagus (Folate, chlorophyll) [Store in cool, dark pace and steam vertically]
- Avocado
- Bamboo shoots
- Bananas (Vitamin B-6, potassium)

- ☺ Barley
- ☺ Beans+ (Folate) [Kidney, black, pinto, aduki, garbanzo, lima, fava, navy, lentil, mung]
- ☺ Beets [peel and chop before steaming lightly]
- ☺ Bell peppers* [Red-Vitamin C, yellow, green]
- ☺ Blueberries+
- ☺ Bok choy
- ☺ Broccoli (Vitamin C, chlorophyll) Western or Chinese [Wash and cut before steaming]
- ☺ Brussels sprouts (Vitamin C, chlorophyll) [Cut an X into the bottoms of stems before stir-frying or steaming]
- ☺ Bulgur wheat
- ☺ Cabbage (Red, green, napa)
- ☺ Cantaloupe
- ☺ Carrots (Beta-carotene) [Add a drop of cooking oil to your thinly sliced and steamed carrots]
- ☺ Cauliflower
- ☺ Celery*
- ☺ Chard, Swiss
- ☺ Cherries*+
- ☺ Collard greens
- ☺ Cornmeal (polenta)
- ☺ Cranberries
- ☺ Currants
- ☺ Dates
- ☺ Eggplant
- ☺ Garbanzo (chickpea) beans (Folate, Vitamin B-6)
- ☺ Garlic [Crush/chop before roasting up to 3 minutes at no more than 390 degrees]
- ☺ Ginger

- Grapes [imported*] (red, white)
- Grapefruit
- Hazelnuts (Vitamin E)
- Herbs: fennel, peppermint, lemon balm, sage, valerian, rosemary, turmeric, chamomile and lemongrass, for example
- Kale
- Kiwi (Chinese gooseberry)
- Lettuce (Romaine)
- Lentils (Folate)
- Lotus root
- Mushroom (Shiitake, straw, Japanese and Chinese, golden oak, oakwood, maitaki, black, and so on)
- Mustard greens (Chlorophyll)
- Nectarines*
- Nuts: Pistachio, walnuts, Brazil, pecans, and so on
- Onion [Cut into chunks and bake red, white or yellow onions in foil for 5 minutes at 390 degrees]
- Oranges (Folate)
- Papaya (Vitamin C)
- Peaches*
- Pears*
- Pineapple
- Plums
- Potato*(Russet+) (Vitamin B-6) [Cut colorful ones with skins into chunks before roasting]
- Potato, sweet (yam; beta-carotene)
- Prune+
- Pumpkin (Canned or fresh: beta-carotene)
- Radish

- ✪ Raspberries+[red*]
- ✪ Sea vegetables (chlorella, spirulina, kelp, nori and so on)
- ✪ Seeds: pumpkin, sunflower, flax
- ✪ Strawberries*+
- ✪ Spinach* (Frozen: beta-carotene)[Steamed or blanched]
- ✪ Sunflower seeds (Vitamin E)
- ✪ Tomatoes [Splash cherry tomatoes or whole tomatoes with olive oil and roast until skins break]
- ✪ Watermelon
- ✪ Zucchini

*Member of the "Dirty Dozen" (as named by the Environmental Workers Union for having the highest pesticide content when commercially grown.

+Has top cancer-fighting antioxidants (source: USDA)

You've probably recognized that almost every common fruit and vegetable is mentioned. Add others available to you and which are native to your region or country to complete the list. Don't hesitate to use frozen vegetables when they are out of season as they are just as nutritious as when fresh.

Be sure to wash all your fresh vegetables and fruits in a mild sea salt and hot water solution and a vegetable brush to rid your food of surface pesticides. Apples, peaches, nectarines, celery and sweet bell peppers are especially susceptible and need more careful attention. Make it customary to peel your fruits and vegetables before cooking and eating them. Better yet, buy organic and locally grown produce.

Wash your hands first before handling, preparing and cooking your food. Use hot, soapy water to clean the cutting board, knives and utensils between cutting meats and vegetables

Discover where and when the farmers' markets are held in your neighborhood and nearby communities and patronize their vendors. Locally grown fruits and vegetables are fresher and therefore more nutritious. You can pick and choose your own produce, much of which may be organically grown.

Buy organic meats, dairy and egg products because you cannot remove contaminants in these products if they are commercially grown. Ask and even visit the farms to support them and spread the word to your network of family and friends.

You'll also find merchants who make their own honey, baked goods, natural soaps and cosmetics, arts and crafts such as soy and beeswax candles and other one-of-a-kind home-made goodies.

Go green by bringing your own reusable shopping bags and leave the paper and the plastic in the recycling bins at home. Go out and meet your neighbors, friends and local entrepreneurs and have fun shopping.

Keep in mind when you shop, that coconut, flaxseed, olive and grape seed oils are the best sources of the healthy Omega-3 fatty acids and that you should avoid or minimize canola, corn, peanut, safflower, sunflower and vegetable oils and animal fat in your diet.

21 Eat seasonal foods

To live a balanced life, one needs to be aware of the cycles of nature and follow their flow. In nutrition, this means practicing the Chinese tradition of eating seasonal foods to align your body with nature's rhythms and the five elements: spring (wood); summer (fire); late summer (earth); autumn (metal); winter (water). Each of these also represents the major organs that we must nourish and keep at their top efficiency: the liver, heart, stomach, lungs and kidneys.

Take your cue on what to eat from your local farmer's market or grocery store produce section and avail yourself of the cornucopia that awaits you. Drink lots of water year-round, regardless of the season.

Spring in almost every culture around the world represents new life, new growth and new beginnings. It is a time of rebirth and renewal after winter's rest. We begin to look and see with fresh eyes and perspectives, feel rejuvenated and hopeful, and look into ourselves and perhaps even experience transformation.

This is the time to eat lightly, to rid yourself and your body of waste and fat, shunning heavy, salty foods and seasonings. Beets, carrots, fresh greens, all kinds of sprouts, legumes, garlic, onions, seeds, grains, and cereal grasses such as wheat and barley can be seasoned with fragrant herbs such as rosemary, dill, basil and bay leaf. The best way to cook your food in the spring is to stir-fry it, using high heat and very little cooking oil.

Try to eat a little bit of raw food daily to strengthen your liver, which is the organ that is responsible for most of the detoxification in your body. A well-functioning liver is reflected in a calm person who does not become easily stressed or tense.

Summer is a time of outward strength and activity, expansion and development, creativity and light, growth, joy and productivity. It is a time to enjoy the abundance of life, whether it is from soaking in the sun's rays or partaking of the fruits and vegetables that are bursting with color and variety during this season.

Serve lighter and smaller meals that cool the body and lighten and boost your heart's health, especially with fresh vegetable or fruit salads, cucumbers, apples, lemons and celery. Drink flower teas such as Chinese chrysanthemum (try this drink after it has cooled and sweeten with a small amount of honey) or try Western chamomile flavored with mint, anise or lime, or make your own lemongrass tea.

Fill your grocery cart with lettuce and sprouts such as soy, alfalfa and mung bean. Add all summer fruits such as peaches, strawberries and nectarines, which fill the produce department at this time of year. Season your food with spices that are heat-generating as the resultant perspiration helps to eliminate waste from your body through your skin as well as cool it.

Avoid heavy foods such as seeds, meats and dairy products, nuts or grains, all of which can make you lethargic. Minimize the use of refined sugar, coffee, refined salt and flour, and tobacco. And in the good ole summertime, watermelon is believed to have a wonderfully cooling, cleansing effect inside your body. The light summer soups made with the white part of melons found just under the rinds are prized for their liver-boosting qualities.

Late in the summer, a subtle change starts taking place as we and the earth prepare ourselves for a change in the seasons. This is the time to aid your stomach and digestive system in its transition to heavier foods.

Meals should still be light without heavy seasonings, and the best ingredients are those that are yellow or orange in color or round in shape. All are believed to help us to stay grounded, and include corn, beans of all kinds (especially soy and garbanzo), millet, cabbage, cantaloupe, yams and sweet potatoes, long and string beans, peas, black beans, squash, zucchini, oats, potatoes and apricots.

Fall (Autumn) is the time of harvest around the globe, a time to put aside food and store it for the coming colder months, to dress in warmer clothing and begin planning for the oncoming, less productive months of winter.

We, the earth and nature together start pulling ourselves inward, even as all three store energy in various ways. The season of fall is related to the lungs and involves consuming more sour and fermented foods, such as those which have been salted or pickled, (but only in small quantities), which cause us to contract just as we inhale to breathe, or to "pucker up."

Food and drinks that are appropriate during this season include soy and almond milk, barley and millet, apples, peanuts, seaweed, pine nuts, shellfish such as crab, clams, oysters and mussels, rice and rice porridge, mushrooms, daikon, turnips, red radishes, watercress, chard, cauliflower, spinach, pears, papaya, and persimmons.

Winter approaches and both the earth and we prepare to rest, storing up fat and energy to see us through this season. It is the time to focus on the kidneys, and consume foods that enhance our appetite. Salty and bitter are the tastes best suited for this time of year.

Ideal foods are vegetable soups with lots of celery, turnips and carrots, as well as other foods such as sweet rice, watercress, bitter melon, quinoa, oats, alfalfa, most kinds of beans, asparagus, winter squash, cranberries, melons, chlorella, wheat berry, ginger, seaweed, fennel, water chestnut, various berries.

With the cold and flu season predictable each winter, start helping your body to fight back. Eat more mushrooms of any kind, fish with Omega-3 fatty acids, such as salmon, mackerel or herring. Consume lots of garlic, using up to three fresh cloves daily in your cooking or even taking garlic in capsule form. This ancient food helps your body to fight the first signs of a cold. Drink up to five cups of green or black tea a day for two weeks, which provide ten times the average amount of interferon protein to stave off flu and cold germs.

22

Watch what you put on your skin

Whether you shower or bathe at night or in the morning, be careful what you put on your skin, which is the largest organ of your body. Convert to using only natural products, especially those that have fewer chemicals. Read the ingredients listed on the labels of your soap, shampoo, conditioner, foundation and other cosmetics, lotions, creams, and so on. Remember that anything that you put on your skin will be absorbed into your body.

Notice that most of the ingredients are man-made chemicals with names you cannot pronounce. Moreover, the majority of skin care products have a list of ingredients that often cover a good portion of the container and are carcinogenic.

In the July 2010 *Time* magazine article entitled "About Face," about two journalists, Siobhan O'Conner and Alexandra Spunt, who investigated toxic components in many cosmetics. These included: sulfates and preservatives such as parabens, which disrupt hormones and are present in shampoos and conditioners; mercury and coal tar that are in mascara; 1,4 dioxane, which may contaminate eye shadow; sunscreens that contain another hormone disrupter called oxybenzone; carcinogens such as formaldehyde in hair treatments; and lead and BHA that may contaminate lipsticks.

Read labels religiously and start looking for and using beauty products for your skin, hair or nails that contain five or fewer natural ingredients listed. Think about Pacific Islander inhabitants who cook with locally available coconut oil, or the folks in Mediterranean countries who have used olive, grape seed and argan oil for centuries. In both geographic regions, people use native plant oils for their cooking and on their skin, hair and nails naturally healthy.

 You can store these oils in larger bottles in your refrigerator after opening to prevent spoilage, and pour out a small amount to keep handy for smoothing right onto your skin after you bathe or shower as they are easily absorbed.

Years ago I owned a book that preached, "If you wouldn't put it in your mouth and eat it, don't put it on your skin." It made much good sense then and applies, even more so today, three decades and tens of thousands of new chemicals later.

So many current choices in bath, bed, eye, hair, skin, hair and body products have been created from a plethora of synthetic substances, it is no wonder that there is an alarming increase of all sorts of skin disorders, allergies, illnesses and cancers.

Through technology today, you can easily access information from the Internet about how to make your own skin care products from fruits and vegetables. Make small quantities when you are preparing your meals and keep them refrigerated in a glass jar until ready for use. How more chemical-free and natural can you get?

For generations, slices of cucumbers have been used to reduce puffiness in and around the eyes. Coconut, grape seed and olive oil can be smoothed right onto your skin after a bath or washing your face or hands. Avocado or yogurt can be face masks. Lemon juice can lighten your hair. To cover your white or grey hairs, a mixture of henna powder with water makes a paste that replaces hair dye that has ammonia and chemicals that irritate or damage your hair and scalp. While making breakfast, spread leftover egg white straight from the shell, right onto your face and neck for an inexpensive and soothing mask than tightens your skin.

Cantaloupe, papaya, strawberry, tomato, potato, peach, watercress, watermelon, rose, walnut, sunflower, saffron, turmeric, sandalwood, and countless other natural ingredients help to keep you healthy from inside, by eating them often, and outside, by applying them on your skin.

23 Remove toxins from your environment

In the United States alone, there are only several hundred chemicals proven safe from a list of 80,000-plus chemicals, to which many of which we are exposed to in every imaginable way and form.

Here's a short list of toxins in your home now: carbon monoxide, radon, chlorine (in many household cleaners), (volatile organic compounds (VOCs), building materials, carpeting, furnishings, paints, chlorine, composite wood products, vinyl, upholstery, solvents, tobacco and second-hand smoke, pet dander. Dust mites, 100,000 to 10 million dead ones and their droppings, can add 10% more weight to a used pillow or mattress, which should be replaced after eight to ten years. Mold spores are everywhere, growing where there is moisture and a food source. According to *Environment, Health and Safety Online,* wallpaper paste, for example, is caviar to mold!

Synthetic materials not made from natural ingredients all have the potential to pollute, such as those listed below:

- ☙ The air we breathe (solvents, bacteria, smog, chemicals, mold, fumes, glues),
- ☙ The water we drink (metals, chlorine, trihalomethanes),
- ☙ The food we eat (pesticides, mercury, flavorings, preservatives, colorings, additives) and

⊛ What we put into (pharmaceuticals) and onto our bodies (cosmetics, dyes, chemicals).

These include everything from plastics and man-made fibers in our clothing that we wear next to our bodies, petroleum products, food storage containers, food wraps, fast food and drink containers, and the packaging for much of our food and dry goods. We are surrounded by all these in our homes, workplaces and vehicles, in which we spend the majority of our time.

Even being inside your car is unhealthy! I saw a 3½ x 3½ inch label attached to the driver's side window of a new Mercedes E-class sedan recently. On it was the following:

WARNING: Motor vehicles contain chemicals known to the State of California to cause cancer and birth defects or other reproductive harm." This was followed by a long list of materials and substances that were in the vehicle or associated with its use, all of which could be hazardous to the health of the driver or passengers.

Remove or replace as much processed materials in your overall environment as possible. Choose instead to "go green," using natural materials such as wood (for example, plank, not pressed), bamboo, wool, cotton and silk in your home and your clothing.

Recent research has revealed the chemical bisphenol A (BPA) found in rigid plastic water and drink bottles and which coats the inside of soda, beer and other drink cans, interferes with female hormones and causes aggression in young girls.

24 Use natural cleaning products

Did you know that plain, white vinegar is great for removing stains, deodorizing, disinfecting and dissolving mineral deposits? It's cheap, handy and probably already in your home. Use vinegar in a half and half mix with water to clean chrome, faucets, glass, tile and tea kettles.

A quarter of a cup of vinegar mixed with water in a spray bottle and wiped dry with plain old newspapers has been a low-cost favorite for streak-free windows for generations. Pour 3 cups of white vinegar into your toilet for a couple of hours to do its disinfecting and cleaning magic before scrubbing the bowl and then flushing. Add a half cup of white vinegar to your laundry's rinse water to remove soap residue from your laundry.

Here's just a sampling of a few more nifty things you can do with ordinary, non-toxic products found in your home.

- Scrub pots with coarse sea salt or baking soda.
- Soak your gemstone jewelry in club soda and gently use an old, soft-bristled toothbrush to bring out the sparkle. You can also use club soda to remove a wine spill from carpet or a fresh food stain from your clothing.
- Take off your makeup with a cotton ball dipped in a thin paste made from mixing a little water with non-fat powdered milk.

- Clean your kitchen and bathroom countertops with lemon juice.
- Shoe shine, mister? Get out that old tube of lip balm from your purse, pocket or bathroom drawer and run it over your leather shoes before gently buffing them with a soft cloth.
- Use biodegradable shampoo to remove oil stains on ties and shirt collars and for other emergency laundry needs. Use it to wash your car, greasy hands, hairbrushes and combs or create a bubble bath.
- Save money by reusing and refilling foam-dispensing bottles by making your own solution: 4 parts water to 1 part of liquid soap.
- Eliminate fish odors by rubbing a mere teaspoon of lemon juice or vinegar onto your hands and under your fingernails.
- Use a lemon juice and honey mixture as a disinfectant on a cut, or do as the troops in the field did in an emergency: use a smashed garlic poultice on a wound to fight infection.
- Keep a chalkboard eraser in your glove compartment or trunk to clear up a foggy windshield instead of an aerosol or pump spray, or run a small cake of soap over glass and then spread it over a windshield or bathroom mirror with a paper towel to keep them from fogging up in the first place.
- Use a little hotel bottle of hair conditioner as an inexpensive shaving cream for your face or legs — it's environmentally friendly without the use of aerosol.

There are thousands of tips like these to make your home, eco-friendlier ("greener") and cleaner without the use of the 100,000 known chemicals (most of which have not been tested) found in everyday products that we use in our home.

Check out your local library, bookstore or the Internet to find as many natural and environmentally friendly solutions for keeping your body and home free of harmful substances.

25 Keep the air clean inside your home

Open the windows in your home and let in the fresh air. This simple practice pushes out the dirty air as well as its contaminants. Just by keeping two inches of a window open most of the time keeps the clean air circulating within your home, and prevents odors, moisture and the potential for mold growth from accumulating.

Invest in an air purifier that has a HEPA (High Efficiency Particulate Air) or carbon filter rather than one that produces ozone, which is harmful to humans in the lower atmosphere, especially as it may produce more concentrated levels than in the outside air.

When dusting, use a damp cloth to pick up anything that you might be inhaling. If your dust cloth is dry, you are just stirring up and breathing in the dust as well as whatever is floating around in it.

Avoid aerosol cleaners, which create and disperse tiny chemical particles that are easily inhaled and very unhealthy for your lungs. Instead pour a small amount of a liquid cleaner onto a rag or dust cloth, keeping windows open and a fan to remove any fumes.

Before winter arrives, clean your fireplace and chimney, and check that the flue is in good working order to draw out wood smoke and fumes. Be sure to use hard woods such as birch, maple or oak, rather than soft wood such as pine, and better yet, burn logs made from compressed sawdust to minimize wood smoke, which is damaging to your respiratory system.

After you vacuum, remove and dispose of the paper bag (with all the dust, dirt, pet hair and everything else in it) *outside* your house or you will be undoing all your hard work when the dust gets back into the air and you breathe it in as you empty the bag indoors. When emptying bagless vacuum models, wear a dust mask and even keep a special pair of rubber gloves to use when you discard the contents in your home's outside garbage bin.

Just think where your shoes have been during the day and what you may have stepped on or into. Use a coarse doormat outside the main entrances to your home to catch pollutants on your footwear before you enter your residence, especially those leading from the garage or street.

It is a common Asian custom to leave one's shoes outside the front door or stored just inside the entrance of a home. Changing into slippers is a sensible front-line defense to keep all sorts of nasty things from getting into your home.

You will find that your home is cleaner and even more so, if you install hard surfaced flooring that can be swept and mopped. Rugs and carpeting attract and trap dirt and dust inside your home. Also, by taking your shoes off, you are symbolically and literally, leaving the outside world outside as you enter your private space and refuge you call home.

26 Keep your home and work space germ-free

Regardless of the season, you are susceptible to getting sick, but taking simple precautions can boost your immunity and keep you and your family well throughout the year. Start with your home and start germ proofing right away by establishing new habits.

Illness prevention starts even before you enter your front door. Keep antibacterial wipes or alcohol swabs handy in your car. Use them frequently to wipe off your steering wheel, knobs and door handles, both inside and out, as well as the metal parts and latch of seat belts. Do the same for other hard surfaces, such as stroller and car seat parts, touched by your or other people's children during the day. Vacuum your car mats and home's doormats often.

When you come home, make a habit of washing your hands with soap and hot water as soon as possible for at least 15 seconds (the time it takes you to sing "Happy Birthday" two times).

Make sure you clean both the backs and palms of your hands and under your nails by applying soap to your palms and then lacing your fingers together, using them to scrub the backs of opposite hands. Use a fingernail brush to get underneath your nails where germs and dirt accumulate. Dry with paper towels or if you use cloth towels, be sure to change and put them in the laundry to wash them frequently in hot water and laundry detergent.

Keep cotton balls and alcohol in your bathroom to wipe down your cell phone and case nightly. Studies have shown that phones have more than 18 times more germs than a toilet seat.

Speaking of work, that particular environment is a minefield of bacteria and germs. According to a University of Arizona study, women's offices have bacteria levels almost three times higher than offices of men.

While you cannot control the re-circulation of stale or germ-laden air coming out of the ventilation system that may be moving all those germs around your workplace, you certainly have control over your workspace. Germ-proof it daily.

Start with your briefcase or handbag, which is as personal as you can get. Don't put it anywhere on the floor, but rather on a shelf, inside a cabinet or closet, or hang it on the back of your office door with your coat or on the back of your chair. Wipe the exterior of your bags, cases or purses often, especially the bottom, with alcohol, which does not damage leather.

Use antibacterial wipes at least weekly outside your workspace to clean on all those surfaces that you remembered touching: faucets, computer keyboards and mice, light switches, copier, elevator and telephone buttons, and so on.

Eating at your work desk is dangerous to your health. The average work desk tested as having 21,000 germs *per square inch* on it and that there are 1500 germs per square centimeter of hands. A University of Arizona research study further showed that the average desk surface had 400% more bacteria than a toilet seat.

Speaking of eating, use disinfecting wipes on the refrigerator and microwave doors, table and sink faucets in the break or lunchroom. An April, 2001 Minnesota Department of Health report revealed that frequently used faucets hide 229,000 germs per square inch. Before sitting down to eat at the table, use a paper towel or two as a handy placemat.

Don't let your food touch any public surface and keep at least five feet away from a coughing or obviously sick co-worker. During the flue and cold season, discreetly ask your employer to distribute a memo to remind sick employees to stay home so as not to infect their colleagues. Bring your own coffee or tea in a car mug for use at work, taking it home nightly to wash it in hot, soapy water.

In the restroom, use toilet paper to avoid touching the handle when flushing a toilet and again when exiting a stall. After washing your hands following a toilet break, use paper towels for quadruple duty: turning on the handles at the sink for drying your hands, holding the handle of the restroom door open and also wrapping around the office restroom key as you make your way back to your work space.

Dispose of the paper towel in the trash, or better yet, if there is an electric hand dryer in the restroom, use it instead for drying your hands. Get a paper towel, several squares of toilet paper or a toilet seat liner to keep your hand clean as you open that restroom door to leave.

The U.S. Center for Disease Control reports that only 77% of people wash their hands after using the toilet, but 64% of the women and only 32% of the men *used soap*. Water alone does not kill germs, soap does. Carry a small hotel-size bottle of biodegradable shampoo for a multiple uses, including getting food stains and grease off clothing and hands.

Just remembering all the places that your hands have touched outside your home should be motivation enough for you to get used to doing this and will easily take up those 15 seconds.

27 Personal health habits in public places

You can't escape them — germs are everywhere. A Minnesota Department of Health study listed the worst hiding places for germs to lurk:

- ✿ Work desk
- ✿ Kitchen sink (worse than bathroom)
- ✿ Dishcloth, sponge
- ✿ Garbage can
- ✿ Refrigerator
- ✿ Bathroom doorknob
- ✿ Keyboards
- ✿ Escalator handrails
- ✿ Shopping cart handles
- ✿ Picnic tables
- ✿ Light switches
- ✿ Remote controls
- ✿ Toys
- ✿ Bathroom cups
- ✿ Pens, pencils and crayons
- ✿ Pet cages

Don't forget ATM machines, mall doors, file cabinets, shopping carts and even car, bus, subway handles, telephones, desk surfaces, elevator and copy machine buttons, money, video game controls and remotes, computer, portable and cell phone keyboards.

Flu viruses can survive for 8 to 12 hours on paper or cloth, 24 to 48 hours on non-porous surfaces, and up to 72 hours on wet surfaces such as towels and faucets, according to Dr. J. Owen Hendley, an infectious disease expert.

Hand cleaning gels (use those marked as being sanitizing or disinfecting) became hugely popular after the SARS outbreak in Asia in 2002 and their manufacturers claimed that using them kills 99.9% of bacteria. However, when I asked my immunologist and allergy doctor what happens to the dirt, she told me that the dirt remains on your hands. If you don't believe this, try it by washing your hands after you use the sanitizer and you'll see dirty water in the sink and going down the drain.

Even in the worst flu season of 2009–2010 as H1N1 (swine) flu spread all over the globe, the first, most critical and best advice and line of defense was still washing our hands frequently. But then, we've always known that a person can catch more colds from the germs transmitted while shaking hands than from kissing another person.

I even discreetly use a hand sanitizer before taking communion at church, especially when the holy supper follows the offering as you may be handling or touching paper money. More often than not, the meeting and greeting of fellow parishioners involves handshaking with strangers as you wish them peace.

Ironically, people who are more sociable, even if they are exposed to more germs, have been found to get fewer colds, especially if they also get out and walk for exercise at least 20 to 30 minutes daily. On the other hand, be sure to eat properly because your body needs fuel to have the energy to fight infection and to keep you from getting sick.

Avoid smoking or drinking too much and get enough sleep at night (8 hours or more). Include downtime in every day to reduce stress, which lowers your body's immune system, making you more vulnerable to bacteria and germs that make you ill.

If you feel that you are coming down with a cold or the flu, please be considerate and keep your germs at home. Do yourself, your co-workers and your company a favor by staying away from work when you aren't feeling well.

What are you saving those illness days for anyway? What are sick days for if not to take care of yourself when you need to? Besides, wouldn't you rather be feeling miserable and resting comfortably at home than getting dressed, traveling to work, feeling unwell and ill all day and then making the trip back home again? What better reason do you have for staying at home than when you are feeling burned out, need to recharge, get away from it all or are just sick of work?

If you are visiting a doctor's office or a clinic, be observant and vigilant. I noticed the practice of some lab technicians who first disinfects a patient's skin with an alcohol swab but then tears off the tip of one of the fingers on the rubber glove to get a better feel for the location of where to draw blood, without wiping either their own finger or the patient's skin once again before inserting a needle for a blood draw.

In another scenario, I watched a receptionist sneeze, covering her nose and mouth, and then use the same hand to offer me a pen and clipboard with a form attached for me to complete. I took out a pen from my own purse and used it, rolling the offered, bacteria-laden pen onto the counter.

It is acceptable and responsible to call attention to or report such unsanitary practices to the person who is doing it, or to avoid embarrassment and be more effective, to the office manager or even your doctor. It is shocking that infections contracted in hospitals are the fifth most common cause of death in the United States.

At your gym or health club, these same good habits and lots of disinfecting wipes will serve you well as you clean weights, walking machine handles, exercise and other mats and other equipment used by countless other people.

Be aware and vigilant of surfaces where other people's hands have touched at other public places: that gas nozzle at the service station pump and all door handles and knobs at malls, government, offices, schools, hospitals, stores or restaurants. The list is endless.

At the airport, department or grocery store or restaurant, carry and use your *own* pen, even when the establishment provides one for you to sign a rental car contract or a credit card slip. And take advantage of the no-charge antibacterial gel dispensers in hospitals and clinics, as well as the grocery store's free bacterial wipes to clean the shopping cart handles.

At the ATM, ticketing machine or in an elevator, use your knuckle, the corner of the credit or ATM card or taking a cue from Michael Jackson, wear gloves to operate the buttons. You may even revive an old custom or start a new fashion trend!

28

Staying healthy while traveling

The following advice came from a flight attendant friend of mine. When traveling, don't touch any aircraft lavatory surface with your bare hands. Always protect yourself by using paper hand towels to handle everything from the door lock, faucets, drain and toilet handles and switches.

Even if you're on an aircraft's first flight of the day, avoid using the pillows or blankets. Use three full sheets of paper towels to drape over the top of the airline seat so your head doesn't touch the headrest. Just think of how many other, countless passengers' hair with possible head lice, dandruff, skin or scalp infections and other "nasties" have rested on that head rest before yours made contact there.

Dress in layers of clothing that you can add if you need to warm up or remove to cool down: a tank top, T-shirt, long-sleeved knit shirt, lined vest or jacket that can double as your blanket.

Ask to change your seat, moving at least three rows away, if the passenger sitting next to or near you is sneezing or coughing. If you cannot change seats, at least sleep or read, turning away from your seatmate.

At the hotel, again wipe down everything from the light switch when you first enter to door knobs, faucets, windows, door knobs, hair dryer, toilet handles and especially clock radios, television remote controls and telephones, which are almost never cleaned.

Do not use the bedspread as a blanket, as research has found an alarming amount of bacteria on hotel bedspreads. Since 1995, there has been a reappearance of bedbug infestations in offices and hotels around the world. These blood-sucking parasites hide in small crevices in beds, couches, luggage, furniture and clothing so it is prudent to make a visual check when you reach your hotel room. Report any sightings or evidence of these pests to the management and insist on changing your room if necessary.

Call housekeeping or the front desk to deliver a clean blanket upon your arrival at your hotel. Invest in and bring your own lightweight "sleep bag" found at travel, bed/bath/linen or online stores, to use in hotel beds and put it into the hotel's free plastic laundry bag to take home to wash in hot water. You can recycle the plastic laundry bag in your home's recycling bin.

Bring and use your own inexpensive and disposable slippers, (as provided free in hotels in Asia) or lightweight slip-on sandals or flip flops, but never walk around the hotel room or to the pool in your bare feet. When you get home, remember to walk on the doormat first and wipe down the handles and zipper tabs of your suitcases, purses, bags and briefcases before you unpack.

Last but not least, launder or dry clean all clothing you wore on a trip as soon as possible after returning home.

29

Get rid of poisonous people in your life

Your mental and psychological health is as important to your well-being as your physical health is. Just as substances can be toxic, the people around you can be toxic, too. Each of us has an energy field surrounding us, which you can sense and feel. You might think of it as body heat, static electricity or even personal space. I would bet most all of you have experienced this sensation.

Whether by word, attitude or actions, someone annoys you and you feel a natural resistance or antipathy, discomfort or dislike toward that person. The negative energy (or "vibe" as it was called in the 1960s) originates from certain people. It doesn't take long for you to decide that you just don't want to be around or associate with them.

Merely being in their presence, whether they are family members, colleagues, associates or just acquaintances, seems to drag you down or drain your energy. Avoid these petty, contrary, grumpy or unkind, crude or generally unpleasant folks as much as you can as they will surely tow your thoughts, energy and morale down to their level.

Believe that you are a person of value to yourself and other people so that you can choose to associate only with others who lift your mind and spirit, treat you like the unique and special human being that you are and who make you feel good.

Avoid those around you who are toxins in your life. They can poison your spirit and mind as surely and pervasively as chemical or environmental pollutants do.

30

Don't let "dirty electricity" ruin your health

Was it only five or six decades ago when radio and television were uncommon in the average household? Electrical appliances are now an integral part of our daily lives but who could have imagined that can openers, hair dryers, light dimmer switches, circuit breakers, vacuum cleaners, juicers, fluorescent light tubes and microwave ovens would become hazardous to our health? For example, do you know that it is recommended that we keep at least six feet away from a microwave oven while it is in use?

The explosion of advances in technology has brought a multitude of new electronic gadgets and toys to our 21st century lives, from electric air fresheners to plasma televisions and countless other electronics used for entertainment, instant information, communication, health testing and treatment.

Other culprits include: air conditioners, energy-saving light bulbs, refrigerators, desktops and laptops, routers, modems, printers, monitors, video games, cell and cordless phones, music storage devices and DVDs.

Regretfully, we are paying a steep price for the convenience, benefits and enjoyment of these devices. A 650-page report citing over two thousand studies found that constant exposure to even low-levels of electromagnetic radiation (EMR) by-products known as "dirty" or transient electricity, emitted from various electronics, charges up the electrons in our bodies. Research has shown this process is known to cause cancer, dementia, heart disease, Alzheimer's, and diminished immunity to illnesses.

Articles appearing in the December 2009 and January 2010 issues of *Prevention* magazine (written by Dr. Michael Segell and others) warned people of the adverse effects of being exposed to these electromagnetic fields (EMF) surrounding common, modern-day electrical appliances and electronic devices.

Because a child's brain is smaller and more sensitive than an adult's, it absorbs much more radiation, so do not let children use cell telephones. More studies are being conducted, including the cohort study following mobile phone use and health (COSMOS) over twenty to thirty years. This major international endeavor was launched in March 2010 in the United Kingdom and will involve up to a quarter of a million people in five countries in Europe to determine the effects of regular cell phone use and how hazardous is it to people's health.

A Swiss study of 10,000 people in thirteen countries indicates that the risk of getting brain cancer is five times greater if children begin their cell phone use while in their teens or continue to use them for ten years or more. Leonard Hardel of Sweden followed cell phone use among teenagers and discovered a 400% increase in the incidence of brain tumors (glioma) among this age group.

Keep informed and support efforts to put health warning labels on cell phone packaging, just as was done on cigarettes back in the 1960s.

On another note, did you know that research has shown that today's doctors are requesting three times as many CT scans for their patients than back in 1993? Just one of these scans themselves can each be equal to having 442 chest x-rays and can cause cancer by itself.

As a patient you have the right to question and refuse the use and number of treatments using bone scans, MRIs and other radioactive tests to which you are subjected and exposed. Ask your doctor about their safety and research the harm they may cause to your body or health.

Moreover, both the EMR and heat that emanate from a laptop computer supported on one's lap has been linked to male infertility and interference with cell function, as well as the diminished quality and count of sperm production.

The following list includes cautionary tips on how to minimize one's risk regarding the hazards of constant exposure to EMR or being within electromagnetic fields(EMF):

1. Avoid wireless devices when possible.
2. Pick safer light bulbs, e.g., non-fluorescent. Avoid using dimmer switches.
3. Keep your distance from circuit breakers, computers and electrical outlets.
4. Choose a liquid crystal display (LCD) television over a plasma type.
5. Choose a landline phone instead of a cordless that charges on a base unit and has extensions.
6. Avoid using over-the-ear cell headsets.
7. Wait to use your cell phone if the service is weak or spotty.

8. Put your cell phone in your purse or briefcase, not clipped at your waist. If you do clip your cell phone at your waist, be sure the keypad, not the battery, faces your body.

9. Avoid holding a phone to your ear. Use ear buds, a speaker phone or redirect it to your car radio speaker.

10. When using a wired earpiece, turn it off when it's not in use.

11. When using a wired headset, clip on a ferrite bead to absorb radiation.

12. Use a hollow-tube earpiece that has no wire under the plastic.

13. Switch your cell phone frequently to opposite ears.

14. Minimize the length of your cell phone chats.

15. Avoid using your cell phone in cramped settings.

16. Text when it is safe to do so, instead of talking. Do not allow your children to use a cell or cordless phone except in an emergency, as both emit similar amounts of radiation.

17. Do not use your laptop on your lap, especially if it is plugged into a power source. Instead, put your laptop on a table in its battery mode.

18. Have your home tested for electromagnetic field levels and reduce them by unplugging electrical appliances and other electronic equipment when they are not in use.

31

Get a good night's rest

Relax and enjoy your home with restful activities as you wind down from your day. Follow regular bedtime routines and keep the habit of going to bed at the same time daily. Create a peaceful and harmonious sleeping environment that helps you to fall asleep quickly, whether it is achieved by installing block-out window treatments, reading, or listening to soothing classical or easy listening "elevator" music (which also reduces pain, vomiting and nausea during chemotherapy). As soon as you feel drowsy, stop what you are doing and turn off the lights.

Limit the number of electrical and electronic devices in your bedroom, including digital clock radios with red numbers, televisions, cell or wireless telephones and their chargers, lamps, electric blankets and heating pads, laptop computers on battery mode or connected to a wall outlet, massage devices that plug into electrical outlets, humidifiers, air filters, light switches, lighting dimmers and remote controls.

Try to position your bed so that your head does not share a wall with electrical outlets or an exterior power line leading to your home from a power pole.

If you stay up past your regular bedtime, after two or three days, your body quickly becomes sleep deprived. Quality sleep is much like making deposits in your "sleep bank." Skipping good rest several days in a row is the equivalent to making large withdrawals each time. Sleep-deprived people are not as alert in their work, tend to forget things, gain weight, make mistakes, and are generally less efficient, effective and productive.

To prevent being too over-stimulated to fall asleep avoid exercise for at least three hours before you go to bed Also, wait a while after you eat before you take your bath or shower, as your body needs time to properly digest your food. When you bathe immediately after your meal, the hot water diverts blood flow to your skin's surface and away from your digestive system, which would have been breaking down your food for your body to absorb.

If you wake up during the night and cannot fall asleep, try not to fight it. Without looking at the clock, read, listen to the radio or watch television until you feel sleepy again. Then turn off the lights right away. Your goal is to get at least seven hours of sleep per night, and eight hours is even better. Your rest is paramount in helping you recharge, mentally, physically and psychologically, to effect optimum food absorption and to repair your body's tissues.

Canadian researchers found that people who only got five or six hours of sleep a night were 35% more inclined to gain over ten pounds and were over 60% heavier in belly weight than people who got seven to eight hours of nightly rest. Amazingly, thinner people only slept 17 more minutes a night than those who were overweight.

Avoid nicotine, sugar, any caffeine and alcohol for six to eight hours before you retire for the night. Caffeine alone takes between three to five hours to move out of your body, and foods such as ham, bacon, sausage and others that have the amino acid tyramine interfere with your body's ability to produce serotonin, which helps you to sleep.

Do not use paraffin candles in your home or bedroom, not only because of the fire danger, but because the soot they produce is detrimental to your lungs. Use soy or beeswax candles instead.

There are some natural remedies that seem to foster restful sleep. Among them are: passionflower, valerian, calcium, chamomile, melatonin, kava, magnesium, and using aromatherapy oils in diffusers or directly on your body.

You can even snack on dates, tuna, bananas, any nut butter, whole grain crackers or figs at night, at least an hour before you go to bed. They all have tryptophan, which is the substance in turkey that makes you drowsy after your Easter, Thanksgiving or Christmas dinners. The best thing is you can eat any of these year-round to help you to fall asleep faster.

32 And for our planet

Reduce, reuse, recycle and pre-cycle! Take an active role in preserving our planet for future generations.

Get into the habit of pre-cycling, which is conscious, deliberate consumerism, *before* you purchase anything. Reduce waste by limiting your consumption in the first place.

Let's face it, we rarely wear clothing until it becomes threadbare or use an item until it breaks down. Donate perfectly good but out-of-style clothes, handbags, jewelry and accessories you don't want, wear or need anymore. Do you really need to go out and spend full price on a new clothes when you can either make your own or have your favorites altered to fit your new body shape?

Let go and gain valuable real estate inside your drawers and closets at home. When you're feeling down, exercise C and C: *clean your closets.* Get out large plastic bags and start purging your closet of everything that is too small, big, out of fashion or hasn't been worn or used for a year. Or get into the habit of keeping a donation bag handy so that if you buy something new, discard something in your closet that it has replaced. Do you really need nine (or more) pairs of black slacks?

There are many people who cannot afford the latest fashions but would be satisfied with the clothes donated to thrift shops that are in gently used, practically new and perfectly wearable condition.

Bring your own coffee mug to work and use it instead of a disposable plastic, paper or Styrofoam™ cup each time you drink coffee, tea or water from the water cooler or fountain. Ask the manager, owner, waiter or waitress at a restaurant *not* to bring you that automatically supplied cup of water when you are seated.

It is up to you to do your part to conserve this most precious resource on our planet. Remember that it takes seven gallons of water to wash a used restaurant water glass.

Bring your own food-storage containers to a restaurant and use them to carry your leftovers home. Bring your own shopping bags to the market and to the mall. Put all plastic grocery bags into one to add to your home or grocery store's recycling container.

You will never need to keep more than a dozen of these in your home and 19 *billion* plastic bags are used annually in the United States alone. Unfortunately most of them end up in our landfills and even many in the ocean where they cannot decompose quickly or easily.

Be vigilant in your recycling efforts in your own community. Patronize and support retailers who take back and properly dispose of their own waste, especially electronic waste such as cell and wireless telephones, computers, fax machines, video cameras, DVDs, inkjet, toner and laser cartridges, printers, monitors, keyboards, scanners, remote controls, cameras, gaming consoles, old or worn-out electrical power strips and cords, lamps, and other electronics.

Purge your bathroom cabinets of expired and unused cosmetics, prescription drugs, over-the-counter medications, beauty products for hair, skin and nails, toiletries, hair dryers, shavers and small electrical items. Collect all toxic cleaners, paints, motor oil and other potentially dangerous substances found in your garage, under your sinks and in cabinets.

But please do not dump any of them in your trash. Save them to support and participate in hazardous waste round-up days in your community or deliver them to your municipal hazardous waste collection sites where they will be properly and legally disposed of.

Join the green revolution today.

Secrets to Happiness

Where have you been?
Where are you now?
How long have you been here?
What are you doing about it?
—Anonymous

33

Be true to yourself

Most of us have found out over the years what is really important in our lives. We now know what has value, both in ourselves and in other people, and we naturally gravitate toward those who share our values as life partners and friends.

Honesty, integrity, kindness, respect, dependability, compassion, responsibility, caring, dignity and decency are qualities of good character. Most likely, they became the components of our personal compasses, fixed and unwavering as we grew older.

During whichever stage or age you are in life today, savor and enjoy the journey of discovering of what you care for and feel passionate about. Take time to discover each layer of your own uniqueness to find what makes you feel fulfilled and happy.

Years ago during my first cancer experience, I attended a Wellness Community meeting at which all attendees were asked to write a list of all the things that made us feel happy. We did not have to share the list, but were instructed to take it home, tape it on our bathroom mirrors and do at least two to six activities from it every day.

Imagine that even if you can manage to do at least one thing from the list that makes you happy, you will have done something for yourself each day. Make the time and effort to carve out personal time daily. Treat yourself, you're worth it!

Whether you take a daily walk, read, listen to music, watch a favorite show or movie, cook, play an instrument, take a class, soak in the tub, do *nothing* for 30 minutes, talk to a friend or family member on the telephone, or whatever makes you happy that is legal and not harmful to yourself or others, you are affirming that you are worthy of doing something special for yourself.

Of course you should, because you are special.

Doing these things, you will be recharged and re-energized. Without doing them, you may feel tired, resentful, burned out, deprived, bitter, depressed or angry at yourself or others. Remember that if you keep giving and giving, without replenishing your mind, body and spirit, it won't take long for you to scrape bottom.

Take rest; a field that has rested gives a bountiful crop.
—Ovid

Think of taking care of and being kind to yourself as refilling the pot, so to speak, so that you *can* continue to give to others. You are also affirming that you are deserving of the love of others as well, whatever your background, upbringing, social or financial circumstances.

To be loved, we need to love and take care of ourselves first. Often that begins with forgiving ourselves and others for all real and imagined slights and hurts, past and present. You may be surprised to find that forgiveness is liberating and can bring you peace.

Every day our lives may be crammed with activities, duties and responsibilities involving ourselves, immediate and extended families, jobs, interests and hobbies. It is critical for our mental, psychological and physical health to take care of ourselves first.

Make a conscious choice to do those things that truly are important and matter to you, your family and friends by learning to say no to everything else. Don't clutter your life with activities that you only feel marginally interested in or take on tasks that nobody else wants or do.

Choose to live a balanced life and strive to be the very best you can be.

WHAT YOU THINK OF YOURSELF
IS MUCH MORE IMPORTANT
THAN WHAT OTHERS THINK OF YOU.
—SENECA

34   Love what you do

The often-quoted and misquoted Chinese philosopher Confucius, who lived over 2500 years ago, was truly a wise man and the following is one of his many sayings could make a huge difference in your perspective about life.

> *If you love what you do, you will never work a day in your life.* —Confucius

Having discovered what is the closest to your heart, written it down and given your list more thought could be the springboard to doing what you *really* enjoy. Research has shown that 70% of people are unhappy at work. That is a lot of disgruntled folks out there who get up each morning to earn their paychecks but are most likely wishing that they were doing something else for a living.

If you haven't yet discovered what you have an aptitude for what your interests are, or where your skills or abilities lie, make time to visit a career center and take one of their assessment surveys. These can be very enlightening and valuable in determining what vocations and professions you would do well in.

There is an excellent chance that what you *like* to do is also what you could be doing and moreover, possibly generating income from it. It is remarkable really when you think about it how one small decision or choice can change your life.

Simple questions such as the following can help to direct your thoughts constructively:

- Do you like working alone, with other people, or with plants or animals?
- Are you a creator, hands-on person, care-giving soul or someone who likes to fix up cars, computers, machinery, bicycles, furniture and so on?
- Do you like to work inside or outside, with wood, fabrics, metal, stone or none of these?
- Would a desk job appeal to you or a position that allows you the flexibility to move around during your workday?
- Are you good with technology or are you a "people person?"
- Are you a left-brain person, analytical and logical? Or perhaps you are a right-brainer, creative and intuitive.
- What type of communicator are you a thinker, feeler, intuitor or a sensor?

Your potential in different areas is boundless.

But the more you know about what gives you enjoyment, the closer you are to finding the right spot for yourself in the world. Your economic survival, and mental, psychological and emotional well-being may boil down to your creativity, innovation, problem-solving skills, teamwork and flexibility, not your education or knowledge.

Think hard about what you know and how you could capitalize on that knowledge or skill. What do you know or can do that someone else is willing to pay you to do? All of us know something about anything that may be or is valuable to someone else in a business or industry.

Once you know what makes you tick, you're already on your way. It is actually an excellent time to think outside the box and outside the way things have always been done because monumental changes have taken place in society, in your country and the world's economies.

None of these will ever be the same again. Technology, science, politics, culture, societies, and all aspects of life, including work, jobs and families, have transformed and will continue to be in flux. During your lifetime, things will be unrecognizable from how they existed during in the twentieth century or even from a few years ago.

Consider, for example, that there are over seventy-eight million Baby Boomers in the United States alone born between 1946 and 1964. The younger Boomers are reaching middle age while the older ones are entering their 60s. This group belongs to the "sandwich generation," caught between still raising their children while caring for aging parents.

These older Boomers have great and varied needs: healthcare, home-health and elder care, financial planning, higher education for their children, and event planning for graduations, anniversaries and such. Imagine how many nurses, health-related technicians in every medical field, caregivers, hospital workers, financial planners, insurance representatives, and retirement-related and recreational personnel will be needed in the next century.

Do your research and analysis, using the latest statistics, information and news in a variety of fields and professions, especially those that interest you. Consult reliable sources such as publications like *American Demographics* magazine, which has been on the forefront of population trends since the mid 1990s and offers valuable insight into all segments of the population.

Keep current with business news in various media - online, print and broadcast and avail yourself to the treasure trove of information that is accessible to you.

> *I not only use all the brains I have, but all those I can borrow.* —Woodrow Wilson

> *The secret of business is to know something that nobody else knows.* —Aristotle Onassis

From this research, you can see into the future, even without a crystal ball. The general population in North America is aging, so goods and service related to retirement, aging, health and medical care will be at a premium.

Look in unlikely places and think creatively "outside the box." Your computer skills, love of solving puzzles and reading detective stories may be the ticket for a new direction: law enforcement. The number of cases of identity theft, fraud, scams, child endangerment, stalking and many other criminal activities conducted via the Internet are increasing. Even the Internal Revenue Service is seeking employees to assist in finding tax evaders.

A September 2010 *Los Angeles Times* article showcased an emerging new career opportunity in the medical field — that of a medical scribe. This person accompanied a doctor during visits to patients and listens as well as records the comments made during an examination, treatment plans and options, follow-up instructions and prescriptions, laboratory tests, referrals to specialists and other pertinent information.

During recovery from one of the worst recessions since the Great Depression, many jobs, industries and businesses will have changed or even disappeared, never to be restored in any way, shape or form. But once you have found your passion, you can still find a rewarding vocation or even re-engineer, reinvent or create your own job or business. Don't overlook opportunities in the ethnic markets, a hidden gold mine if you grew up in and understand other cultures or are fluent in other languages.

Be flexible. Be willing to change, retrain or go back to school in a new or emerging field. When you're out of work is an opportune time to do so. This may be your golden chance to enter a new profession or learn that skill that you've always wanted to try but never had the chance to do in the past.

When making decisions regarding your future, follow your heart, but use your head. Research and do your homework regarding any position, profession or endeavor you consider pursuing. Without doing your homework and evaluating the sacrifices you are willing to make to attain your goals, you are putting yourself, your family and your economic future at risk.

Don't skip any steps as you develop your business plan, strategize and execute the re-engineer your future or launch an entrepreneurial start-up. As the fable of the hare and the tortoise taught us, taking short cuts will surely sabotage your success. Remember that only in the dictionary does success come before work.

Where will the jobs be? A recent *Time* magazine article identifies the sectors that will be most likely to recover or grow:

- Business: real estate, rental and leasing; professional, scientific and technical companies; finance and insurance
- Durable goods manufacturing: machinery, wood products, transportation equipment, electrical equipment

and appliances, computers, electronics, primary metals, furniture and related goods
- ❧ Retail: motor vehicles and parts
- ❧ Education and health: health care, social assistance
- ❧ Leisure and hospitality: arts, entertainment, recreation, accommodation, food services
- ❧ Government: state and local
- ❧ Natural resources: logging
- ❧ Other: construction, transportation, warehousing

Acquaint yourself with reliable sources of information regarding demographics, psychographics and consumer trends, especially as the eco or "green" revolution gains momentum globally. There is a burgeoning awareness of and commitment to the environment, ecology, recycling, sustainable energy sources and resources, conservation and the green movement both in North America and globally. That focus will generate a lot of creativity, interest and investment in green technology, innovation and invention, and in new sources of energy such as solar, wind and more.

The greatest advantage of democratic societies is their citizens' freedom to express themselves. For those of us who are so lucky and blessed, I believe that our greatest resource is creativity, unfettered by traditions and old-fashioned thinking.

Imagination is more important than knowledge.
—Albert Einstein

After all, one can always acquire knowledge and learning, but creativity, innovation, ingenuity and imagination are priceless to the future of any country. Even during an economic downturn, there are opportunities available. Remember that throughout history, much of the world's immigration has occurred during times of famine, economic, political or religious turmoil in many countries. Those people had courage, took risks and made sacrifices, were resourceful and willing to work hard were able to survive and even thrive in new lands.

Downsizing, job loss, scrimping and saving, doing without discretionary income enjoyed in the past, husbands staying at home with their children while their wives become the primary breadwinners in their families. These are just the tip of an iceberg. Everyone is affected in some way when the world's economy stalls.

Like the message I read on a sticky notepad declared: Opportunities are never lost because somebody will take the ones that you missed or passed up.

WHEN LOVE AND SKILL WORK TOGETHER,
EXPECT A MASTERPIECE.
—*JOHN RUSKIN*

35   **Your purpose in life**

In my school author visits, one point I always make to young people is that they should learn as much as they can from everyone they know and meet. Each one of those people with whom they, and you, come in contact daily has knowledge or a skill about something else that you do not. By listening, asking and watching, you can learn something new every day. This is how we all grow and develop.

Who knows, perhaps one of these encounters will spark the interest or passion in you.

Admire those who attempt great things, even if they fail.
—Seneca

On the other hand, you know something or many things that others don't. Everyone has something that they do well, know more about than another person or something to share. Share what you do best.

The multi-millionaire J. Paul Getty once said, "Money is like manure. It's no good unless it is spread around." I say that knowledge is no good unless it is spread around.

Do you have a purpose in life? After all, there is and will only be one of you ever to live. There is a reason why you were given life and put on this planet, at this time. Discover what gifts, abilities and talents you were born with and what you were meant to share with other people.

You are the sum of a unique equation. —Benvido Cruz

Ask yourself what you want out of life and then make it happen. Do something every day toward your goal. Be ready to adapt and change according to circumstances or conditions. After all, what you believed was your purpose in life when you were sixteen years old will undoubtedly be different or inappropriate as you grow and mature.

We must always change, renew, rejuvenate ourselves, otherwise we harden. —Goethe

Perhaps you were not meant to follow family tradition and drop out of school or on the other extreme, attend a four-year university, but rather become a craftsperson, inventor or artist. Your future may not lie in being employed by another person or company, or require an advanced degree. Maybe, just maybe, after learning about yourself, work, self-discipline and ambition while "learning the ropes" by working for others, you discover that your destiny is to be your own boss.

Think about investing in or becoming an entrepreneur or starting your own business. But don't try to do everything yourself. Find investors or honest and hardworking partners, silent or active, who share your vision.

Start small and engineer your business and reputation slowly, carefully and deliberately. Hire the best people you can. Remember that you can always train a new employee, but recognize that energy and enthusiasm are more valuable. Neither of these can be faked or bought.

*The best executive is the one who has the sense enough to
pick good men to do what he wants done, and self-restraint
enough to keep from meddling with them while they do it.*
—Theodore Roosevelt

Learn to be and stay frugal. Be willing to take risks but
don't gamble. Never, ever compromise your integrity, reputation,
character or core values in your personal or professional conduct.
Once lost, none of these can be saved or recovered.

The five top megatrends of the twenty-first century are:
convenience, environment, ethnicity, fun and nutrition. What can
you think of, create or build that could make life easier or more
comfortable for someone or millions of "someones?"

If you have an idea about something that meets a consumer
demand or relieves pain, i.e. emotional, physical, mental, and so
on, you are already on the right track. The key is that while there
are already many ideas, services and products already, there is
always opportunity to improve on any of them.

*If you build a better mousetrap, the world will beat a path
to your door.* —Ralph Waldo Emerson

Like Emerson's mousetrap, another idea has evolved through
thousands of years. It began with the ancient Romans who first
used solar energy to heat water in glass bottles. The idea led
to the invention of the glass vacuum bottle to store liquids by
James Dewar in 1892. In 1904 the German company Thermos
developed what is now commonly known as the thermos bottle.

Someone clever then improved on the design with a thumb-
operated cap with a cork, spout and handle. This "warm water
bottle," literally in Chinese, was a staple in homes and offices, to

keep boiling water readily available for drinking, brewing tea, storing and cleansing.

Along came wide-mouth thermoses manufactured with plastic or stainless interiors, replacing glass for safety and to hold chunky soups and meals. About fifteen years ago, the first electric thermos for keeping water hot all day appeared, and was soon followed by the non-electric air pot, a container that dispensed hot and cold liquids by pressing down on a button pump incorporated into the cover.

To accomplish great things, we must dream
as well as act. —Anatole France

Years ago, take-out coffee was first served in thick paper cups and then graduated to being served in a new product called Styrofoam™. Shortly thereafter, someone invented a simple plastic cover to retain heat and prevent spills. My husband would make two parallel tears from the cover lip and fold the resulting flap back to enable him to drink from the cup without spilling his coffee as well as to keep it hot. I thought he had a brilliant idea but it never occurred to us to take action on his idea. Consequently, another smart person did, and made money from it. Today you can see how others have ingeniously improved on the lid design for both hot and cold liquids.

But it didn't stop there. Another idea followed the massive lawsuit against a famous fast-food franchise whose coffee temperature was so hot, a spill caused a burn on a customer's hand. Thus was born the corrugated cardboard sleeve that slipped onto a cup to protect hands from the hot liquids inside. The latest innovation reflects the increase in environmental awareness. It's back to the future - a light cardboard eggshell exterior covering a *paper,* rather than a non-biodegradable Styrofoam™ cup.

> *Take an object. Do something to it. Do something else to it.*
> —Jasper Johns

There are many places to find inspiration and ideas, from print to broadcast media to online. Discover the fascinating stories behind thousands of inventions such as the compass, Velcro, adhesive tape, sticky notepads, the zipper, the paper clip, Worchester sauce, and thousands of other items that have improved and changed our everyday lives.

Often, the best solutions or ideas are those which are the simplest. British Petroleum (BP) used a device to remove spilled oil that inventor Gerry Matherne made from parts he obtained from a hardware store. His was among tens of thousands of ideas submitted to BP after the tragic April 2010 explosion and devastating oil leak in Louisiana.

How can we not admire the exuberance and perseverance of one of the greatest inventors of all time?

> *I never allow myself to become discouraged under any circumstances.* —Thomas Edison

> *Everything comes to him who hustles while he waits.*
> —Thomas Edison

> *Results! Why man, I have gotten a lot of results. I know 50,000 things that won't work.* —Thomas Edison

Edison reminds us to keep plodding along, not give up, make things happen while you "wait," and increase your knowledge from unsuccessful attempts. There is much to be learned from failure, the most important is that you can either let it defeat you or you can overcome your disappointment and forge on. Notice that Edison said he never *allowed* himself to become discouraged.

But remember, your service or product must meet a consumer need, or you must cleverly create a need for it. You must do your homework and know the market you are trying to reach. Learn about and study the trends that are driving business. Be aware that research shows that it takes at least $27,000 to bring a product to market and even then it still may be unsuccessful.

Failure can be divided into those who thought and never did, and into those who did and never thought. —W.A. Nance

I thoroughly enjoy exploring street fairs, local marketplaces, arts and crafts shows, swap meets, and hardware and general goods stores wherever I travel in the world. Unique, new products are often field tested at special events such as these. Most have never been the subject of something called a focus group which evaluates a product before it goes into mass production. You can judge the potential for almost any service or product by introducing it to ordinary people first as they would be using it. Their common sense responses, comments and suggestions are invaluable.

Who would have imagined purses made from metal license plates or shopping bags made from rice and wheat bags from Asian countries? And have you seen the $3 telescoping cover that covers a wet umbrella when closed and has a water reservoir at its end?

Who thought of creating and selling a spongy ball for exercising our fingers to relieve the cramping from typing on a computer keyboard for too long or for patients to grasp and pump before a blood draw at a lab? And then another creative person was the first to expand on that thought and create the hand exercisers in unusual and colorful forms such as animals, buses, hearts, airplanes, and other fun shapes? Company and product names were printed on these to give away as promotional items.

Mannix Delfino took over her husband's business upon his retirement and her company hand sews vestments, accessories, banners and other furnishings used by priests and clergy. The San Antonio Winery, the only one remaining within Los Angeles City limits, survived during Prohibition by making wine for the numerous Catholic churches in the city.

When I first saw it, I thought the four-inch round piece of thin rubber was to help me open the lids of bottles. But a man dreamed up a new use for it. Wrapping the little mat around a clove of garlic and rolling it within could easily remove the skin. It was a handy kitchen gadget for the elderly and those with arthritis. A friend invented one of the first folding bicycles that could be carried easily by hand or fit into the trunk of a car. Another friend's son parlayed his childhood hobby of collecting soda bottle caps into a profitable business of supplying bottled sodas from around the world to various events.

"I want to work and travel until I'm thirty," our youngest son Steven told us after his university graduation with a double major in business and environmental studies. He took one look at the awful duck- poop green drapes with their gold fleur de lis pattern laying on the floor of our new home and asked if he could have them. The next time I opened his website home page, there were my discarded drapes. They had been transformed into a stunning bicycle bag, lined inside with used billboard vinyl and sporting a shoulder strap crafted from car seat belt remnants. The bag proudly sat atop a matching upholstered loveseat.

"Do you have more of those drapes, Mom?" he asked the next time we spoke, "That pattern was my best seller." Eventually he supported himself and his love for exploring new places for years in San Francisco. When now roaming the globe, he hand-sewed and sold customized bicycle bags, made exclusively from recycled materials.

You can learn a lot about a country and its people by poking around a bit in neighborhood shops and discovering tools, utensils, kitchenware and other items devised and designed locally. It is always inspiring to see the results of other people's creativity, imagination, ingenuity and resourcefulness.

Necessity, the mother of invention. —Plato

Everything man-made has evolved from a need of some sort, from the first primitive tools and weapons of pre-historic men to the most sophisticated scientific and technological inventions through-out the planet. Even the lowly seagull knows to use a beach's rocks or hard sand as a tool. The bird finds a clam, carries it in the air and then drops it to crack it open to access the meal inside.

But just having a brilliant idea is not enough, there are many other factors involved before a new product or service is acknowledged and accepted or becomes popular. Why did VHS take hold and leave Beta in the dust? In the history of auto-making, why did so many models never appeal to the public and others became the standard?

While the big-name automakers in the United States kept manufacturing gas guzzlers for over half a century for the general public, creating a dependency on foreign oil to this day, Japanese automakers "got it" long ago. They looked into the future and began designing and developing affordable, fuel-efficient cars to fill a void in the American market. The products that Nissan, Honda and Toyota introduced to the car-buying public became popular decades before it was hip to own environmentally friendly automobiles.

Just tracing back to the evolution of the camera, computer, cell telephone and the global positioning system (GPS) since their inceptions, you can see that to stay ahead of the wave, companies must spend tremendous sums of money for research and development.

It is not enough to aim, you must hit. —Italian proverb

Since the 1800s, there has developed a great deal of interest and research in identifying and quantifying what form intelligence takes. In 1983 Dr. Howard Gardner of Harvard University developed the idea of multiple kinds of intelligence: spatial, linguistic, logical-mathematical, kinesthetic, musical, interpersonal, intrapersonal and naturalistic, added in 1999.

Thomas Armstrong put it in simpler language: space smart, word smart, number/reasoning smart, body smart, music smart, people smart, self smart and nature smart. Daniel Goleman in 1994 developed the idea of emotional intelligence.

But the loveliest way I ever heard intelligence explained came from a teacher. When I told an audience that I had math anxieties and was technically challenged, she told me, "Your head is filled with pictures and words, not numbers."

What kinds of "smarts" do you possess? How can and will you make the best of them?

Your talent is God's gift to you. What you do with
it is your gift to God. —Leo Buscaglia

Perhaps you're a disaster in the kitchen but can play any piece of music by ear. Can you do square, line or belly dancing, take apart and re-assemble any piece of equipment or machinery, decorate your home with items you have knitted, quilted, painted, sewn, hand crafted in wood, stone, metal, clay, glass or another material?

Are you a whiz in the garden and can grow anything but have two left feet on the dance floor? Maybe you can shoot baskets, ski down a black diamond mountain slope, swim a hundred laps or run a marathon? Or perhaps you have a gift for public speaking, working or communicating with people, telling jokes or writing an article or media release in a jiffy.

Maybe you can identify every bird on sight, or stars and constellations in the night sky, or plants or flowers in your region.

You may be able to tell a gripping story or have the empathy or patience to take care of or nurse someone with special needs or give comfort to a patient with a terminal condition. Or perhaps you possess a special affinity with animals or can turn a satisfying profit on any investment you make.

What makes you a one-of-a-kind human being?

Believe that you were born with "a purpose unto heaven." You were put here on earth for a specific purpose, to make a positive difference, or as Mahatma Gandhi said: Be the change that you want to see in the world.

It is your challenge to find what that purpose is because, as the saying goes, "God doesn't make junk."

EVERY INDIVIDUAL HAS A PLACE TO FILL
IN THE WORLD AND IS IMPORTANT IN SOME
RESPECT, WHETHER HE CHOOSES TO BE SO
OR NOT. —*NATHANIEL HAWTHORNE*

36

For everything, there is . . .

I am a firm believer that there are no accidents in life, that we were all created for a reason and purpose, and all that happens is a minute component of a grand, universal master plan. You can call it destiny, the will of God, or attribute it to any higher power you believe in.

In my feng shui work, I often told my clients that the right home came to them at the right time in their lives. We would then explore together the details of how they found it. Their recall of the ease or difficulty, positive or negative experiences that were associated with their search, decision and move-in provided a pattern for what they were going through when they engaged my services.

This examination also holds true for other aspects of our lives. It is a blessing to learn the lessons of life and gain our maturity and wisdom, whether they were profound and joyous experiences or great challenges. In hindsight, those that were the most excruciating, painful or traumatic may turn out to be the ones from which we emerge stronger and most transformed.

A few years ago I had an exhibit booth in Los Angeles Chinatown during the celebratory launch of the Metro Gold Line from Union Station to Pasadena.

"People and things come into our lives at different times," said the woman who was in the adjoining booth, "just when we need them."

Her words gave me food for thought and amazingly, not long after that, an entire passage arrived in my email, the source and author unknown, but it appeared to be a modern-day adaptation of Ecclesiastes 8:6.

Everything, including people, come into your life . . .

Everything, including people, come into your life for a *reason*, a *season* or a *lifetime*. When you know which one it is, you will know what to do for that person to meet a need you have expressed. They have come to assist you through a difficulty with guidance and support, to aid you physically, emotionally or spiritually. They may seem like a godsend and they are. They are there for the *reason* you need them to be. Then, without any wrongdoing on your part, or an inconvenient time, this person will say or do something to bring the relationship to an end.

Sometimes they die. Sometimes they walk away. Sometimes they act up and force you to take a stand. What we must realize is that our need has been met, our desire fulfilled, their work is done. The prayer you sent up has been answered and now it is time to move on.

Some people come into your life for a *season*, because your turn has come to share, grow or learn. They bring you an experience of peace or make you laugh. They may teach you something you have never done. They usually give you an unbelievable amount of joy. Believe me, it is real. But only for a *season*.

Lifetime relationships teach you lifetime lessons, things you must build upon in order to have a solid, emotional foundation.

Your job is to accept the lesson, love the person and put what you have learned to use in all other relationships and areas of your life. It is said that "Love is blind but friendship is clairvoyant."
—Author unknown

STAND WITH ANYBODY THAT STANDS RIGHT WHEN HE IS RIGHT AND PART WITH HIM WHEN HE GOES WRONG.
—*ABRAHAM LINCOLN*

37 Missing the gold

How could you not be a pessimist in today's world? You are bombarded by bad news from the media with technology, natural and man-made disasters, death and destruction, global warming, wars and conflicts, pollution of every sort, poverty, illness, calamities, hunger, disease and pestilence.

Is there good news anywhere to be had anymore?

The greater part of our happiness or misery depends on our dispositions and not our circumstances.
—Martha Washington

Someone once said that if you are trying to solve a problem, don't consult an accountant or attorney, both of whom are trained to *find* problems! But then, that is their profession for which they are trained and through which they make their living. Likewise. if you are always looking for or expecting the worst, that's exactly what you will find and get.

You can complain because roses have thorns, or you can rejoice because thorns have roses. —Ziggy

If you are always looking for dirt, you will miss the gold. Examine your own outlook on life. Are you a person who always sees the glass as being half empty and looking at and for the worst in people, situations, or in your life? You will never be disappointed!

The law of attraction contends that people who send out negative energy, attract it and their darkness becomes a self-fulfilling prophecy. If you think that something or the worst will happen, it almost always becomes true.

> *Do not anticipate trouble, or worry about what may never happen. Keep in the sunlight.* —Benjamin Franklin

Recent research has even shown that negative people get sick more often and for longer than those who have a happy disposition. Dr. Stephen Sinatra contends that cancer patients who believe that they will recover, actually do, and that "their belief is 50 percent of the battle."

On the other hand, if you see things positively and with optimism, you will almost always discover the good around you. After all, life is not constantly made up of momentous occasions and major events, it's more like a quilt comprised of many small pieces stitched together.

> *A multitude of small delights constitute happiness.*
> —Charles Baudelaire

Moreover, you will attract people to you as surely as being around negative people repels or repulses others. Nobody enjoys being around people who are always grumpy, complaining, unhappy, angry, emotional or overly dramatic.

Norman Vincent Peale wrote that those who emit negative thoughts and engage in negative activities, become more mired in doom and gloom, attracting further troubles and darkness.

Sow a thought, reap a word;
Sow a word, reap an action;
Sow an action, reap a habit;
Sow a habit, reap a character;
Sow a character, reap a destiny.
—Anonymous

Or the short version . . .

Our life is what our thoughts make it. —Marcus Aurelius

Buddha, Gandhi, Wayne Dyer, James Allen and countless others have stressed the power of one's mind and expressed variations on the same theme.

Choosing happiness means giving thanks for what you have, not focusing on what you don't have or had yesterday. Robert Schuller advised us: "Let your hopes, not your hurts, shape your future." Enjoy your memories, but don't dwell or live in the past.

Even if we can't be happy, we must always be cheerful.
—Irving Kristol

Keep in mind that the most precious things in life are free: going to the beach; a walk in the woods or park; enjoying time with family, friends and neighbors; visiting a library; engaging in a favorite hobby or an act of kindness; feeling and showing compassion or love for someone.

Start small by taking little steps or shuffling along. Let go of small hurts and big grudges. Begin *thinking* positive thoughts with your head, *feeling* with your heart and *doing* with your hands. Start a new habit of indulging in a single random act of kindness a day.

It could be as easy or simple as smiling or greeting a co-worker or a stranger.

Say thank you to somebody during the day and mean it. Feel grateful when you find a parking place or a shorter grocery or gas station line. Pick up the phone and tell someone that you love, miss or appreciate them.

Then, each day increase one positive thought, word, or action to two a day, and then three, four and more, until being positive becomes a habit.

There is a positive health and social benefit for you in choosing to be happy. Research shows that happy people are perceived as and are more optimistic, confident, long-lived, competent, and have many other positive characteristics that attract people to them.

Make happiness a goal you'd like to achieve.

> WHEN ONE DOOR OF HAPPINESS CLOSES,
> ANOTHER OPENS; BUT WE OFTEN LOOK SO
> LONG AT THE CLOSED DOOR THAT WE DO
> NOT SEE THE ONE WHICH HAS BEEN OPENED
> FOR US. —*HELEN KELLER*

38

Ways to be rich

"There are two ways to be rich: work harder or desire less," proclaimed the message I read on a T-shirt in a Honolulu souvenir shop years ago.

We've probably all done it in our lives at some time or another because it is such a human thing to do - comparing ourselves, conditions and circumstances with that of others around us. Once you get seduced into counter-productive thinking or into the "rat race," it is difficult to pull out.

There will always be someone who has more of something than you do, and you can make yourself pretty miserable and bitter if you are always pushing yourself to attain what others have. While you're making comparisons, there are far more people who have less than you do.

Your life is not theirs, or vice versa. Everything about someone else's life and material wealth cannot be duplicated, even if you own exactly the same *things*. If you envy another's possessions, you will never be satisfied. If you are jealous of another person, you will leave yourself open to a plethora of negative emotions. You can keep working harder and longer for the remainder of your life and still not achieve or possess everything that the other person has or what you want.

Before we set our hearts too much upon anything,
let us examine how happy they are who already possess it.
—La Rochefoucauld

Riches enlarge, rather than satisfy appetites.
—Thomas Fuller

Those who want much are always much in need.
—Mohammed

It is more important to have what you need than what you want, as many during an economic depression or recession have found out. Working harder might not necessarily generate more income, merely more disappointment, anger or frustration, all injurious to your health and relationships.

The pessimist sees difficulty in every opportunity.
The optimist sees opportunity in every difficulty.
—Winston Churchill

Families have had to make very difficult and painful choices. When their lives are reduced to the basics, people around the world at every economic level, discover what in their lives is truly worth having and keeping. As Friedrich Nietzsche said: "Necessity is not a fact, but a matter of interpretation."

What one person or family considers as basic needs represent luxuries to another. Designer clothing, vehicles, bottled water or going out to a movie don't even factor into the choices of a family that just needs to put food on the table or shoes on their children's feet.

In the words of Henry David Thoreau: "That man is richest whose pleasures in life are the cheapest." Many people would rather have more time than money. Of course it didn't help prevent a recession when the U.S. president George W. Bush urged Americans in 2006 by saying, "I encourage you all to go shopping more" which further exacerbated a dire economic situation.

By desiring less, your life can become easier and simpler. The simple act of divesting your life of unnecessary things can give you the feeling of greater freedom, empowerment and liberation. If you really want to feel rich, make a list of all the things you have that money can't buy.

When was the last time you read the U.S. Constitution, the Bill of Rights and the ten amendments? Reflect on your freedoms of speech, to vote, to assemble peaceably, of religion and to petition.

But back to wealth and riches. A recent AARP article about being thrifty revealed that for many "cheapskates," the formula was simple: spending less money created more time. Often, just delaying a purchase can diminish the desire to buy. If your children are clamoring for you to buy them something, ask them if they would spend their allowance or be willing to work to earn the money for it. Many things lose value when they are free and conversely, are treasured when a person's time, money or other resources are personally involved in their acquisition.

Think about the example you set. Do you refuse to buy an item for your child and then spend money on something for yourself? What are the spending priorities or how do you model financial responsibility in your household?

Perhaps you desire and imitate the lifestyles of the rich and famous, even though you do not have the means to do so. Maybe the result will be losing your job or home, the failure of your business or employer, depreciation of your portfolio, or a change in the economy, either national or worldwide.

Or maybe you put more value on material things rather than on yourself.

PRAY NOT FOR GOLD.
PRAY FOR GOOD CHILDREN
AND HAPPY GRANDCHILDREN.
—*CHINESE PROVERB*

39

When you're feeling down

Want to feel better about life and yourself?

"I believe that every human mind feels pleasure in doing good to another," was Thomas Jefferson's answer.

Doing something for or giving something to another person, whether you're involved in hands-on volunteerism or writing a donation check, makes you feel good. Research has shown such activities give you a sense of joy, and feelings of warmth, wellbeing and more energy, creating something called "the helper's high." There are studies that actually show that community volunteers feel better, live longer and are generally healthier. Even watching films of people doing generous acts for others improved the immune systems of audience members.

Noble deeds and hot baths are the best cures for depression.
—Mark Twain

It may feel impossible to do when you've just received sad or bad news, or have experienced or are still reeling from a devastating loss, betrayal or disappointment in your life. You may have just lost a job, loved one, cherished dream or something you've saved, struggled or worked hard for. You may be feeling traumatized, numb, weary, disheartened, insignificant or depressed. Your health may be suffering and you just plain don't feel like doing a darn thing.

If you can make it out of bed in the morning and put on your clothes, you have already accomplished two things for the day. Make no mistake, because every subsequent action you take is moving forward to your healing.

Consider that if you do one small or simple thing a day to direct your attention, thoughts or preoccupation away from yourself and toward another person, your single act of kindness or thoughtfulness could make a significant difference in someone else's life.

Think of your family and friends or somebody who could use cheering up or a hug across the miles, or anyone who might come to mind who is less fortunate than you. It could even be someone you don't know.

It will help you to appreciate what you have, rather than focus on what you don't have. Then pick up the phone or a pen, sit at your computer or send a message to someone in or out of your life just to say, "I love/miss/thank/forgive/want to see/reconnect with you."

If you don't have charity in your heart, you have the worst kind of heart trouble in the world. —Bob Hope

Decades ago, I peeled and shared an orange with a friend during a work break. It wasn't a large, expensive or flamboyant gesture or gift, and I didn't think much of our short visit. But years later upon meeting her again, she told me that she always remembered me and that day.

When asked the reason, she said that it had been one of the darkest days of her life and that visit and those orange slices we shared uplifted her like nothing else could have.

I wrote the following poem after she thanked me, and included it in my book *A Woman's 4-Minute Bible:*

A DAILY GIFT

*If you can't give money
give your time.
If you can't give your time
give listening.
If you give listening
give your heart.
If you can't give your heart
give your spirit.
If you can't give your spirit
give hope.
If you can't give hope
give love.
If you can't give love
give thanks.
If you can't give thanks
give forgiveness.
If you can't give forgiveness
give a hug.
If you can't give a hug
give smiles and laughter.
What can you give today?
It will nourish your soul,
renew your spirit and
someone will cherish your gift
whatever it is.*
—Angi Ma Wong

You do not have to join any formal organization or group to do something for others, but if you are inclined to, you could. You may never know what may bloom from your small act of kindness or generosity of spirit. You may never know how it may transform someone's life. You can act on your own or become a volunteer today as a member of a service organization in your community.

You may not even realize that you are already a volunteer, especially if you have helped out in any way at your place of worship, at a library, a school or a community center. Have you read to a child lately or practiced speaking English to a new immigrant at a park, at a bus stop, grocery store or library; delivered food or good cheer to someone in a hospital or given a ride to a friend for his chemotherapy treatment?

The life you improve may very well be your own.

NO ONE IS USELESS IN THIS WORLD
WHO LIGHTENS THE BURDENS OF ANOTHER.
—*CHARLES DICKENS*

40 How to be happy

A lot of people have it all wrong. While "life, liberty and the pursuit of happiness," is part of the United States Constitution, it does not guarantee happiness. You could chase after happiness throughout your life and never find it.

Happiness does not come from success Success comes from happiness. If you are happy, you will be successful.
—Buddha

Many folks believe if they are successful, they will be happy, but it is not true. One has only to hear or read about fabulously wealthy people who are lonely, friendless or miserable.

While they may accumulate and surround themselves with status symbols that represent success and material wealth such as homes, cars, planes, jewelry, designer clothing and accessories, and so on, but they are *spiritually* impoverished. They may have all the money to spend on themselves and do, but are stingy with spending it on others. They are not happy.

Happiness is where we find it, but rarely where we seek it.
—J. Petit Senn

On the other hand, there are those who do not possess material wealth but are rich in the love of their family and friends and those who they respect. They are doing what they love and earn enough money to live modestly, simply or comfortably. They enjoy the satisfaction and contentment resulting from doing meaningful work of which they are proud, and living the life they want on their own terms.

Don't waste another day feeling sorry for yourself or envying what others have. Wake up every morning and see each day for what it is — a gift and new opportunity to take action and make change happen in your life and in your world.

You might respond by telling me that you don't know how to be happy. Maybe you haven't figured out who you are yet or what you really want. One day over ten years ago after feeling particularly misunderstood and unappreciated by my husband, I sat down and poured out my feelings and later shared what I had written with some friends. They read it and told me they could truly relate and requested copies so I made it into a poster to give away as gifts.

Here it is:

WHAT WOMEN WANT

Women want to be and feel cherished. As daughters, wives, and mothers, we want to know that we have worth to our parents, partners, children, families, and friends. We want to be secure in the knowledge that we are important in the lives of those around us. We want to feel convinced that we are valued, that we are respected, and that we truly matter.

We want to be told and shown in great and small ways, on special days and drudgery, everydays, that we are appreciated. We want our words not only to be heard, but for the messages behind them to be listened to, and responded to with dignity. We want to be spoken to in softer, quieter tones because our hearing, psyches, feelings, and emotions are fragile. We become deaf to high volume, aggressiveness, roughness, crudity, and profanity.

We want to know and believe at all times that we are loved, just as we love those around us. We want to feel safe and nurtured and cared for, even as we nourish, nurture, and care for those around us. We want commitment to us and our relationships. We want to be valued for who we are, our individual, personal worth, and not for what income, status, or outer beauty we possess, or what we might or might not become, for we are precious in our own right as human beings.

We seek most, other human beings who acknowledge our humanity, special gifts, uniqueness, originality, and are sensitive to all of our needs — spiritual, emotional, intellectual, sexual, mental, and physical. We will gravitate to such kindred spirits, even as we respond most to caring, compassion, kindness, generosity, and humor. These are the qualities that empower and embolden us to sacrifice as well as to dream, try and achieve great and wondrous things.

We care little whether the people who have these qualities are rich, poor, young or old, abled or disabled, for we possess the unique ability to see into hearts and souls while disregarding the outer physical layers. Those who are rich in spirit and willing to share even a small measure of that wealth with us, are rewarded a thousand-fold, with our loyalty, friendship, affection, respect, and love.

—Angi Ma Wong

Come to think of it — isn't this what men want too? I guess we aren't so different after all. The way we make each other feel good about ourselves inside is what makes us happy.

HAPPINESS IS NOT SOMETHING
YOU POSTPONE FOR THE FUTURE;
IT IS SOMETHING YOU DESIGN
FOR THE PRESENT. —*JIM ROHN*

41 Keep score of your successes

From the time you start your first or a new job or position, or learn a new skill, however small or unimportant it may seem at the time, start a file. Document, make a list and a collection of your performance reviews, letters of appreciation, thanks from clients and customers, and other correspondence. Print out complimentary messages and emails and add them to your collection.

As the years pass, keep including updated resumes, but keep the old so you can track your personal and professional growth. Add certificates from classes you have taken and courses completed. Don't forget those hard-earned diplomas, commendations, awards and accolades, news clippings, photos and digital images of you in action.

Make a list of all the skills that you have as well as another of the projects you have participated in, including the nature and extent of your involvement, and continue to add to both lists.

Start another list of things that you like about yourself, things that you can do, things that you have achieved or accomplished. Put each on a piece of paper and collect them in a jar. Whenever you are feeling vulnerable, uncertain, rejected or unappreciated, take three of these out and read them.

Frame and hang on your wall those plaques that have the most significance, personally or professionally, or those that represent special achievements or accomplishments. If you are a homemaker or work from home, you still can surround yourself with the proud results of your labor and skills. It could be a piece of handmade art or craft work, a digital recording or photograph, or any memento of something you have created, made or done.

Don't hoard or hide these things but take them out from time to time, and frame, hang or display them to remind yourself what you have accomplished. They will also define precious moments in both your professional and personal life. Take time to reflect on the path you have traveled and record in a journal or diary the progress of your self- development.

There will be times in your life during which you may feel unappreciated or useless. You may have been demoted, laid off from or replaced at your job. Your morale may be at an all time low and you may feel you have no value to anyone or any company. Your future may look bleak and you may have lost hope.

At times like these, take out your success file to relive and bask in those glory moments. These will validate how worthy you are and how your life is really one of success and of which you can be proud.

Moreover, with your updated skills list, you can see which could be transferrable to a new job. You can craft and rewrite to adapt them to the requirements of a position in an emerging industry especially if the one you held before has been eliminated. Be flexible and examine how your experience can benefit an employer, be it a for-profit or charitable organization.

CHERISH ALL YOUR HAPPY MOMENTS;
THEY MAKE A FINE CUSHION FOR OLD AGE.
—*CHRISTOPHER MARLEY*

42

How to choose a mate, friend or partner

We who recently attended the Rotary District 5280 conference in La Quinta, California were privileged to hear Michael Josephson, founder of the Josephson Institute, speak at the first breakfast meeting. His minute-long "Character Counts" features are heard on the air and sent daily to tens of thousands of email subscribers, and his training seminars are provided to educational institutions, businesses, industries and organizations around the globe.

His "Six Pillars of Character" provide an exceptional guideline for making solid choices as you decide with whom you would like to surround yourself — those who possess strong moral character. These could include your lifetime mate, friends or business partner(s).

In his "Six Pillars of Character," Mr. Josephson lists the following core values that comprise good character: trustworthiness, respect, responsibility, fairness, caring and citizenship. They clarify a person's moral obligations "that make us better people and produce a better society." His yardstick can be a useful measure as to whom in your life you may rate as "keepers," those who are worthy of your attention, love and loyalty.

From his father Joshua, former UCLA basketball coach John Wooden was handed a seven-point creed when he was in grammar school in 1948. He later developed it into his now-famous "Pyramid of Success" by which he trained his college, and later, professional teams.

Coach Wooden placed success at the pinnacle of his pyramid, with industriousness and enthusiasm forming its two keystones. "The cornerstones of success to me in anything," he said, " are hard work and enjoy what you do."

Enthusiasm fuels the hard work, which in turn becomes its own reward and riches, which may not necessarily be monetary.

YOU CAN PREACH A BETTER SERMON
WITH YOUR LIFE THAN WITH YOUR LIPS.
—OLIVER GOLDSMITH

43 Be kind to yourself

Each morning I walk out my front door and literally stop to smell the roses. Those fragrant Double Delights were deliberately planted by the front steps for me to sniff on my way out.

I cherish the solitude and serenity of my 2.5 mile walk, even if it does take me to the top of a hill and back down again. Communing with nature daily makes up for missing the camping and hiking trips we used to take all over California in different seasons when our children were young.

The peace and quiet that follows the rush of a passing car allows me to savor the stillness and hear the various twits, tweets and chirps of the birds, squirrels and other critters in the trees and bushes flanking the road, in neighborhood gardens and along the rows of Chinese pepper trees lining the neighborhood golf course. Sometimes the silence is broken by the soft clinks of golf clubs in their bags as their owners stroll through the grass, their shoes' rubber cleats clunking lightly on the cart path, or by the gentle swishes of the oscillating sprinklers watering the greens.

Occasionally, in the bushes or leaves, there is a sudden rustle or I hear an unfamiliar scraping sound made on the bark of a hidden tree nearby. In the spring, I pass under the drapery of those pepper trees and hear the soft humming of hundreds of bees, hidden as they seek the pollen within tiny, green pepper buds. If a birdsong is unfamiliar, I reach into my jacket pocket, pull out my little telescope and try to find the source.

Through the years of walking in my neighborhood, I have learned a valuable lesson from observing the pervasive peacocks that roam free throughout the Palos Verdes Peninsula. During the mating season, the males literally shake their tail feathers to attract the females.

Sometimes there is one female pea hen in their audience, sometimes several, and often there are none nearby at all. Those male peacocks are still there strutting their huge tails which are fanned out in shimmering colors and unbelievable beauty. Sometimes it is only I, a mere human, walking by to see the show. Just watching them is a lesson in perseverance!

What I described above is my routine daily walk that sets me in the proper frame of mind to face every day. That walk keeps me feeling grounded and my life balanced Every step I take is a step to maintaining good health. An added benefit is that many ideas for my writing surface during the walks.

What do you do for yourself each day? Here's what one teenager wrote in her diary:

> I don't think of all the misery, but of the beauty that still
> remains…My advice is: go outside, to the fields, enjoy
> nature and the sunshine, go out and try to recapture
> happiness in yourself and in God. Think of all the beauty
> that's still left around you and be happy! —Anne Frank

It is said that we are our own harshest critics. The cure is to stop criticizing yourself by being your own best friend. That means not to do anything to yourself that you would never do to your closest pal or buddy.

Psychological Science reports that those who acknowledge both their strengths and weaknesses feel better about themselves and have higher self-esteem and confidence than if they had only treated themselves to positive affirmations.

Self-examination, setting high goals and standards, having lofty dreams, being focused and ambitious enough to reach for your dreams are all well and good. But don't be guilty of being so busy making a living that you forget how to live.

Avoid trying to plan or control every single thing in your life. You are sure to be frustrated or miserable when things don't go your way or people don't act the way you wanted them to. Being mature means accepting the truth that you cannot and should not control every little thing in your life.

Surround yourself with folks who like as well as love you, accepting you for who you are, imperfect, like all of us are. Keep close those who boost your confidence, help raise your self-esteem and appreciate your worth. With them, you can truly relax and be yourself. Among them, you can feel strong and self-assured, be spontaneous but not impulsive, fun but not frivolous, childlike but not childish.

Even by standing with your back straight, your shoulders pulled back and stomach pulled in, you can physically feel and breathe better (from your diaphragm) and look more poised and attractive.

You must also deliberately plan and do things for your own well-being. In today's high-pressure, fast-paced and competitive world, scheduling time for yourself is imperative to your mental and psychological health.

A day out of doors, someone I love to talk with, a good book, and some simple food and music. That would be rest.
—Eleanor Roosevelt

Once you have set your objectives, write them down in the form of attainable goals. Goals need to have timelines, be measurable to be effective and are useless if they are ambiguous and sit gathering dust. "Failing to prepare is preparing to fail," basketball coach John Wooden, "the Wizard of Westwood," and Mike Murdock have both declared.

Next, list the activities or action items you need to do to attain those goals. You do not have to do or finish *all* of them every day, as some may take days, weeks, months, or are long-term or ongoing. What is important is that you do *something* every day, however small or large a task, toward your personal and professional goals. And don't forget, being happy can be a goal too.

It does not matter how slowly you go, as long as you do not stop. —Confucius

Take a lesson from Dr. Steven Covey, the best-selling author of the *The 7 Habits of Highly Effective People* and categorize all your tasks for each day. These are a) Important and urgent; b) Important but not urgent; c) Not important but urgent; and d) Not important and not urgent. If you always take care of Group B first, you will be able to avoid crises and emergencies.

Do the following little exercise and then prioritize the list:

- Read your mail
- Meet a work deadline
- Pay bills
- Read to your child tonight

- ꙮ Fix a leaky pipe in your kitchen
- ꙮ Exercise
- ꙮ Schedule an important meeting with a client
- ꙮ Put air in your car tires
- ꙮ Buy a gift for your spouse's birthday (a week in advance)

Know yourself well, arrange your activities to be the most effective and efficient during your day and always keep in mind what is important in your life. These would be yourself; your family; your mental, physical, spiritual, intellectual and sexual health; your goals and dreams; your friends; and the values and causes that you care about the most.

Then learn to say no. De-clutter your life of people or things that mean little or nothing to you, or those you really don't care about. True happiness may be as simple as creating the life you want so you can do the things you truly love.

Be aware that your life and resources, including time, energy and money are finite. Don't let your yesterdays undermine your todays and sabotage your tomorrows. Banish negative thoughts, emotions and activities from your life. Live every moment in the present. It's all any of us has.

Nothing should be prized more highly than the value of each day. —Johann Wolfgang von Goethe

Being kind to yourself means that if you are feeling out of sorts, asking yourself the following questions:

- ꙮ Am I getting enough sleep?
- ꙮ Am I drinking enough water every day?
- ꙮ Am I eating properly?
- ꙮ Am I getting the proper nutrition from my meals?

⊛ Am I exercising daily?

⊛ Am I at peace with myself?

Take responsibility for your own health first. Without it, you will not be able to enjoy what you have worked hard for or be happy. Remember that Howard Hughes was once the richest man on the planet, but he died in poor health, miserable and alone.

Love yourself and take care of your own mental, emotional, intellectual, physical and spiritual needs above those of others. To do so is not being selfish, but being smart. Know that you are a worthy human being and that you have a purpose in life.

Be sure to schedule in some time, at least half an hour, for yourself every day, doing something for you that lifts your spirit, heart or mind. It could be as simple as stopping everything to enjoy a phone call to a friend; buying a bouquet of flowers; spending time doing nothing in your garden; watching half an hour of a favorite TV program; listening to music; taking a walk in the park; creating something; or treating yourself to a break, a cup of coffee or tea. It could be anything that recharges your inner batteries, but do it and do it once or several times a day. Those mini breaks will keep your spirits, energy and enthusiasm up.

You cannot expect to be good at what you do if you are not good to yourself. You cannot help others if you do not help yourself. You cannot keep giving and giving to others if you do not give something to yourself each day. And we are not talking about material things here, like buying something, but rather engaging in activities that refresh, reward and replenish your body and spirit.

There are many ways to move forward. What's your style of

getting things done, of accomplishing your goals, of actualizing your dreams? Your way is not my way, and thank goodness we are not all the same. The world thrives on diversity of every sort.

Here are some words of wisdom and hope to guide you along the way.

Every day do something that will inch you closer to a better tomorrow. —Dough Firebaugh

Wisely and slow; Them stumble that run fast. —William Shakespeare

One's objective should be to get it right, get it quick, get it over. You see, your problem won't improve with age. —Warren Buffet

To know the road ahead, ask those coming back. —Chinese proverb

It is not because things are difficult that we do not dare, it is because we do not dare that they are difficult. —Seneca

The longer we dwell on our misfortunes, the greater is their power to harm us. —Voltaire

Our greatest glory is not in never falling, but in rising every time we fall. —Confucius

Enthusiasm releases the drive to carry you over obstacles and adds significance to all you do. —Norman Vincent Peale

As you go through your day and your action items or to do list, put a check next to or cross out each one that has been completed. Even if you have done only a single or a few things listed, you have moved forward. Take time to review the list at the end of your day and feel good about yourself and what you have accomplished. You owe yourself that sense of satisfaction, reward, achievement, progress and a pat on the back.

Don't beat yourself up about those tasks you were unable to do or complete. You are not and don't have to be perfect. Although you may have high expectations for yourself, be reminded that there are always reasons beyond your control that prevented you from accomplishing everything on that day's plan.

Evaluate your list by Dr. Covey's guidelines and start a new one for the next day before you leave your office or retire to the night. You will have something to give you a sense of purpose in the morning as you begin a new day.

Epictetus said: "Today is the first day of the rest of your life." Do what you love and love what you do . . . whatever it is.

MOST OBSTACLES MELT AWAY WHEN WE MAKE UP OUR MINDS TO WALK BOLDLY THROUGH THEM. —*ORISON SWETT MARDEN*

44 Response-ability

There will come a time in your life when you will realize that there are few things that you can control. You have no control over the weather, stock market, traffic, death, taxes, politics, and other people's thoughts, feelings or actions.

You cannot force another person to be happy, content or angry, just as you are unable to change their other emotions, moods and feelings. You may be able to provide material things, or comfort or try to help them, but there is no guarantee that your efforts will bring about changes or the response you anticipated. In fact, your actions may even cause a totally opposite reaction or response than what you had hoped or planned for. You may even be resented or not appreciated for your involvement or efforts.

How other people treat you is their karma. How you react is yours. —Author unknown

Accept that you cannot control everything in your life, but you can control your *response* to whatever happens to you personally. It could be a simple thing like dropping something on the floor or as major as a business error that costs you or your business a great deal of money. It could be missing a bus or an opportunity to do something you wanted.

For example, you are driving along and a person cuts in front of you, almost causing a rear-end accident. You can choose to get angry or just let it go, telling yourself that the other driver was just plain rude, distracted or just really a jerk. You can choose to yell at the other person or make a rude gesture. Or you can choose to remain calm and remind yourself that you are lucky that you were a good enough driver to have avoided an accident and just dismiss the incident.

In another scenario, your child, spouse or friend has just said or done something hateful or hurtful to you. You can choose a knee-jerk reaction by retaliating verbally, emotionally or physically. Not surprisingly, the situation will most likely escalate into something so damaging to your relationship, perhaps temporarily or even permanently beyond repair.

Forgiveness does not change the past, but it does enlarge the future. —Paul Boese

On the other hand, should you choose to forgive the other person for offending you, you can exercise self control, remain calm and walk away, perhaps even asking that both or you take a time-out. Such a mature and gracious gesture could go a long way to defusing a potentially injurious or risky situation.

Hide your offended heart. Keep your treasured friend. —Chinese proverb

It takes courage, resolve, strength, respect for the other person and the power of love to remove yourself from a touchy, delicate or explosive situation. But remember that you are in control and your power lies in your freedom and ability to choose your response to any and every situation or circumstance.

You have the strength to take charge of your life. Make it whatever you wish it to be. —*Kate Jenkins*

45

Don't put your dreams or life on hold

Over twenty years ago, I was told that a lump in my breast was malignant. Upon returning home from a stay in the hospital for a lumpectomy, I walked through my front door and experienced an epiphany. In one glance, I saw my lovely home through new eyes.   All of a sudden, it occurred to me that everything within my sight had less value than my family and friends. The furnishings and accessories, even the house itself, could never replace the love and support of those around me.

Immediately another realization dawned. Life was too precious and short to waste and only God knew how much longer my life would be. Cancer could have easily taken my life and by golly, I had things I had dreamed of doing, places to go and people to meet. It was at that very moment that I decided that I had better get moving to make those dreams real.

> *When you look back on your life, you will regret the things*
> *you have not done more than those you did.*
> —H. Jackson Brown

Look around you, near and far, and it doesn't take much to see that most people are putting off their dreams. You hear folks saying things like, "When I retire, my husband (or wife) and I will _____" or "When I save this much money, I'll _____."

The trouble with this line of thought is that life is unpredictable. From one moment to the next, we have no clue what it will bring. Right now you are enjoying a perfectly ordinary day but within the next few seconds, you could be downed by a heart attack or stroke, or lose a family member, friend or your job. Within minutes, a hurricane, earthquake, fire, tsunami, flood, a terrible disaster (remember 9/11?) or freak accident could strike.

I put the following words on our family's holiday card one year as well as used it in a Rotary speech, both times resulting in positive and poignant responses.

> *To realize the value of ten years:*
> *Ask a newly divorced couple.*
> *To realize the value of four years:*
> *Ask a graduate.*
> *To realize the value of one year:*
> *Ask a student who has failed a final exam.*
> *To realize the value of nine months:*
> *Ask a mother who gave birth to a still born.*
> *To realize the value of one month:*
> *Ask a mother who has given birth to a premature baby.*
> *To realize the value of one week:*
> *Ask an editor of a weekly newspaper.*
> *To realize the value of one hour:*
> *Ask the lovers who are waiting to meet.*
> *To realize the value of one minute:*
> *Ask a person who has missed the train, bus or plane*
> *To realize the value of a second:*
> *Ask a person who has survived an accident.*
> *To realize the value of one millisecond:*

Ask the person who has won a silver medal in the Olympics.
To realize the value of a friend:
Lose one.
Time waits for no one. Treasure every moment you have.
—Author unknown

What dreams are you putting off?

Is it learning a new skill, taking your dream trip, reaching out for your dream job, or being your own boss as an entrepreneur and starting up your own business? Whatever it is, don't delay. Even doing something as simple as setting aside a jar with a "Trip Fund" label taped on to collect your spare change each night or setting up an automatic deposit from your paycheck into a savings account qualifies as your taking the first step.

Enjoy life. It's later than you think. —Chinese proverb

Articulate your own dreams and live them, not someone else's. Write your dreams down as your goals. Put them in a time frame of 1, 3, 5, 10 and 20 years from now, as you make your plans to actuate your dreams. Plan your work and then work your plan. Find mentors and solid role models. Emulate those whose ethics, actions and character you admire.

Be flexible, adaptable and as resourceful as you can. Be willing to adjust your plans as circumstances change, as they surely will. When encountering challenges en route, find ways to go over, under, through, around or whatever you can to get the other side to continue to your destination.

Let us watch well our beginnings, and results will manage themselves. —Alexander Clark

Leave your past behind, especially any attempts that have been unsuccessful. There will be times when something you do will be unsuccessful, but this does not mean that you are a failure. Do not think, believe or label yourself as such. The time, situation, idea, opportunity or any of many other factors may not have been receptive or conducive to your success, plans or projects.

> *Notice the difference between what happens when a man says to himself, 'I have failed three times,' and what happens when he says, 'I'm a failure.'* —S.I. Hayakawa

The telephone, television, Internet, and untold thousands of other significant discoveries, inventions, human and historical landmarks in every field of endeavor all began with somebody's flash of inspiration, a random thought or idea or a seemingly impossible dream. Both dreamers and realists have been ridiculed, ostracized, ignored and scorned.

> *Big ideas are so hard to recognize, so fragile, so easy to kill. Don't forget that, all of you who don't have them.*
> —John Elliott, Jr.

But as the old cliché goes: "When the going gets tough, the tough keep going." When life hands you lemons, make lemonade, and I add: open a lemonade stand with it!

Having second, third and fourth thoughts is helpful to keep you stay realistic, but do not allow in doubt in yourself or your abilities to hijack your determination to succeed. Have faith in yourself and in the grace of a higher power, no matter what you conceive that to be.

Believe in yourself and what others think won't matter.
—Ralph Waldo Emerson

Don't dwell on mistakes or allow yourself to be dragged down, especially by naysayers, but pick yourself up and keep trying and learning. Be patient and persistent. Do not allow your yesterdays steal your tomorrows, but let today light them. Avoid the would-haves, should-haves and could-haves. Don't get mired in unproductive or negative thoughts of what you cannot do. Focus on what you can do. Achieve and accomplish all you can on your own terms and do it your way.

Don't be afraid of opposition. Remember a kite rises against, not with the wind. —Hamilton Wright Mabie

You and only you, are solely responsible for your own happiness, so don't blame anyone else if you aren't happy with your life. You are guaranteed to be disappointed or frustrated sometime in your life if you depend on other people for your happiness. Nobody can make you happy. It is within you.

Live every act fully as if it were your last. —Buddha

Keep in mind that nobody cares more about you, your health, happiness, well-being, dreams and destiny than you do. You cannot grow without taking some risks in life. Watch a baby who is learning to stand, then to walk, constantly falling backward on his rump or forward onto her knees or face.

Fall down seven times, stand up eight. —Japanese proverb

A baby repeatedly gets back up, over and over again, first standing by holding onto something, and then letting go, a bit off balance. And then in one unique moment, a shuffle of a little foot becomes a slight lift of a heel off the ground. The child wobbles again, swivels a hip and shifts his weight to another foot, which in turn barely lifts up. It is magic.

You can make your own magic too, whatever your age or circumstance. Not only must you want it, you must understand and accept the sacrifices involved. You will need to take risk because without it, you cannot grow.

Wherever you go, go with all your heart. —Confucius

Do not allow age to be a handicap or limit your dreams.

Octogenarians and those in their nineties and up are the fastest-growing segment of the U.S. population today. They play golf, dance, earn high school and university degrees, jump out of airplanes, manage businesses and continue healthy, active and productive lives.

Consider the fact that Colonel Harlan Sanders founded Kentucky Fried Chicken at the age of 70 and our Uncle Art typed the manuscript for his first book at age 80 and penned his second, a family saga about his immigrant grand-parents, at 93. **Bitter Roots: A Gum Saan Odyssey** later won two book awards, including the Mom's Choice honor.

Remember that everything worth having is worth working for. Remember never to compromise your values, reputation or integrity because every morning and night, you must face the man or woman in the mirror. Remember that a journey of a thousand miles begins with the first step. Remember never to give up. Remember to believe in yourself.

Get up and make your move today to meet your destiny. Enjoy every moment of your journey and truly embrace life.

GO AND WAKE UP YOUR LUCK.
—*PROVERB*

46

How to make smart decisions

In 1932 Herbert J. Taylor, a businessman of faith and high moral character, took over as the president of the nearly bankrupt Club Aluminum Company. He carried around a small notebook in which he kept his notes and from it developed the idea of an ethics statement for business people to keep on their desks.

From a hundred words, Taylor pared his ideas down to share with his department heads, each of whom belonged to different faiths. All four of them agreed that the final version of four simple questions concurred with their beliefs.

These easy-to-read and understand but nevertheless powerful words became something very special.

1. Is it the truth?
2. Is it fair to all concerned?
3. Will it build goodwill and better friendships?
4. Is it beneficial to all concerned?

What Taylor called the 4-Way Test became the guideline by which his employees were asked to conduct the company's business. As a result, it gained a reputation for truth, integrity and goodwill and within a few years, the company paid off its debts and became a very profitable business.

In 1943, Rotary International, the oldest and largest humanitarian and community service organization in the world, adopted the 4-Way Test as an ethics principle for its members, most of whom were business people.

Twenty four words make up the creed and the number matches that of the cogs found in Rotary's famous wheeled logo, reminding members of the principles by which they live. It is a constant and reliable set of moral guidelines Rotarians use to make daily choices and decisions in their personal and professional lives. The 4-Way Test applies to everything that Rotarians think, say and do, and it is the most translated and quoted code of ethics around the globe.

Imagine what a profound and positive difference it would make if families, employers, businesses, schools, cities and countries operated by these words? It would surely change the way we think, how we speak to and how we treat one another. It would help us better decide how organizations and businesses would be conducted, and who would be worthy to be our leaders.

Employ the 4-Way Test in one decision or choice today, and increase its application over time until it becomes a habit for the rest of your life. Try it and see how it can become the gold standard for every aspect of daily living and the difference it makes in your life.

> CHARACTER IS LIKE A TREE AND REPUTATION
> LIKE ITS SHADOW. THE SHADOW IS WHAT WE
> THINK OF IT; THE TREE IS THE REAL THING.
> —ABRAHAM LINCOLN

47

That I may serve

Who is someone, living or dead, who you admire? Who is somebody you view as a role model? Who is a person you would tell, "I want to be like you when I grow up" no matter what your age is today?

There are heroes who live among us with whom we have contact every day. They are not necessarily known celebrities, very famous or wealthy or people whose names are in the news.

Examine the folks with whom you interact during a week's time and take a closer look. Think of how those people affect your life and you may be surprised. You may not have thought of a single parent raising children alone, a community volunteer, a colleague, neighbor, co-worker, fellow club or church member, or even a member of your family.

> *Do all the good you can,*
> *In all the ways you can,*
> *In all the places you can,*
> *At all the times you can,*
> *To all the people you can,*
> *As long as ever you can.*
> —John Wesley

You have the potential to be a role model or leader too. You don't have to consciously work to do so. Your life can be an example to others. By living your core values, you can be the person others would like to emulate.

Do everything with pride because your words, actions and work comprise your calling card. Conduct yourself and your business with self-respect, honesty and integrity. Expect the excellence and the best from yourself and those around you. Maintain high standards but don't put pressure on yourself by demanding perfection from yourself or others.

Consider that some things will never be accomplished if you wait for perfection. Do the best job you can because word of mouth from your satisfied customers and clients is the best advertising you can invest in and it doesn't cost you a cent.

We are what we repeatedly do, excellence then is not an act, but a habit. —Aristotle

The secret of greatness is simple: Do better work than any other man in your field-and keep on doing it.
—Wilfred A. Peterson

You need not possess material riches to share them. To take the time to teach a child a skill that you know, to open his or her eyes to new things to appreciate the world or the environment, to help him experience something that affected your life in a positive way or to help him realize and appreciate his blessings — this is the stuff of which role models are made.

The greatest good you can do for others is not just to share your riches, but to reveal to them their own.
—Benjamin Disraeli

As an adult, you can become a mentor, taking someone under your wing, guiding him or her in your profession, giving that person the benefit of your knowledge, expertise and experience.

> *When you climb the ladder of success, take someone with you.* —Mary Hurst

Outside your work or business, there are many skills that you can teach to others. There are countless community organizations that need volunteers to reach out to youth, the needy, seniors and the less fortunate. Take to heart the motto of Virginia Polytechnic Institute and State University: "Ut Prosim-That I May Serve" and make it your own.

Whether you give your time to a hands-on project or your attention to someone on a one-on-one basis, there will always be a person who will appreciate you. There is much to do in your own community and the opportunities for involvement are infinite. Most kindnesses does not involve giving money but your heart, as my poem *A Daily Gift* indicates.

> *Not what we say about our blessings, but how we use them, is the true measure of our thanksgiving.* — W.T. Purkiser

You don't need wait for Earth Day or to join a community service organization to walk the walk. Here are just a few suggestions but you, your family and friends can brainstorm and come up with many ideas to help others.

- Organize a beach cleanup
- Knit winter caps for the homeless or prayer shawls for the residents of a women's shelter

- Serve food in a soup kitchen
- Roast turkeys or assemble food baskets for underprivileged families during the holidays
- Lead a group to play musical instruments or serenade seniors at a convalescent home
- Collect and distribute socks, books and gifts at the local veterans' hospital or to our troops and/or their families serving abroad

One life to live will soon will be past, but only what we do for others will last.
—Westwood Village Rotary Club newsletter

In the service of others, you can reclaim your soul or find your true self. Discover the reward and riches of giving unconditionally to make a difference in someone else's life.

What can you think of that would benefit someone who is less fortunate than you are?

ONE THING I KNOW: THE ONLY ONES AMONG YOU WHO WILL BE REALLY HAPPY ARE THOSE WHO WILL HAVE SOUGHT AND FOUND HOW TO SERVE. *—ALBERT SCHWEITZER*

48   **Fight fear**

It's happened to every single one of us so you are not alone. You may be approaching the lectern to deliver a speech, just received a call regarding the results of your biopsy or mammogram, decided to start your own business, leave a bad or abusive relationship, discovered that you are pregnant or have a terminal disease, made a new investment, prepared for your first day at a new job or new class.

Fear cripples you, fills you with doubt, immobilizes you, crushes you, leaves you lonely, feeling faint or nauseous, totally helpless, breaking out in a sweat, knees knocking and your heart pounding in your chest. No matter how hard you try, you cannot think or force your way out of it.

Ironically, that same terror sent the adrenaline pumping through the bodies of human beings millions and millions of years ago. The physical reaction caused us to prepare for a "fight or flight" response in order to survive. Our brains and bodies were primed to fight or flee the danger we encountered, which in those days, was most likely a prehistoric creature that wanted to make a meal of us.

In today's world, we no longer have to fear becoming the snack of a Tyrannosaurus Rex as we hunt for food on land or of sharks as we wade into the ocean to spear fish to feed our tribes.

But our bodies, the marvelous creations that they are, still prepare us to face our fears, whether they are real or imagined.

The mind is a double-edged sword that is mighty powerful. On one side is that thoughts can be so strong that they help crime and abuse victims and prisoners of war survive the horrific atrocities, cruelties and humiliation they suffer. The flip side is that thoughts being out of control can bring misery and exacerbate feelings of fear.

There were many times during my high school and university days when I thought so obsessively about death and dying until mere thoughts brought about panic attacks. When my cousin Colleen died, everything changed. During the visitation at the mortuary, I looked down at her body and a realization came over me all of a sudden.

"That's not Colleen," I thought to myself, "that is the shell of who she was." It was a profound revelation that liberated from my fear of death.

By comparison, other scary moments for me were minor, such as being a candidate for Tech Princess in college, going on a job interview or embarking on new project, such as investing my own money to launch my own business start-ups, making excruciating family decisions during turbulent times, and even now, being buckled in my seat in an aircraft and feeling each bump during flight turbulence.

But the most frightening of all were the three times when I was told that I had cancer. I remember vividly each time how my heart dropped to my stomach and jumped back up, pounding in my chest and causing me to hyperventilate. My first thought was, "I am going to die" and I felt frantic and sad, and then morbid thoughts started again.

After the initial shock had passed, I told myself that while we all have to die sooner or later, I wanted to fight to stay alive. I resolved to do everything in my power to help my body fight back the disease as well as heal because I had many things to live for. There were places to travel to which I had never seen, my children and unborn grandchildren to love and enjoy and things I had not done yet and all those entries in my life's To Do or Bucket List that hadn't been checked off yet.

In short, I *chose* life.

I *chose* to take action. I chose not to sit around, feeling helpless and vulnerable and asking "Why me?" I *chose* to fight cancer with everything I had so that even if I lost the battle, I could tell myself that I did all that I could. I *chose* not give up and just let myself fall victim to the same disease that each year claimed the lives of relatives and friends. Most importantly of all, I *chose* to believe that each time, God was giving me yet another chance to get it right and continue His work.

"Fear is not trusting your own power," Oprah Winfrey once said. But the truth is that you *do* have power and you must trust it. You are not helpless and you do not have to be a victim of fear or anything else. You have freedom and choice, intelligence and knowledge, moral and physical strength. And if you feel the lack of any of these, you can make changes or do things to attain them. Don't just sit and barely exist each day, do something, anything.

Courage is holding on a minute longer. —George Patton

Nothing is impossible. Look at that word again in a different way. It says *I'M POSSIBLE.*

Here's what worked for me at different times when I felt afraid. I call them the **Four Fs**: faith, facts, family and friends.

FAITH is believing that the sun will rise tomorrow, whether you can see it through the clouds or not. It is believing that there is a power greater than yourself that has a better plan that you, a mere mortal, can ever dream of. It is believing that, "This too, will pass." Perhaps whatever frightens you will take time to overcome, but as the saying goes, tough times don't last, but tough people do. Faith is believing in yourself, your network of family and friends around you, your doctors, and the dedicated researchers who devote their lives to finding or developing new treatments.

Faith is believing, as I do, that the accumulation of empirical knowledge of other cultures and civilizations, both ancient and present, has great value and merit. While courage is the nudge to get you to take the first step in a new endeavor, it is faith that keeps you moving to take the second, third and further steps in your journey.

Faith is believing that yes, if you can keep taking those steps forward, everything will turn out okay and you will reach your goal. Faith is giving thanks for what you have, not praying for what you don't have, whether it is peace, success, fortune, fame, or whatever you desire.

Faith is knowing that a higher power is watching over you, whether you believe in one or not and that you were born for a purpose and finding what it is, however long it takes. Faith is the conviction in your heart and in your soul that even if you don't reach your original destination or goal, you *always* have choices at all times and at every step of the way. You can stick to your plan, keep going, turn back, start again, change direction, take another path, make corrections or modifications, or carve out a completely new trail.

Faith empowers and liberates, enriches and rewards, and most of all, is the root of hope. Ultimately, faith is the peace you gain in knowing deep down inside, that by giving your very best, you fought the best fight you could.

Do your best. Say a prayer. Let go and let God do the rest.
—Author unknown

FACTS: Most of the time, fear is caused by ignorance. Whatever throws you into panic can be tackled. Start today and learn more about what alarms you. It is one of the first steps to conquering whatever you causes your terror.

Gather as many facts as you can about your situation, problem or challenge, and then analyze them. Without knowledge and accurate information, without second and third and fourth opinions from professionals, mentors and other reliable knowledgeable sources, you cannot make informed decisions in your life.

Acknowledge your fear. Accept that you feel frightened and it is okay to be afraid. Everyone is scared of something, although the cause or source may not be the same. There are people all around you who experience the same or other fears. Please take comfort in and believe that you are not alone.

Depending on which list you consult, you may be surprised to discover what scares your fellow human beings. For example, did you know that *glossophobia,* fear of the public speaking, is the number one phobia among people in the world? It means that more people on the planet are afraid of speaking to or in front of others, whether to one person or a thousand, than they are of dying! Fear of dying, *necrophobia,* is in second place globally so I know that I was not unique.

There are hundreds of thousands of sites online where you can get information, find support and help. Arm yourself with knowledge. Begin facing and fighting fear now.

FAMILY: We did not choose them, but inherited them and for better or worse, they're ours for life. Yes, they are our relatives. You may love, hate, feel indifferent to or just tolerate them, hold them close or push them away, but imperfect as they are, they're here to stay. Even as a very young child, you knew who shared and influenced your life.

When you are feeling afraid is an ideal time to surround yourself with people who you trust, love and feel close to. If you are blessed to have such a family, most likely them to whom you will turn first. If you do not, all is not lost, because you can find comfort and support around you if you look.

You have immediate or extended family members, but if none of them has ever personally experienced the fear you are going through, whether it is giving birth, facing cancer, surviving a car accident or divorce, he or she can still provide sympathy and empathy.

Other people who have lived through the same or similar circumstances or experience that you have can truly know and understand the uncertainty and panic that you are living through. This is where you can seek comfort and understanding with fellow survivors who are going through or have been through what you are feeling now.

Every one of us has family in some form, but don't make the mistake of limiting your concept of family only to those who share your bloodlines, home or name.

That's what friends are for.

FRIENDS: If you aren't connected to your family of origin, create your own or adopt one by making lasting friends.

Sometimes those folks with whom you have grown up and lived with - your parents and siblings, for example, are not the best people with whom to share your deepest secrets and greatest fears. It is very possible that you love them dearly, but do not really feel comfortable talking to them about your issues. With relatives, there is often too much emotion and history interfering with good communication between and among you.

It is natural for most creatures, including humans, to group together, for survival, work, companionship, protection or a plethora of other positive and negative reasons. Your family of friends is what and who you believe it is. The members could be united by culture, gender, heritage, ethnicity, nationality, a common goal, interest, cause or experience.

You can bond with different people both near and far because you share something in common with them. You may even be able to share your feelings and words with friends that you would otherwise be unable to do with your own family members.

Friendship is a sheltering tree. —Samuel Taylor Coleridge

Find these people and become friends with them. Attend a conference, seminar or convention, or join a class, group or organization that is composed of other people who share your experiences, interests or values.

Make new friends but keep the old. The first is silver, the other is gold.
—Entry from the author's high school yearbook

The most beautiful aspect of friendship is choice, yours, theirs or mutual. While you cannot choose the family you are born into, you can choose your friends by taking the advice of Ralph Waldo Emerson: The only way to have a friend is to be one.

You know the feeling of camaraderie and can identify it accurately right away.

What is a friend? A single soul dwelling in two bodies.
—Aristotle

They are the ones who can give you spiritual strength, provide warm hugs, understanding and wisdom, and share your good times and bad, perhaps when your family members cannot. You might forgive a friend's brutal honesty while being unable to accept the same from a sibling or parent.

If you have a friend or friends, you will never be alone. And if you have relatives who are also people you would choose to be your friends, you are doubly blessed.

COURAGE IS DOING WHAT YOU'RE AFRAID TO DO. THERE CAN BE NO COURAGE UNLESS YOU'RE SCARED. —*EDDIE RICKENBACKER*

49 Riches that cannot be stolen

Learning is a treasure that nobody can steal.
—Chinese proverb

Imagine that! You can lose your fingers or toes; your car, house or you job; all your material possessions; family or friends; but the knowledge and skills you have today can *never* be taken away from you. There are many people who have lost everything due to circumstances beyond their control, both natural or man-made. But they still possess the knowledge or education they have acquired.

During my author visits to schools, I remind young people that it is not their physical appearance that will get them ahead in their lives, but what is inside their heads. One day in the future when the time comes to find a job, someone will pay them for what they know, and what they can do with that knowledge and their skills.

While models, television and film stars and professional athletes are paid high wages for their looks, superior talents and skills, most people are not so blessed. The rest of us mortals must rely upon our "smarts" to get somewhere in life.

What do you know or can do that somebody else will give you a paycheck for?

"Every artist was first an amateur," opined Ralph Waldo Emerson. Think outside the box of those who are artists in their own right, those who are the most skillful at what they do-in every sport, business, creative or humanitarian endeavor. There is art and magic being made every day.

Your life's path and fulfilling your destiny is a journey, to be enjoyed, savored, proud of and *experienced*.

I will prepare myself then when my opportunity comes, I will be ready. —Abraham Lincoln

Be thankful when you don't know something for it gives you the opportunity to learn. —Abraham Lincoln

Failure is the opportunity to do something over again, only this time more wisely. —Abraham Lincoln

You will make mistakes as we all do. Learn what you can from them. In your lifetime you will take detours, because no journey is a smooth, straight path. It is certain that you will encounter bumps in the road, but they're not enough cause to abandon your trip.

You will pass through weather, both fair and foul, and you will survive it all. You will have discouraging and challenging times along the way, but nothing so awful to make you abandon your destination.

You will also experience marvelous, awesome and breathtaking times when everything feels like you are in the "zone" and going with the flow. You will meet the good, the bad and the ugly along the way and live to tell about it. You will see new things, meet new people and try things you've never done before and be enriched for each encounter.

> *Learn as if you are going to live forever, live as if you are going to die tomorrow.* —John Wooden

Find ways to do so. There are few obstacles to acquiring new knowledge or skills these days. Can't afford a computer? Thanks to Benjamin Franklin, we have public libraries with books and computers with Internet access. We can barely keep up with technology and the marvels it brings to us: instant communication and news, global social networking and medical and scientific breakthroughs. No business or industry is untouched. Our world keeps changing at breakneck speeds. It is thrilling but also stressful to try and keep up with it all.

> *You are the same today that you are going to be five years from now except for two things: the people with whom you associate and the books you read.*
> —Charles "Tremendous" Jones

Thanks to the kindness and generosity of visionaries before us, there are low-cost and free classes, technology and computer labs available in your community or neighborhood, at your local adult school or community college or university. Thanks to the caring compassion of volunteers, you can learn to read, or write or do just about anything you choose.

> *As a rule . . . (s)he who has the most information will have the greatest success in life.* —Benjamin Disraeli

If you think education is expensive, try ignorance.
—Derek Bok

You will never get old if you keep learning new things. Imagine what potential you have if you could keep learning for the rest of your life.

Why not? Why not now?

| IF YOU REST, YOU RUST. —*HELEN HAYES* |

50 Enjoy the peaks and the valleys

The top of the mountain can be cold, lonely and barren, while the valleys can be the most peaceful and most fertile. From the highest point on the mountain range, you can see the horizon in every direction. In the deepest part of the canyon, it may be so dark and inhospitable that nothing can grow.

It is the same in life, for you have to experience the lowest points to appreciate the highest. Without the rain, how can you gasp at seeing the beauty of a rainbow or delight in the sunshine and the flowers? Without living through the dark and cold of winter, could spring be more welcome when it arrives? Doesn't the anticipation of an event prime you for its enjoyment?

You cannot keep living on adrenaline highs constantly.

It only takes one day during which everything goes wrong, for you to savor another when all goes well. Sometimes it will be just a small thing that trips up all your plans — locking yourself out of your car, an accident on your way, a doctor's appointment that runs late, a phone call, communication or email that did not reach its recipient.

Life is filled with ups and downs. It is what it is, full of contrasts: the yin and yang, dark and light, sorrow and joy, rain and sunshine, passive and active, bitter and sweet, shade and sun. Just like the scenery depicted in a Chinese brush painting, the mountains are hard and by contrast, the waterfalls and rivers are soft. The familiar, and pervasive color combination of red and black in Chinese art, accessories and furnishings represents fire and water.

As you have discovered, most things are beyond your control so you have learned good time management, for example, to factor more time in when you drive to your appointments. You realize that you should carry change for bus fare or a parking meter, keep your car in good working order, have an umbrella handy, and not allow important things such as bills, licenses, passports, medications and so on. become overdue or expire. Being prepared for a myriad of situations is one of the best ways to avoid stress and emergencies.

On the other hand, when you are able to get through your to-do list for the day with no glitches, be thankful! Take a deep breath and pat yourself on the back for what you were able to accomplish. Enjoy the feeling of satisfaction and accomplishment of a day well lived.

THE TRAGEDY OF LIFE
IS NOT SO MUCH WHAT MEN SUFFER,
BUT RATHER WHAT THEY MISS.
—*THOMAS CARLYLE*

51

How to be remembered

Who was the gold medalist in the 100-meter track and field competition during the past summer Olympics? Which man made the winning goal at the last World Cup championship game? Who were the last three governors of your state? Who holds the title for being the richest man or woman in the world? Which man and woman won the Oscar for the best performances this year?

Now name your favorite teacher in high school, a special person who made a difference in your life or a friend you have known more than ten years with whom you still keep in touch.

Our emotions are powerful and it is human nature for us to avoid pain more than seek pleasure. We have evolved to remember people and experiences in our lives according to the impact they left on us, both positive and negative.

> *The heart has its own memory like the mind, and in it are enshrined the precious keepsakes.*
> —Henry Wadsworth Longfellow

Memories last longer if associated with feelings. People may never remember your words, actions or even your name or face but they will always remember how you made them feel. Remember: It's nice to be important, but more important to be nice.

Reprove thy friend privately; commend him publicly.
—Solon

We recall easily and vividly the defining moments in our lives: special days such as the arrivals of our children, or somebody who became special or influential in our lives. We remember weddings, anniversaries and other significant moments too. Who can ever forget the day we were offered your first job or the first day on the job, closed the biggest sale we'd ever made or signed up an important client.

Within our own countries and around the world, we have shared emotional experiences with strangers too — those days or moments we will never forget. For various generations, it was Black Friday followed by the Great Depression, the start of world wars, the day that Pearl Harbor was attacked, V-E and V-J days and when the Japanese surrendered, or when you heard that President Franklin Roosevelt.

For the Baby Boomers, Generation X and Y, it was remembering what you were doing when you heard the news that Martin Luther King, Bobby or John F. Kennedy had been assassinated or the day the Challenger exploded. Maybe you will never forget the dot-com crash, when Hurricane Katrina hit or the day that Princess Diana was killed in an auto accident. And around the globe, September 11 will be etched in our collective memories for the rest of our lives.

Think back on your own life and to those people who made an impression or a difference to you. Were they associated with a moment of negativism such as embarrassment, anger, humiliation or pain, or do you remember a time of kindness, learning, dignity, love, compassion, understanding, truth, or enlightenment?

How would you like to be remembered?

It is never too late to be what you might have been.
—George Eliot

Who are you? Where are you now? How long have you been here? What or who do you want to be? How will you transform yourself into that person you aspire to become? As Abraham Lincoln said, "Whatever you are, be a good one." Just as your mind and body changes with time, the person you are changes too. Self-development is an ongoing project and re-engineering yourself takes time and effort, and you will always be a work in progress whether you are nineteen or ninety.

Keep away from people who try to belittle your ambitions; small people do that, but the truly great make you feel that you too, can become great. —Mark Twain

Aspire to be someone who others want to know and keep company with, who your family members and friends respect and admire, who lives according to his or her own basic values, who dreams big and then actuates them, who defines and achieves success in his or her own terms and who wants to be a better person.

Build your character in a way that will define your reputation. Then work hard to maintain both.

SEEK OUT THAT PARTICULAR MENTAL
ATTITUDE WHICH MAKES YOU FEEL MOST
DEEPLY AND VITALLY ALIVE, ALONG WITH
WHICH COMES THE INNER VOICE WHICH
SAYS, "THIS IS THE REAL ME."
—*WILLIAM JAMES*

52

How to measure your life

*Life is not measured by the number of breaths we take but
by the number of moments that take our breath away.*
—James W. Moore

Turning a corner to see my first glimpse of the Garden of
the Gods in Harmony Springs, Colorado. Remembering one of
my birthday picnics at a Marina del Rey park when a stranger's
dog grabbed and ran off with my sandwich. Sunsets over the
Pacific Ocean from the bluffs at the Pt. Vicente Interpretive
Center. Standing at Pike's Peak which inspired Katharine Lee
Bates to pen the lyrics to "America the Beautiful." Crying my
eyes out during the same four minutes every time I watch the
movie *Up.* Stars reflected on the golf course lake in Copper Cove
in central California. Watching in wonder from the beach as
bands of hungry dolphins break the ocean's surface as they follow
schools of sardines. Seeing a full moon against a blue, eastern
daytime sky with the sun shining from the same sky in the west.
Observing a flame tree visited by orioles, hummingbirds, white-
wings and butterflies from my office window while working on
my manuscript. Riding a bicycle on the beach. Attending morning
worship on sand and joining the drum circle on the same
morning at Hermosa Beach.

One morning I picked up a peacock feather from the road

along my daily walk. As I held it in my hand, it bounced gently with each step. I happened to look down at the brilliant colors as the sun's rays hit the feather and rolled the hollow end between my thumb and index finger in the sunlight. As I watched in wonder, the feather's vibrant hues changed with every angle, taking my breath away.

Five years ago, just for the fun of it, I bought several crayfish with my fresh water fish. Amazingly, within a year, they developed miniature grape-like clusters underneath their tails. First the eggs were off-white in color, then they turned to a dark pink and at last, became more and more transparent with tiny black dots. A magnifying glass showed that the dots were their eyes! Pretty soon I had over sixty baby crayfish in their individual sacs dangling under their mother.

Over the years, I learned how to save and care for the eggs through the mother crayfish's several pregnancies. During the writing of this book, a third generation of tiny babies have been born from that single mom!

What simple pleasures do you find in life and which bring you joy? Cultivate them carefully and take joy in them. You can find and see beauty everywhere if you really look. Beauty is not only physical, but also in the soul.

Sir Thomas Browne said, "All the wonders you see are within yourself."

IT IS NOT THE YEARS IN YOUR LIFE
BUT THE LIFE IN YOUR YEARS THAT COUNTS.
—*ADLAI STEVENSON*

53 Choose your battles

It is only sensible to remind ourselves constantly that none of us are perfect people so it is unfair and unrealistic to expect perfection from others or in our relationships.

An ideal wife is any woman with an ideal husband.
—Booth Tarkington

I remember telling my daughters many years ago to do three things before they decided on a life partner: shop, travel and go home with the person they may be becoming serious about.

Shopping can reveal tastes, spending habits and generosity to others. Journeying together shows a man's flexibility, patience, tolerance and consideration to fellow travelers as well as to strangers and service providers. And by going home with a man and meeting his family, you can get a first-hand look and feel of how he treats the women in his life.

Are caring, kindness, responsibility, thoughtfulness and good humor evident in his relationships with his mother, sisters and other female relatives? What you observe will give you clues as to the way he will probably treat you in the years to come.

Speaking of relationships, how do you get along with the folks in your life such as your significant other, children, parents, friends, co-workers, employer, employees and business partners? Are you easy to get along, live or work with, to talk to and confide in?

Must you have your way some, half, most or all of the time? Are you willing to be flexible and understanding for the common good? Are you in a relationship with hopes of changing another person?

Do you share values, ethics, dreams, goals and activities with those you live or work with? Do you impose your will on other people? Can you still like, love, live or work with others who do not share your opinions, views or tastes? Do you acknowledge and appreciate generational differences in "the way things are said and done" in this day and age? Do you acknowledge and respect the fact that society and the world has changed and you need to change with it to get along with others who share it with you?

My mom Renee and my aunt Matilda, were born in China but were educated, married (both for over 60 years) and stayed in the United States for the rest of their lives. They each gave me the following advice decades apart regarding marriage and raising children, but I found the expression "Choose your battles" helpful to remember in other aspects of life too.

One time when I was home in Washington, D.C. from Virginia Tech, I asked my mom how she could put up with some of the annoying things that caused friction between her and Dad. Her answer was so simple but wise that I remembered it often as I matured.

"It's not worth getting angry or sick over," she told me. Mom was wise and right. Most things were not worth the time and energy expended on disagreement or conflict. However, other real concerns are imperative to acknowledge, discuss, agree or compromise on before they become true crises.

Thank you, Aunty Matilda, my dad's sister, who once made two unrelated off-hand comments at the same time that I never forgot. They made a lot of sense and profoundly changed my perceptions about finance and raising children.

"Don't save your money, invest it," she remarked, and then added, "Don't battle your children over small stuff. Save it for serious stuff." These two simple statements liberated me.

The first statement was advising me not to sweat the small stuff, because most of life is small stuff. It is about taking care of priorities and the inconsequential will take care of itself.

As an oldest child and a first-time mother, I felt quite insecure, agonizing and over-analyzing almost every parenting decision. The result was my being rigid and a perfectionist.

In contrast and at the other extreme was my husband, who was the youngest child of two and an only son in a Chinese family, and who was far more lenient than I in our childrearing practices. Some of the things that got me very upset seemed and felt important at the time. Only later after hearing my aunt's words, it occurred to me that they were not critical issues and I didn't have to make such a fuss or be so rigid about them.

It was all about letting go of ordinary, everyday, typical age-appropriate behaviors and focusing on serious, larger issues, such as those having to do with morals and issues, drug and alcohol use, unwanted pregnancy and so on.

In matters of principle, stand like a rock. In matters of taste, swim with the current. —Thomas Jefferson

I also realized that we all make mistakes as a child, a parent, an employee, or in any of our many roles in life. But the important thing for us is to learn from mistakes, not to repeat them and then move on. Strive to create or resolve situations with a win-win outcome for all concerned.

It is also never too late to apologize or right a wrong. It doesn't get easier with the passage of time. The old saying "Better late than never" also applies to forgiving yourself or someone else for anything, real or imagined.

> *No matter how far you have gone on a wrong road, turn back.* —Turkish proverb

> *Experience is the worst teacher. It gives the test before presenting the lesson.* —Vernon Law

> *In giving advice, seek to help, not please your friend.* —Solon

> *Love truth, pardon error.* —Voltaire

If I had possessed Mom and Aunty 's wisdom earlier to guide me from the time I became a parent, this mother would have been more relaxed and confident in her ability to be a good parent over time.

Each of us has free choice as how we respond to others and situations.

We get to choose what to skirmish or fight for and about. It's not about winning or losing because in choosing unimportant things to argue or fight about, nobody wins.

GOOD JUDGMENT COMES FROM EXPERIENCE, AND EXPERIENCE, WELL, THAT COMES FROM POOR JUDGMENT. —*ANONYMOUS*

54   Love is . . .

Love is _____. (Fill in the blank.)

It is safe to say that this one emotion is the subject of more books, poetry, songs and music than any other feeling.

Start with loving yourself. It means that you recognize your own worth. Accept who you are but be open and proactive to self-development to be all and the best that you can be. Constantly challenge yourself to improve in some aspect of your life. You are an ongoing work in progress. Keep working at it. In the year 8, the Roman poet Ovid said: If you want be loved, be lovable.

All, everything I understand, I understand only because I love. —Leo Tolstoy

Next, love other people, starting with those who are closest to you: your family, friends or a higher power in which you may believe. Then begin extending your love to colleagues, acquaintances, people you don't know or who are in need. Let it be manifested in your kindness, compassion, caring and understanding to others.

When you love, you wish to do things for. You wish to sacrifice for. You wish to serve. —Ernest Hemingway

Surround yourself with people who love you, things that you love and be sure to see, do, hear, touch and taste what you love as much as you can. Travel to new places and try unfamiliar foods; listen to music, engage in your hobbies; go out and see different scenery; watch ballet, old or new films and shows, sport events and experience nature. We only travel the path of life once, so fill your heart with love, spread it around by sowing its seeds and enjoy its harvest. Embrace and love life itself by showing and sharing the joyous gift of each new day.

> *Do you love me because I am beautiful or am I beautiful because you love me?* —Oscar Hammerstein II

A fascinating thing about love is that the more you demonstrate and send it out, the more it returns to you. You cannot force it on another person. When you try to give it away, it keeps coming back. And the human heart, although only about the size of a hand, has the capacity to love an infinite number of people.

> *Love's gift cannot be given, it waits to be accepted.* —Rabindranath Tagore

From the 1970 movie *Love Story* came a line that was simple but profound: Love means never having to say you're sorry. It reminds us that if love is the foundation for your words and actions, you would never have reason to apologize for what you say or do.

> *Love, you know, seeks to make happy rather than to be happy.* —Ralph Conner

To love means to give, and to give means to build, while to hate is to destroy. —Anwar El-Sadat

A loving person lives in a loving world. A hostile person lives in a hostile world: everyone you meet is your mirror. —Ken Keyes, Jr.

Love is patient and kind; love does not envy or boast; it is not arrogant or rude. It does not insist on its own way; it is not irritable or resentful; it does not rejoice in wrongdoing, but rejoices with the truth. Love bears all things, believes all things, hopes all things, endures all things. Love never ends. —1 Corinthians: 4-8, English Standard Version

One word/Frees us of all the weight and pain of life:/ That word is love. —Sophocles

Love is the only gold. —Lord Tennyson

THE BEST AND MOST BEAUTIFUL THINGS
IN THE WORLD CANNOT BE SEEN
OR EVEN TOUCHED. THEY MUST BE FELT
WITH THE HEART. *—HELEN KELLER*

55 Last words from a saint

People are often unreasonable and self-centered
Forgive them anyway
If you are kind, people may accuse you of ulterior motives
Be kind anyway
If you are honest, people may cheat you
Be honest anyway
If you find happiness, people may be jealous
Be happy anyway
The good you do today may be forgotten tomorrow
Do good anyway
Give the world the best you have, and it may never be enough
Give your best anyway
For you see, in the end, it is between you and God
It never was between you and them anyway

—Mother Teresa

Recommended Reading

Ades, Terri; Alteri, Rick; Gansler, Ted; Yeargin, Patricia, senior editors *Complete Guide to Complementary and Alternative Cancer Therapies* (2nd edition): American Cancer Society, 2009.

Campbell, T. Colin; Campbell, Thomas M. *The China Study: Ben Bella,* 2006.

Chan, David, M.D. *Breast Cancer: Real Questions, Real Answers.* Henry Holt, 2006.

Cohen, Misha Ruth. *The Chinese Way to Healing: Many Paths of Wholeness:* Perigee, 1996.

Gottlie, Bill. *Alternative Cures:* Rodale, 2000.

Katz, Rebecca with Mat, Edelson. *The Cancer-Fighting Kitchen: Ten Speed,* 2009.

Lu, Nan. *A Woman's Guide to Healing from Breast Cancer:* Avon, 1999.

Leung, Albert Y. *Chinese Herbal Remedies: Phaidon Universe,* 1984.

Link, John, M.D. *Take Charge of Your Breast Cancer: A Guide to Getting the Best Possible Treatment.* Henry Holt, 2002.

Link, John, M.D. *The Breast Cancer Survival Manual: A Step by Step Guide for the Women with Newly Diagnosed Breast Cancer.* Henry Holt, 2007.

Lipton, Bruce. *The Biology of Belief:* Hay House, 2008.

Lu, Henry C. *Chinese System of Food Cures: Prevention and Remedies:* Sterling, 1986.

McCauley, Bob. *Achieving Great Health:* Spartan, 2005.

McIntyre, Anne. *Drink to Your Health: Delicious Juices, Teas, Soups and Smoothies:* Fireside, 2000.

McWilliams, Peter. *You Can't Afford the Luxury of a Negative Thought* Prelude,1995.

Nelson, Dennis *Food Combining Simplified:* Paperback, 1988.

Ni, Maoshing, Ph.D. *Second Spring:* Free Press, 2009.

Ni, Maoshing, Ph.D. *Secrets of Longevity:* Chronicle, 2006.

Ni, Maoshing, Ph.D. *Secrets of Self-Healing:* Avery, 2008.

Ni, Maoshing, PhD. *The Tao of Nutrition:* College of Tao and Traditional *Healing,* 1987.

O'Conner, Siobhan and Spunt, Alexandra. *No More Dirty Looks.* 2010.

Varona, Verne. *Nature's Cancer-Fighting Foods:* Reward, 2001.

Pitchford, Paul. *Healing with Whole Foods: Asian Traditions and Modern Nutrition:* North Atlantic, 1993.

Robin, Vicki and Dominguez, Joe. *Your Money or Your Life:* Penguin, 1992.

Schor, Juliet, PhD. *The Overspent American: Why We Want What We Don't Need:* Basic, 1999.

Somers, Suzanne. *KNOCKOUT: Interviews with Doctors who are Curing Cancer:* Crown, 2009.

Vasey, Christopher, N.D. *The Acid-Alkaline Diet for Optimum Health: Inner Traditions* International, 2006.

Voderplanistz, Aajonus. *We Want to Live,* 1997.

Wong, Angi Ma. *Been There, Done That: 16 Secrets for Success for Entrepreneurs:* Pacific Heritage, 1997.

Wong, Angi Ma. *Feng Shui Dos and Taboos:* Pacific Heritage, 2000.

Wong, Angi Ma. *Feng Shui Dos and Taboos for Health and Well Being:* Pacific Heritage, 2005.

Wong, Angi Ma. *What Women Want:* Pacific Heritage, 1999. (poster)

Yeagar, Jeff. *The Cheapskate Next Door:* Broadway, 2010.

Yeagar, Jeff. *The Ultimate Cheapskate's Road Map to True Riches:* Broadway, 2008.

Also

Anti-Aging Secrets: Rodale Press, 2001.

Fight Back with Food: Use Nutrition to Heal What Ails You. Reader's Digest, 2002.

Resources

- American Cancer Society, cancer.org

- AARP.org

- Federal Trade Commission Facts for Consumers, ftc.gov/bcp/edu/pubs/
  consumer/health/hea07.shtm (May 22, 2009)

- Foodallergy.org (FAAN)

- National Center for Complementary and Alternative Medicine, nccam.nih.
  gov/research/clinical trials/fact sheet (May 28, 2009)

- Snopes.com

- Urbanlegends.com

- U.S. National Institutes of Health, www.cancer.gov

Index

1 Corinthians: 4–8, English
    Standard Version 186
4-Way Test 155

A
AARP 2, 21, 121, 191
    acorn 49
acupressure 6
    acupressure points 5
acupuncture ix, 6
A Daily Gift 125, 158
additives 15, 25, 32, 61
airport 74
alcohol 26, 33, 68, 69, 73, 84, 182
    alcoholic drinks 20
alkaline xiii, 32, 33, 190
Allen, James 117
almonds 49
amaranth 13, 30, 49
anger 7, 120, 175
anise 55
antibiotics 32
antioxidant 33, 47, 52
apples 30, 49, 52, 55, 56
apricots 49, 56
Archives of Internal Medicine 2
argan oil 16, 59
Aristotle 157, 167
Armstrong, Thomas 109
artichokes 39, 49
artificial sweeteners 15, 33
Asia 9, 72, 76
Asian ix, 23, 44, 45, 67, 106, 190
asparagus 33, 49, 57
ATM 71, 74
Aurelius, Marcus 117
avocado 49, 59
A Woman's 4-Minute Bible 125

B
baby boomers 96, 175
baking soda 63
balance xiii, 1, 6, 7, 8, 10, 32, 33, 152
bamboo 62
bamboo shoots 49
banana 13, 42, 49, 85
barley 33, 50, 54, 56
Baudelaire, Charles 116
beans 19, 38, 39, 50, 56, 57
    aduki 50
    black 38, 50, 51, 56
    fava 50
    garbanzo 50, 56
    kidney 50
    lentil 50
    lima 50
    mung 50, 55
    navy 50
    pinto 50
bedbug 76
beets 50, 54
bell peppers 39, 50, 52
berries 39, 57
beta-carotene 50, 51, 52
bicycles 4, 95, 107
bitter melon 42, 57
Bitter Roots: A Gum Saan Odyssey 152
blood pressure 5, 11, 25
blueberries 50
body v, ix, x, 1, 2, 3, 4, 5, 6, 10, 13,
    16, 17, 26, 27, 29, 31, 33, 36, 37, 38,
    39, 40, 45, 47, 48, 54, 55, 56, 57, 58,
    59, 65, 73, 77, 81, 82, 83, 84, 85, 86,
    92, 109, 141, 161, 162, 176
Boese, Paul 145
Bok choy 50
Bok, Derek 171
bones 9
bread 12
breakfast 10, 34, 46, 47, 60, 134
British Petroleum (BP) 105
broccoli 30, 33, 39, 50
Brown, H. Jackson viii, 147

Brussels sprouts 33, 50
Buddha xvi, 117, 127, 151
Buffet, Warren 142
bulgur wheat 50
Buscaglia, Leo 110
Bush, George W. 121
butter 16, 40
    almond 13, 46
    cocoa 16
    nut 85
    peanut 30
    sunflower seed 46

C

cabbage 50, 56
caffeine 33, 84
calcium 85
C and C 86
canola oil 16
cantaloupe 50, 56, 60
carbohydrate 5, 13, 29, 31, 39, 40, 47
Carlyle, Thomas 173
carrot 30, 41, 42, 50, 54, 57
cauliflower 30, 39, 50, 56
celery 16, 30, 41, 52, 50, 55, 57
cell devices 3
chamomile 51, 55, 85
Character Counts 134
chard 50, 56
    Swiss 50
cheese 16, 22, 23, 30, 33, 38, 40
    cottage 16, 30
    string 30
    Swiss 38
chemical bisphenol A (BPA) 62
chemotherapy vii, viii, ix, x, 22, 27, 83, 126
cherries 50
chestnuts 38
chickpeas 38
chi gong 6
China vii, 6, 22, 23, 24, 35, 181, 189
Chinese gooseberry 51
Chinese medicine ix, x, 5, 6

Chinese proverb 13, 46, 122, 142, 145, 149, 168
chlorophyll 33, 49, 50, 51
cholesterol 3
chrysanthemum 55
Churchill, Winston 120
cinnamon-honey-apple cider vinegar 10
Clark, Alexander 149
coconut oil 16, 53, 59
colds 2, 4, 72
Coleridge, Samuel Taylor 166
collard greens 50
computers 3, 81, 83, 87, 95, 99, 170
Confucius 1, 94, 139, 142, 152
Conner, Ralph 185
cornmeal 50
corn oil 53
cosmetics 53, 58, 62, 87
COSMOS 80
cotton 62, 63, 69
couscous 13, 30
Covey, Dr. Steven 139
cranberries 50, 57
Cruz, Benvido 102
cucumbers 39, 55, 59
currants 50

D

daily walk 3, 92, 137, 179
dairy 16, 18, 19, 22, 24, 38, 42, 47, 53, 55
dates 50, 85
Delfino, Mannix 107
diabetes 5, 25
Dickens, Charles 126
Disraeli, Benjamin 157, 170
Dyer, Wayne 117
dyes 62

E

edamame 38
Edison, Thomas 105, 106
egg 13, 47, 53, 60

eggplant 50

eggs 15

electromagnetic fields (EMF) 80

elements 6, 7, 54

Eliot, George 176

Elliott, John Jr. 150

El-Sadat, Anwar 186

Emerson, Ralph Waldo 103, 151, 167, 169

emotion 5, 6, 7, 119, 129, 140, 144, 174

energy v, 1, 3, 6, 7, 19, 36, 39, 40, 46, 56, 57, 73, 77, 79, 99, 102, 103, 116, 123, 140, 141, 181

enriched 12, 14, 15, 170

enriched wheat flour 14, 15

Environmental Workers Union 52

exercise vi, 3, 4, 5, 6, 7, 40, 72, 74, 84, 86, 139, 140, 145

F

fall (autumn) 56

faro 13

fears 8, 161, 164, 166

feng shui xi, 6, 112

fiber 15, 19, 29, 34, 37, 38, 62

filter 10, 66

Firebaugh, Dough 142

fish oil 13

flaxseed oil 13, 53

flu 2, 57, 72, 73

folate 49, 50, 51

folk cures 6

food absorption 4, 10, 84

food label xiii, 14, 17

France, Anatole 104

Frank, Anne 137

Franklin, Benjamin 116, 170

free-range 18

fruit viii, ix, 7, 18, 19, 25, 29, 30, 31, 33, 34, 39, 42, 43, 47, 48, 49, 52, 53, 55, 59

frustration 7, 120

Fuller, Thomas 120

G

Gandhi, Mahatma 110, 117

Gardner, Dr. Howard 109

garlic 40, 41, 50, 54, 57, 64, 107

germs xiv, 4, 57, 68, 69, 70, 71, 72, 73

Getty, J. Paul 101

ginger 41, 42, 50, 57

global positioning system (GPS) 109

glues 61

glycogen 5

Goethe 102, 140

Goldsmith, Oliver 135

Goleman, Daniel 109

grains 13, 15, 19, 25, 33, 39, 54, 55

   amaranth 13

   couscous 13

   faro 13

   quinoa 13, 30, 49, 57

granola 46

grape 16, 42, 51, 59, 179

grapefruit 39, 51

grape seed 13, 16, 59

grape seed oil 13, 16

grass-fed 18, 38

green tea 10

grocery store 17, 54, 74, 87, 126

H

H1N1 (swine) flu 72

ham 19, 84

Hammerstein, Oscar II 185

Hardel, Leonard 80

Harvard University 109

Hawthorne, Nathaniel 111

Hayakawa, S.I. 150

Helen Hayes 171

hazelnuts 51

hearing vi, x, 8, 129, 182

heart viii, 1, 2, 4, 7, 11, 16, 25, 54, 55, 80, 94, 98, 107, 120, 117, 124, 125, 129, 141, 145, 148, 152, 158, 160, 161, 163, 174, 185, 186

heart attack 4, 11, 148

heart disease 2, 16, 25, 80
Hemingway, Ernest 184
Hendley, Dr. J. Owen 72
HEPA (High Efficiency Particulate
  Air) 66
herbal cures 6, 189
herbal supplements 26
herbal tea 10
herbs 7, 41, 43, 51, 55
  basil 55
  bay leaf 55
  chamomile 51
  dill 55
  fennel 51
  lemon balm 51
  lemongrass 51
  non-salt 40
  peppermint 51
  rosemary 51, 55
  sage 51
  turmeric 51
  valerian 51
herring 30, 57
high-fructose corn syrup 14
Hong Kong vii, 22, 23, 24
Hope, Bob 124
hormones 4, 18, 32, 33, 58, 62
Hurst, Mary 158
hydrogenated oil 14
hypertension 16

I

ice cream 16, 19, 22, 29
immune system viii, 1, 5, 46, 73, 123
Internet ii, 8, 20, 59, 65, 97, 150, 170
intestines 10, 44
Italian proverb 109

J

James, William 177
Japan 9
Japanese 23, 44, 51, 108, 151, 175
Japanese proverb 151
Jefferson, Thomas 123, 182

jerky 19
Hopkins, John 18
Johns, Jasper 105
Johnson, Enez xxi
Jones, Charles "Tremendous" 170
Josephson Institute 134
Josephson, Michael 134
juice 10, 16, 31, 34, 41, 45, 59, 64

K

kale 51
kava 85
Keller, Helen 118, 186
Keyes, Ken Jr. 186
kidneys 8, 10, 54, 57
kiwi 42, 51
Korean 44
Kowloon 24
krill oil supplements 13
Kristol, Irving 117

L

lard 16
La Rochefoucauld 120
Law, Vernon 183
legumes 19, 39, 49, 54
Leigh, H.S. 35
lemongrass 51, 55
lemons 39, 55, 150
lentil 50, 51
lettuce 55
    Romaine 51
lifestyle x, 3, 6, 23, 121
lime 31, 39, 55
Lincoln, Abraham 114, 155, 169, 176
lip balm 64
liver 7, 10, 26, 33, 40, 54, 55, 56
longevity xi, 6, 17, 190
Longfellow, Henry Wadsworth 174
lotus root 51
lungs 7, 54, 56, 66, 85

M

Mabie, Hamilton Wright 151
magnesium 85
manganese 46
mango 42
maple syrup 13, 46
Marden, Orison Swett 143
Marley, Christopher 133
martial arts 6
Matherne, Gerry 105
meditation xi, 6
melatonin 85
mercury 58, 61
milk 15, 16, 18, 22, 23, 33, 39,
    41, 42, 47, 56, 63
millet 33, 56
mind v, xi, 3, 5, 6, 7, 8, 10, 39, 41,
    77, 78, 92, 117, 123, 124, 137,
    140, 141, 143, 151, 161, 174, 176
mindset viii
Minnesota Department of Health
    69, 71
mint 55
miso 16
mobile devices 3
mobile phone 80
Mohammed 120
molasses 46
Moore, James W. 178
Mother Teresa 187
Murdock, Mike 139
muscle 2, 4, 5, 9
Mushroom 39, 51, 56, 57
    black 51
    Chinese 51
    golden oak 51
    Japanese 51
    maitaki 51
    oakwood 51
    Shiitake 51
    straw 51
mustard greens 33, 51

N

Nance, W.A. 106
nature iii, vi, xi, xiii, 3, 4, 5, 8, 10,
    54, 56, 109, 131, 136, 137, 174, 185,
    190
nectarine 51, 52, 55
New Zealand 23
nicotine 84
Nietzsche, Friedrich 120
nori 30, 52
no-white diet 12, 13
nuts 18, 25, 30, 38, 46, 49, 51, 55, 56
    Brazil 46, 51
    chestnuts 38
    hazel 51
    peanut 15, 16, 53, 56
    pecans 38, 40, 51
    pine 38, 56
    pistachio 38, 46, 51
    walnuts 38, 40, 46, 51, 60

O

oatmeal 13, 39, 46
oil 13, 14, 16, 25, 50, 52, 55, 59, 64,
    85, 88, 105, 108
    argan 16, 59
    canola 16, 53
    coconut 15, 16, 59
    corn 53
    fish, supplements 13
    flaxseed 13
    grape seed 13, 16, 53, 59
    hydrogenated 14
    olive 13, 16, 52, 53, 59
    peanut 53
    red palm 13
    safflower 53
    sesame 13
    sunflower 53
olive oil 13, 16, 52, 53, 59
Omega-3 fatty acids 53, 57
Onassis, Aristotle 97
onion 51, 54
orange 42, 51, 56, 124

Ovid 92, 184
oxygen 2, 4, 9
oysters 30, 56
Oz, Dr. Mehmet 14

P

papaya 42, 51, 56, 60
paraffin 85
passionflower 85
Patton, George 162
peach 12, 51, 52, 55, 60
Peale, Norman Vincent 116, 142
peanut 15, 16, 30, 56
peanut butter 30
peanut oil 53
pear 42, 51, 56
pecans 38, 40, 51
pesticides 18, 52, 61
Peterson, Wilfred A. 157
pineapple 42, 51
pistachio 38, 46, 51
Plant, Dr. Janet 22, 23, 24
Plato 108
plums 51
polenta 50
potassium 49
potato 19, 39, 40, 47, 51, 56, 60
    russet 51
    sweet 51, 56
preservatives 15, 25, 58, 61
prevention v, x, xi, 4, 6, 13,
    19, 68, 189
Prevention magazine 20, 80
protein xiii, 5, 16, 18, 25, 26,
    29, 30, 31, 33, 37, 38, 39, 40,
    41, 44, 46, 47, 57
prune 51
Psychological Science 138
pumpkin 38, 51, 52
pumpkin seeds 38
Purkiser, W.T. 158
Pyramid of Success 135

Q

quinoa 13, 30, 49, 57

R

radiotherapy 22
radish 51, 56
raspberries 52
red palm oil 13
reflexology 5, 6
respiratory system 7, 67
restaurant 34, 37, 40, 74, 87
rice 12, 13, 24, 33, 39, 42, 47,
    56, 57, 106
Rickenbacker, Eddie 167
Rohn, Jim 130
Romaine lettuce 51
Roosevelt, Eleanor 139
Roosevelt, Theodore 103
rosemary 51, 55
Rotary International 154
    4-Way Test 154, 155
Ruskin, John 5, 100

S

safflower oil 53
salmon 30, 57
San Antonio Winery 107
Sanders, Colonel Harlan 152
sardines 30, 178
SARS 72
saturated fat (animal fat) 14, 16, 47,
    53
sausage 19, 38, 84
Schweitzer, Albert 159
sea salt 13, 31, 52, 63
sea vegetables 33, 52
    chlorella 52
    kelp 52
    nori 52
    spirulina 52

seeds xi, 18, 25, 30, 38, 49, 52, 54, 55, 185
  flax 52
  pumpkin 38, 52
  sunflower 52
Segell, Dr. Michael 80
Seneca 93, 101, 142
Senn, J. Petit 127
sesame oil 13
Shakespeare, William 142
shellfish 15, 37, 44, 56
Sidney Kimmel Comprehensive Cancer Center 19
silk 12, 62
Sinatra, Dr. Stephen 116
Six Pillars of Character 134
skin xiii, 1, 2, 10, 16, 38, 42, 55, 58, 59, 60, 73, 75, 84, 87, 107
Smaller Portion, Smaller Plate vi, 35
sodium 13, 15, 16, 20
Solon 175, 183
Sophocles 186
soup xiii, 16, 24, 29, 30, 31, 37, 41, 42, 44, 45, 48, 56, 57, 104, 159, 189
sour cream 16, 40
soy 15, 38, 42, 53, 55, 56, 85
spaghetti squash 49
spices 7, 41, 43, 55
spinach 52, 56
spirit v, vii, xi, 5, 6, 7, 8, 10, 77, 78, 92, 125, 126, 129, 141
spring vii, 54, 55, 136, 172, 190
SPSP vi, xiii, 35
Stevenson, Adlai 179
stevia 13, 46
St. John's Medical Center, Santa Monica 23
stomach 7, 10, 26, 31, 33, 34, 36, 37, 54, 56, 138, 161
strawberry 52, 55, 60
stress 4, 7, 73, 173
sugar vi, 12, 13, 14, 15, 18, 19, 20, 25, 29, 31, 33, 34, 39, 40, 47, 55, 84
sugar substitutes 15

summer vii, 54, 55, 56, 174
summer squash 39
sunflower oil 53
sunlight 1, 2, 116, 179
sunshine 2, 137, 172
supplements 2, 13, 20, 26
sweet potatoes 40, 56

T

Tagore, Rabindranath 185
tai chi 6
Tarkington, Booth 180
Taylor, Herbert J. 154
teeth 10
tempeh 38
Tennyson, Lord 186
The 7 Habits of Highly Effective People 139
Thoreau, Henry David 121
Time magazine 58, 98
tobacco 55
tofu 38, 47, 49
Tolstoy, Leo 184
tomato 16, 39, 42, 52, 60
  tomato juice 16
toxins xiii, 38, 40, 45, 61, 78
  building materials 61
  carbon monoxide 61
  carpeting 61, 67
  chlorine 61
  composite wood products 61
  dust mites 61
  furnishings 61
  mold 61, 66
  paints 61, 87
  pet dander 61
  radon 61
  second-hand smoke 61
  solvents 61
  tobacco 55, 61
  upholstery 61
  vinyl 61
  volatile organic compounds (VOCs) 61
  wallpaper paste 61

traditional Chinese medicine (TCM)
ix, x, 5, 6
trans fat 16
trihalomethanes 61
tryptophan 85
tuna 30, 47, 85
Turkish proverb 183
turmeric 13, 51, 60
Twain, Mark 123, 176

U

UCLA 134
United Kingdom 22, 80
United States Constitution 127
University of Arizona 69
U.S. Center for Disease Control 70

V

valerian 51, 85
vegetable ix, 7, 18, 19, 24, 25, 26, 29,
30, 31, 33, 37, 38, 39, 42, 43, 44, 47,
49, 52, 53, 55, 57, 59
vegetable oil 53
Vietnamese 44
vision ix, 7, 102
Vitamin B-6 49, 50, 51
Vitamin C 50, 51
Vitamin D 1, 2
Vitamin E 47, 49, 51, 52
Voltaire 142

W

walnut 38, 40, 46, 51, 60
Washington, Martha 115
water ix, 6, 9, 10, 11, 18, 25, 26, 29,
31, 32, 36, 44, 45, 52, 53, 54, 57, 60,
61, 62, 63, 64, 68, 70, 72, 76, 84, 87,
103, 104, 106, 120, 140, 173, 179
watermelon 42, 52, 55, 60
Wayne State University 47
weight v, vi, 4, 5, 7, 8, 10, 20, 27, 30,
39, 40, 61, 84, 152, 186
Wesley, John 156

Westwood Village Rotary Club
newsletter 159
Wilson, Woodrow 97
Winfrey, Oprah 14, 162
winter 39, 54, 56, 57, 66, 158, 172
winter squash 39, 57
Wong, Angi Ma i, ii, xii, 125, 129
wood 6, 54, 61, 62, 66, 67, 95, 98,
110
Wooden, John 134, 139, 170
wool 62
World Cancer Research Fund —
American Institute for Cancer
Research 19
worry vi, 7, 116

Y

yam 40, 51, 56
yang 6, 7, 172
yin 6, 7, 172
yogurt 22, 23, 30, 40, 41, 59

Z

Ziggy 115
zinc 46
zucchini 52, 56

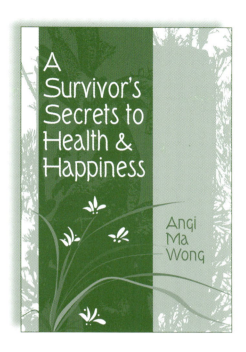

GIVE *A Survivor's Secrets to Health and Happiness to:*

- Motivate your sales teams and associates
- Attract customers, members or donors
- Thank valued supporters, staffs, clients, customers, associates—anyone or everyone!
- Improve your company's image
    . . . fuel your fundraiser
    . . . reach new markets
    . . . show appreciation or gratitude
    . . . increase morale
    . . . reward loyalty or achievement
    . . . share information

Call 1-888-810-9891 to place your corporate order today and your book will be customized FREE!